Came Upon A Midnight Clear

KATIE PORTER

RIPTIDE
PUBLISHING

Riptide Publishing
PO Box 1537
Burnsville, NC 28714
www.riptidepublishing.com

Came Upon a Midnight Clear
Copyright © 2012, 2017 by Katie Porter

Cover art: Natasha Snow, natashasnowdesigns.com
Editor: Carole-ann Galloway
Layout: L.C. Chase, lcchase.com/design.htm

ISBN: 978-1-62649-673-6

Second edition
November, 2017

Also available in ebook:
ISBN: 978-1-62649-672-9

Came Upon A Midnight Clear

KATIE PORTER

RIPTIDE PUBLISHING

About Our Charity

Twenty percent of the proceeds of this title will be donated to the Russian LGBT Network.

A Statement from the Russian LGBT Network

The Russian LGBT Network is an interregional social movement that unites various LGBTQI(+) initiatives across Russia. In the headquarters in St. Petersburg a team of 15 activists work every day to promote human rights, to fight inequality in Russia, and to build a strong and powerful community of LGBTQI(+) activists and their allies.

The Network provides various services to the community: we offer psychological and legal assistance to the people in need. Our Hotline services – land line and on-line chat – function 24 hours a day and provide assistance to LGBTQI(+) people in need across all 11 time zones in Russia.

The Network also provide Emergency assistance to the LGBTQI(+) people, who suffer persecution and prosecution, who find themselves in dangerous situations and fear for their lives and wellbeing.

In April, the world became aware of the fact that LGBT people in the Chechen Republic are being persecuted, unlawfully detained, tortured and killed. We, the team of the Russian LGBT Network, have been working hard to help these people to flee the republic, to restore their feeling of safety and security, and to find sanctuary outside of Russia. It has been especially hard since both Russian and Chechen authorities have continued to deny that this crime against humanity is happening in the North Caucasus. They need to hear our voices. They have to.

We are immensely honored that Riptide Publishing selected us as their Holiday Charity. Our philosophy is that human right defenders and the civil society are capable of ending LGBTQI(+) inequality all over the world. We, the team of the Russian LGBT Network thank you for showing you solidarity with the cause. Right now, we need you, because when we unite our efforts, we can create a better tomorrow.

With love and solidarity,
Russian LGBT Network.

If you are willing to submit a separate donation, please click the donation button on our webpage lgbtnet.org/en

You can also donate using our crowdfunding platforms:
help.lgbtnet.org/en
help.lgbtnet.org/chechnya-en

If you are an organization that is willing to submit a donation, please contact our Fundraising Officer at communications@lgbtnet.org

Follow us on Facebook: facebook.com/lgbtnet

To BV & JR
Here's your rich guy.

Table of Contents

Chapter One

"**H**ey, Christmas cheer, remember?"

Kyle Wakefield looked up from his pint of Carlsberg and smiled at Steph. She was an extreme people person, at times almost obnoxiously cheerful. She even wore a pair of colorful jingle bell earrings.

Steph and her can-do attitude were very good for him and a million times better for their fledgling production company. He knew that on a profound, logical level, which was probably why they'd been business partners since undergrad days at Yale.

But that evening, Kyle was going to have trouble maintaining a happy face to match fifty percent of her enthusiasm.

"I know." He smiled. "But you know how much tomorrow means."

"Sure." She shrugged, then sipped Red Bull and vodka as if she needed external energy. "All the more reason to enjoy tonight. 'The calm before the storm' does not mean dwelling on the storm. It means having a pint and breathing. You remember how to breathe, yes?"

Triggered by her reminder, Kyle inhaled deeply. She was a wonder, helping him to let go of the bad stuff. But not when their future depended on how well the next four weeks panned out.

"Okay, you're in that sort of mood," Steph said. "Spill it and we'll clear it out of your head. *Then* you shut it down and have another pint. That one is depressingly full."

Kyle looked her in the eye. Beautiful blue eyes, with blonde hair she kept in old-time-movie-starlet waves. He'd never seen her less than meticulous, but then the same applied to him.

He took another sip of the pale lager and exhaled. "To shoot the Christmas portion of *Fast Money* during the actual season was my idea. You know Peter wanted a decked-out set later in the winter."

"Only to accommodate his holiday skiing schedule. Snow bunny number three was *very* disappointed. That isn't our problem. Your reasons were sound; otherwise I wouldn't have agreed. You know that."

"Right. What was my bullshit? Something about the ready-made magic of Christmas in London?"

She chuckled. "Something like that. It'll save money. Thousands of dollars on artificial sets saved. You wanting an excuse to get out of your parents' official holiday events was just a bonus. Plus there's the crew—look at them. I mean it. Look."

Kyle settled back against his leather-padded chair and ignored Steph's too-true assessment of his family as he took in the sights. A regular pub with a long, long bar turned at ninety degrees on either end. Glasses hung from the ceiling, with stout on tap. Lush booths, tons of tables, and a fireplace ringed by couches were the final touch. The BBC evening news, soccer games, and some prime-time talk show scrolled in closed caption on flat-screens, while Slade's ubiquitous "Merry Xmas Everybody" added to the noise.

Why were the British so obsessed with that damn annoying song?

More than the details, the pub possessed an unnamable English atmosphere. Modern, and in the midst of an unabashedly urban setting, yet friendly in a small-town way. A warm haven against the damp cold of early December.

The pub had the extra advantage of an upstairs all-purpose function room, where he and Steph had set up shop for their roster of employees. The hotel was fine for sleeping and taking official meetings, but they needed a quiet space to escape when actual work—and the occasional emergency—popped up. The pub was also directly across the street from the boutique hotel they'd entirely booked for the crew.

Not that anyone seemed to mind the hotel's economy accommodations. Kyle recognized maybe fifty faces out of the eighty crammed inside, all smiling and drinking. Three harried bartenders jumped and hustled to serve so many. Kyle had covered that detail, making sure the pub and the hotel staff were prepared for such an influx of patrons, most of whom would keep ridiculously weird hours because of several night shoots.

"They look happy," he said with a wistful smile. "Probably because Peter isn't here."

That made Steph laugh. "Cheeky man. I've always liked that about you." She lifted her glass in mock salute. "We've done well, Kyle. I need you to relax now. Babysitting your anxieties hamstrings me."

"Yup. Promise." He nodded to her empty glass. "Just water, though, Miss Three Minimum. I need you on your game too."

"Not water. Diet Coke. I'm on it."

Kyle watched her weave through the crowd. Men stopped talking to stare at her shapely ass wiggle past while she strutted on banana heel pumps. More of the '40s retro she adored.

It would've been so much easier. *So* much easier. Why not fall in love with Stephanie Penn, his closest friend for the last eight years? His life would've been as orderly as his closets.

But not the one he still hid in.

His body simply didn't work that way.

He caught his fingernails in a coarse gouge on the table's varnished wooden surface. Apprehension that had only a little to do with his business ventures, here on the brink of embarking on Pennfield's third big-budget film, settled like a bonfire under his breastbone. Hiring Second Chances—a fearless stunt crew comprised of ex-cons on the hunt for another shot at life—had been his decision too.

When shooting started, he would see Nate again.

Nathan Carnes. His name didn't waft through Kyle's brain like a ghost, although the man did haunt him. No, it slammed against him like cannon fire. Always did. It was inevitably followed by regret and desire, nostalgia and pain. And a hot, bone-shaking anger that wore away at the best memories of their two years as high school lovers.

Nate had run scared like the fucking stubborn asshole he'd always been. Kyle had left for Yale. End of story.

He needed to get out of this suddenly claustrophobic place. But Steph returned to the table. She wiggled her fingers toward a smokin' guy in a tight black T-shirt.

"Waving up the wrong tree," Kyle said as she sat down.

"What was that?"

"Gay as I am."

She blinked. "Shit. What a waste."

He grinned down at his lager, then tipped her a glance from under his brows. "I wouldn't say so."

"No, I insist. A waste. Because you sure as shit won't go— What is it they say here? Chat him up? I'd cheer you on if you did." She leaned over, hands flat on the table.

Other than past lovers, Steph was the only person who knew Kyle's sexual orientation. It was something he'd needed to reveal to her. Couldn't be helped. They split an LA apartment, an office, and sometimes twenty hours a day of one another's time.

He wasn't in the mood for the cute stranger. Thoughts of Nathan, what they'd shared, what they'd thrown away with both hands, would not leave him be. Kyle had roughly eight hours to get his shit together before a 6 a.m. shoot—before he'd see Nate again.

Steph took his hand. "Kyle. This isn't Virginia. This isn't someplace where your parents will stroll in and turn your life to shit with their goddamn issues."

"Not that they'd deign coming in here in the first place."

Andrew and Vanessa Wakefield were a power couple of the first order. Kyle's dad was a DC lobbyist. His mother tracked her lineage to one of the First Families of Virginia. They traveled to London regularly, but Kyle would bet cash that they'd never been in an actual pub.

His parents weren't the only problem, either. While there were more and more openly gay Hollywood players, few had the success Kyle craved: owning a large-scale production company that operated at the top level, making giant, famous pictures. He refused to settle for anything less than a blockbuster career. If he ever wanted to be free of his parents' looming influence, he *couldn't* settle. That meant he couldn't gamble his future on the whims of an industry that ought to know better than to judge anyone's sexuality.

"That's totally true. But my point stands. This is England. It's *nearly* Europe. Sometimes. Look, no one's giving those guys a second glance. No fuss."

He nodded. "I know."

"But . . . still no go." She sighed. "I hear you, my dear."

"Slumming it with the rabble, I see," came a voice that would make nails scraping down a chalkboard sound like Beethoven's Fifth.

In tandem, Kyle and Steph looked up to find Peter Upton, boy-wonder director, standing beside their table. Fabulous. How about layering ouch on shit on worry? Perfect for an evening meant to be full of holiday cheer.

"Slumming it," Kyle muttered, "would be if we let you sit down with us."

"Shut it," Steph hissed under her breath.

The dull roar in the pub kept their exchange private. Then again, Upton wasn't known for being particularly observant of others' moods. Being so wrapped up by one's ego must be rather smothering.

"Good to see you, Peter." Steph was the master of quick recoveries. Otherwise Pennfield would've collapsed in something like 2014. "And not slumming it, making sure we have the whole crew on board. We're stoked for tomorrow."

"Glad you are. But there's a problem in the hotel. Robert is having a meltdown. He's too drunk. The tabloids will have a field day. Again." His thin face was exceedingly tan, as if holding on to the USC film school vibe he'd perfected to a T. He hid his receding hairline under an ever-present red baseball cap. Only twenty-seven, he was the lucky-ass prodigy of Hollywood—for now. He had as much hinging on this project as anyone. Many banked that his blockbuster success wouldn't last, that he was too young and too full of himself. And enjoyed a little too much cocaine.

Steph took a gulp of her Diet Coke that only Kyle interpreted as a tiny sign of nerves. "Robert Durant has three assistants. Aren't they holding his hand?"

"I want one of *you* to handle it." Peter was in full-on pout mode. "I don't want him hungover on the first day. He's a fucking prima donna, and his shit is the last thing we need."

We. An interesting word, Kyle thought.

Prima donna. That was interesting too.

What an asshole.

He leaned away from the table, one arm hitched over the back of his chair. "We'll handle it," he said calmly. Steph was the public face, but Kyle was the money. And the heavy.

Peter looked down at Kyle with a tiny smirk. "If you don't, losing Durant could shut this whole show down. I won't work without him."

"You won't work without our cash either." Pennfield was a relatively new production company, but Kyle's money helped, as did the backers he brought in through his family connections.

Steph flashed a grin as bright as the Christmas lights strung along the ceiling in a checkerboard pattern. "I think what my crabby-as-hell partner means is, I'll take care of it. Rest easy, Peter."

The man glared at such an undeniable dismissal, but he left anyway.

"You could've handled that with a *little* more tact."

"Nah. Score one for being rude. I don't like it, but you know how the game is played. One half smooth as cream, one half flaming gasoline." He finished his beer. "You're the cream, Miss Penn."

"You're full of shit. You *do* like it. It's the only time you let loose." The laugh in her voice took the sting out of the accusation. "Just . . . watch it. We need him too."

Kyle offered her a chagrined nod. He stretched his aching neck and happened to glance toward the front door of the pub.

And froze. Solid. Except for his heart, which kicked up speed like a jet barreling down a runway.

Steph caught the direction of his gaze and turned. "Oh, cool. The stunt team. Maybe at least one of them won't be gay. You may be a complete stick-in-the-mud, but I'd at least like second base tonight."

"Bull," he said past a desert-dry throat. "You never go to bat without scoring."

"Quippy gay man with his sports lingo. Nice."

"Business requirement."

"C'mon. Let's go introduce ourselves. Talking on the phone isn't the same."

Kyle followed her lead, standing. His legs were like barn-door hinges left too long without oil. "Sure."

Across the crowded pub, his gaze locked with Nate's. Shock registered on that nearly familiar face as plainly as a volcano bursting. Nate hadn't known who backed Pennfield Productions. He'd only ever dealt with Stephanie during negotiations.

Closely shorn dark-blond hair with short, neat sideburns. Canny blue eyes so pale as to be almost silver. Rough features, but classically proportioned, with a brawny bruiser's body suited to a Special Ops stud.

Or an ex-con who made his living defying death.

He wore a midnight-blue wool coat over a white shirt, open to reveal the lean, toned muscle of his neck. Dark jeans clung to thick thighs, and Doc Martens boots added to his bad-boy cool. Only when Kyle and Steph wove closer, pulse slamming in his ears, did he see a new tattoo. Pure black, it climbed like fire to lick beneath Nate's right ear—like an intentional arrow pointing toward his small diamond stud.

He'd never been afraid of wielding his sexuality like a machete.

Kyle swallowed. They stood close enough that he could smell a hint of aftershave. And the scent of the boy he'd once known—the angry, clever boy who'd matured into such a toughened man.

A golden-blond man with a distinct resemblance to Robert Durant stood next to him. Probably the stunt double. Kyle only noticed him when Steph shook his hand.

She turned toward Nate next. "Mr. Carnes. I recognize you from your stunt reel. So good to meet you in person. Let me introduce my business partner, Kyle Wakefield."

Chapter Two

"**W**hat the fuck are you doing here?"

The minute the words left Nate's mouth, he knew how goddamned rude they sounded. It'd be pretty hard to miss. Kyle Wakefield was more than a ghost from Nate's past. He was a demon. Someone he'd thought himself well quit of.

Confronting that demon meant all bets were off.

Jesus, the man had always known how to wear a suit. Charcoal pinstripe, complete with a slim, narrow-collared vest. Tailored. Of course it was tailored. Showing off the body Nate had once known intimately.

Nate sure as hell hadn't expected to see Kyle in London.

Then it dawned. Cold and trickling, like the growing realization of a bad, bad day when things just kept getting worse. Wakefield. Pennfield. The way Stephanie Penn, with whom Nate had conducted three teleconferences, was looking back and forth between Nate and Kyle. Her partner.

Odds and ratios. The distance to the door. How fucking fast could he be up on the tables? The entire densely packed crowd of genial people calculated into how quickly he could jet. He'd be gone. Betraying, hiding Kyle Wakefield would see no more than the soles of Nate's DMs.

Except Second Chances needed this gig. Ethan Raney, Nate's closest friend since prison, stood at his side, heading up their small crew. Doing stunts for a Peter Upton picture would make them once and for all. There was no other reason Nate would drag his team all the way to merry fucking England.

Kyle smiled. He'd never been exactly handsome. His features were bluntly rounded, with lines carving around his mouth. Those full lips though—they were enough to plant dirty ideas in a man's mind. Especially when he knew what pleasure Kyle was capable of offering.

"Nice to see you too, Nathan."

Stephanie's eyes narrowed. She was an attractive woman, if one went in for the overdone look. And women. "You two know each other?"

"Well now, that's a matter of interpretation," Nate drawled. He flicked his jacket back, which was rapidly becoming too warm in the closely packed pub. The fireplace at the far end didn't help. "I used to know someone named Kyle Wakefield. Turned out I knew someone entirely different than the rest of the world."

Kyle's eyes were brown. Just brown. Not rich or fathomless. But once, they'd been so special. Nate couldn't look away.

"Is that really at issue right now?" Kyle asked with the same *everybody please love me* geniality he'd had all those years ago.

Nate ground his teeth. "You tell me. Does Ms. Penn know you like dropping to your knees and—"

"That's more than enough," Kyle said. "If you don't mind, Steph, apparently we need to adjourn to my office and discuss a few things."

The blonde looked stunned. "Apparently *you* do. I'll fix things with Robert and wardrobe."

Kyle nodded, then wrapped his hand around Nate's upper arm. Raney tweaked his chin toward the door in a silent inquiry, but Nate waved him off.

Through the dark-paneled pub, up a narrow stairwell, and down to a single door, Nate let himself be herded. Upstairs, the large multi-use space stretched the entire length of the narrow building. A pool table at one end contrasted with three tables pushed together piled with papers and half a dozen computers. Midway along the room was a grouping of couches that faced a seven-foot screen, probably for running dailies.

Most of all, it was private. Quiet. Through the wooden floorboards and scattered rugs came the muted hum of patrons downstairs. Up here, there was no one except him and Kyle. No sound but their breathing.

Nate curled his fingers into fists at the small of his back. "Your partner. In business?"

"Mostly."

Edgy, still stunned, Nate ranged toward the front of the room. Two slender windows pointed toward the hotel where he'd agreed to stay for the next month. Most importantly, he wasn't looking at Kyle. That moment to recover his bearings was priceless. But he could feel the weight of the other man's gaze on his nape.

"Have you broadened your horizons, then? Used to be you had very narrow tastes."

"Still do." Kyle's voice was hoarse. Almost as if he gave a shit.

Nate had been with plenty of guys over the years—only one in the joint, despite prison's reputation. Didn't mean he'd ever forgotten Kyle's mouth, neither those lips nor the wet heat. More than that, though. The way he'd made Nate feel like the center of the world.

"I need this job," he found himself saying unwillingly. "I've got five of my best drivers, our parkour specialists, and Jimmy, our pyro guy. We turned down two other jobs. The outlay in time alone . . ."

"You've got the job."

"Then why the hiding?"

There were a few quiet footsteps. The shifting of cloth and fine wool. "Would you have taken it if you knew I was involved?"

"Fuck no."

Nate turned. A punch to the gut all over again. Kyle had stripped his jacket. A slim gray vest hugged his trim waist. His shoulders had filled out, wider and thicker. The crisp white dress shirt gleamed in the low light.

Out of Nate's league. He had been, even when they were in school. That had been a hard lesson learned, but Nate had never thought himself dumb. Slow, maybe. Yet he'd been stupidly deluded by Kyle's insistence that so long as they were together, everything would be fine.

His feet moved him toward Kyle, who held his ground. When they were alone, he held firm. They'd come together like two boxers going toe to toe. Not making love.

"I don't much care for working with two-faced assholes," Nate said quietly.

Kyle lifted his chin. He never smelled like anything so simple as soap. Expensive cologne made of musk and spice. "Nine years is a long time."

"You're right." Nate nodded with mock understanding. He was close enough that the small movement brought his mouth in line with Kyle's. The wash of breath over lips made him think of how hot they used to burn. "So maybe I should check in first. Downstairs, did you cut me off because I was rude as fuck? Or does everyone else think the pretty blonde bounces on your dick every night?"

"Stephanie has her own partners."

"That's not an answer."

Kyle licked his lips. Pink tongue, pink lips. Brown eyes, however, remained steady. "I keep my private life private."

Nate understood keeping things quiet sometimes, when necessary. But when a man had a trust fund, a Yale education, and all the privileges available in life . . . he didn't understand. His top lip peeled back from his teeth. "Yeah," Nate said. "If that's what you want to call it."

"I'm trying to do you a favor here, to make the right impression." Kyle's wide shoulders were tense beneath the pristine cloth. "Don't be like this."

"You led me around by the dick in high school, but I'm not your little bitch." He framed Kyle's jaw. The sharp bristle of evening growth abraded his palm. The tender flesh under Kyle's chin was meant for the press of a man's fingers. "Or maybe you can convince me that your financial beneficence is completely unlike your parents' methods of buying the world."

Kyle's tendons twitched, but he didn't pull away. "We each have a job to do here."

"You're playing an angle."

"It's called being a professional. And you're doing really good work with your company."

Nate locked down against the greedy impulse to take that as a real compliment. He'd learned after three years on the inside that ex-cons didn't always get good breaks. Not only did future employers look on a record with disdain, it was a different kind of life. Freer. No regimen to keep the restlessness at bay. Adjustment was slow. People who didn't understand failed to provide the necessary help, which meant more offenders back behind bars.

So Nate had combined the adrenaline he used to get from boosting cars with a better purpose. Stunts. Then he'd set out to hire as many cons as he could reasonably train. They turned out to be excellent stunt people.

Having little to lose helped.

Nate had Second Chances, which meant that pushing made no sense. He couldn't risk this gig.

Well, *shouldn't* risk it. Kyle went to his head. His cock too.

Nate set his jaw. "That's not an answer."

"I need a Maserati to barrel past Big Ben. It's not a bullshit stunt, and neither are the others. They're big. The whole project is big. I need the best." Kyle's dark eyes narrowed. "Steph thought you were it too. It wasn't just me. If we were wrong, say the word. We'll find someone new."

"Don't you dare."

Kyle lifted his eyebrows, carving lines across his forehead. "Or what?"

Jesus, Nate knew that look. That challenge. They'd spent two years hiding in Kyle's fancy, so-huge bedroom. Sweaty and sticky, wrapped up in each other's bodies. All because of challenges thrown down and picked up again. Seeing it repeated, now all grown up, punched Nate in the small of his back. Tense pleasure.

Anticipation.

He took Kyle's mouth. The lips he'd missed were soft under his. He couldn't call it a kiss because it was all explosion. They stroked together, all teeth and tongues and taste. Kyle was bitter beer and memories. Kissing him was like taking back a piece of his youth, when Nate still thought he could be everything Kyle had hoped.

Before Nate had figured out he had a hard-on for self-sabotage.

Which had to be why he was pressing Kyle back toward the center of the long, open room. His hands folded around the other man's face. Abrading and harsh and rough. They bumped against a leather couch.

Leather against Kyle's ass.

Nate drove his fingers into rich honey-brown hair. Pulled his mouth back. "Is this what you want? Is this what you were after?"

"No."

"Really?" He stroked his knuckles down Kyle's body. Warm cloth. Probably not cotton, but something fancier than Nate knew. He was tending to more important matters, like unfastening cool buttons and Kyle's belt. "Because you feel like you're ready."

Kyle's cock was hard—more than hard, swelling against the inside of his fancy trousers. A kiss of precome already dampened the material. But the elegant man didn't bow. His spine didn't curve. "It's been a while. Apparently my prick isn't very particular."

Nate curled his fingers around that girth. "You always did like dark alleys."

Kyle only raised an eyebrow.

In his mind, Nate cussed at his idiocy. He *was* a fucking idiot, because he'd hoped Kyle would deny slumming. Kyle only shoved his hands up the back of Nate's shirt and kissed him.

That was Kyle Wakefield, stubborn to the damn end.

Wrong. So much of this was a bad idea. Mixing business and pleasure rarely worked, even before Nate added the fact that he was kissing his ex-boyfriend—and dropping to his knees before his ex-boyfriend.

Belt and zipper parted.

Dumb, stupid, idiotic moron.

Moron with his hands full of cock.

Kyle had the fattest cock Nate had ever gotten his hands on, made for filling a man's mouth and taking over his airway. The slit welled with a drop of pre-come that Nate licked away. He looked up Kyle's body. Bulky and brutal while dressed in what remained of that fine, well-cut suit.

Nate might be in the supplicant's position, but one glance at Kyle's face revealed that the man was lost. His brown eyes were dark and wide. Shell-shocked. His hands shook the slightest bit as he held them out above Nate's head.

For a moment he thought Kyle might pull away. Push him off. An interesting test of wills. Then Kyle's shaft twitched upward, toward where Nate's mouth hovered over the fat, plum-shaped head.

Nate licked, starting at Kyle's base, with the tip of his tongue in the short-trimmed pubic hair. He traveled all the way up to the defined ridge and line beneath the slit. His mouth filled with the salty taste of skin and man. Smooth hands came down on the back of his head. Gently. Tentatively.

Win. So much made of win that Nate thought he could come in his own jeans.

Not happening though. He'd hold off to the very last, because he had to report to Kyle the next day. On the set, producers were more like gods than bosses.

No way was Nate showing up for work without the fresh memory of his cock up Kyle's ass.

Chapter Three

For about three seconds, Kyle was able to filter the situation through some semblance of logic. It shouldn't feel this powerful or this insanely special. Not after nine years apart. Other lovers should've been able to erase—

Then Nate sucked. His cheeks hollowed as he pulled the head of Kyle's cock between his lips. He swirled his tongue in powerful strokes and flicks, paying special attention to the sensitive ridge underneath.

Kyle couldn't help tightening his hands. He speared into short, silky dark-blond hair. Gripped. Kneaded. He didn't so much intend to guide Nathan, although it might have read that way. He took more and more of Kyle's hard-on into the hot, unforgiving pleasure of his mouth. No, Kyle held tight in order to stay standing, to stay in control of emotions that had erupted upon seeing the lover he'd never been able to forget.

The ending he'd never stopped regretting.

He grabbed harder.

With his hands clutching the backs of Kyle's thighs, Nate rolled his eyes closed. Kyle had been waiting for this moment. The attitude and hesitation slipped away—all the distrust they'd never been able to get past. When his eyes closed and his throat relaxed, Nate meant it. Meant to shatter Kyle's mind.

Maybe that was why, back in high school, Kyle always believed they had a chance. There were times when Nate let him in, and not just sexually.

Old anger made Kyle rougher. He pushed ferociously. His prick hit the back of Nate's throat. Both moaned. Kyle dropped his head back. He knew the ceiling was up there, but he saw nothing. Felt nothing other than Nate's viselike hands and his mouth, poised in that gorgeous middle ground between slack and gripping intent.

Nate popped off. "I'm going to swallow your come, Kyle. You'll give it to me and I'll suck it into me." His icy blue gaze reached up, all mocking arrogance. "You want that."

"Yes," Kyle hissed.

He tried to drag that tempting mouth back, but Nate's strength of will was equal to his. Fucking hell. The thin, eager partner of his youth had matured into a man of brawn and power.

"Tell me." Nate licked his lower lip.

"I want to come in your mouth. God, I want you to taste my come."

"But you're not going to return the favor," he said, still stroking Kyle's slick, engorged cock.

He would've been disappointed. Maybe Nate intended this as punishment or a power play. Yet Kyle recognized dirty fire and the telling smirk that made silent promises. Silent, beautiful threats. "I'm not?"

"No. I'm going to fuck your ass."

Kyle sucked in a breath. Nate took the opportunity to increase the pace of his strokes. His fist was viciously tight. The prospect of coming in his mouth was slipping away. If Kyle didn't hold it together, he'd jerk the fists of hair he held, expose Nate's neck roped with tendons, and come all over that mysterious new tattoo.

"You think I'll let you do that?"

"You will," Nate said. "You'll be begging for it by the time I have you stretched across that pool table. I want to fuck you while you wear that five-grand suit." His grip eased a little. "Goddamn, you could always wear the hell out of a suit."

Kyle only nodded. How was he supposed to take that almost offhanded remark? Compliment? Insult? The tone of Nate's voice sank it right between the two.

"Now lean back." He pushed Kyle to arch his spine against the couch back. To offer support. To thrust Kyle's dick out like a spear. Nate, still on his knees, resumed the dizzying blowjob. He was ferocious now. Licking, sucking, ringing his fingers and stroking.

Kyle was losing it. Especially as his mind floated on the promise of Nate's fat prick up his ass. Mere moments away.

"Jesus." He stretched his arms along the back of the couch for balance. "Take it, Nate. Deeper. I need it all. Everything you can wring out of me. Let me fuck your beautiful face. I want you so goddamn stiff when you push into my ass. I want to feel how much this affects you. I can see it in your eyes. *Take it.*"

He jerked his hips. Thrusting hard. No mercy. No fear that Nate couldn't handle the force. He always had, like a dare. A test of their wills. That made it better. The complete freedom to take what he wanted. No politeness or reserve. Each drive hit the back of Nate's throat, jolting Kyle's swollen, aching head. Every ridge and vein disappeared between his lover's taut lips.

"Now, Nate. *Now*. Swallow me. Take it all. Ah, fuck . . ."

He exploded in a rush of pleasure. The edges of his vision dimmed to black. All he could see was the clear, wicked blue of Nate's eyes. Kyle focused on that color. It was that or lose his goddamn mind. Come spurted from his dick, and just as he'd promised and taunted, Nate gulped it all. His throat worked over a single swallow. He gagged a little, which shot an extra burst through Kyle's brain.

As if he'd won.

Nate surged off his knees. "My turn."

Kyle couldn't resist being dragged toward the pool table, having been blasted by one of the best orgasms of his life. Nate's arms were more robust with muscle, fueled by the unspent desire blazing in his eyes.

He found himself pushed face-first onto green felt. Breathless. Lungs hot. Anticipating all over again, despite the release that had ripped out his spine. He wanted Nate's power. That same lack of mercy.

"Arms out," Nate said sharply. "Grab the sides of the table. Don't you fucking let go. Understand?"

"Yes."

"I want 'yes, sir' out of you while I'm pounding your ass. That's what you get to give me. Big, bad producer calling the ex-con 'sir.'"

Kyle suppressed the unease that scraped in his stomach. Not about calling Nate "sir." They'd played that way before, so long ago. Master and servant. Top and bottom. The truth remained that they'd loved the switch. Power given and power relinquished. No, his unease came because of how angrily Nate had issued his command.

Logic rocketed away again. Nate yanked Kyle's trousers and boxer briefs down to his knees. Shirttails tickled his low back. But it was his ass, naked and exposed, that claimed Kyle's attention.

Nate's hands roamed over and around, under tense hips. "Relax," came a soothing whisper. "Relax, Kyle."

It was the first time all night Nate had used his name, and so quietly. Kyle exhaled slowly and eased into the supporting strength of the pool table.

"Yes, sir," he breathed.

"Oh, God, that's good. And your ass. So good." Nate slipped his fingers up the line between Kyle's cheeks, then grabbed, then pulled them apart. "This rosebud is mine, isn't it?"

"Yes, sir."

For a second Kyle was bereft as Nate fished through his pockets for a condom—a harsh reminder of other lovers. Other casual fucks. Squeezing his eyes shut, Kyle forced himself to stay in the moment. This was a one-time thing, an explosion of passion to cap off nine years of anger. Give it a little vent, if only so they could work together.

"Lube?" Nate asked. "Anywhere?"

"Steph's desk is there, closest. Maybe lotion or Vaseline."

Nate strode across the room. He was still fully clothed, leaving Kyle in such a deliberately vulnerable position. He rifled through Steph's drawers and made a sound of approval. "You'll have to buy her a new tube of lip balm."

"Yes, sir."

Nate grinned, so filthy and lovely. "Watch yourself, Kyle. You'll slip on set tomorrow. I'll have you well-trained in a manner of minutes."

"Fuck off."

A quick swat to his ass broke the shimmering silence. "Watch it, rich boy. No one approves of language like that."

"You do."

Nate took position behind him. Jeans rubbed against Kyle's bare ass in a slow grind. "Yes, I do. I bring out the worst in you. Always have. Just . . . look at you."

There. Definite wonder. No condescension or mockery. Nate petted from thighs to low back, softly, while Kyle soaked in that unexpected tenderness.

That pause amid the storm ended with the sound of a zipper yanked down. Kyle looked back as Nate slipped on the condom, then squeezed the tube of gel lip balm along his huge prick.

"You're bigger," he said, unable to hide his aroused awe.

"Hell yes, I am. Can you take it?"

"Hell yes. Sir."

A nudge. Prick against anus. Just a hello. Just like their reunion down in the pub, the niceties were brief. Nate shoved two lubed fingers into Kyle's tight opening. He gasped and curled his hands around the edges of the billiard table. He looked back, however, not wanting to miss a glimpse of Nate's face. He gave Kyle so little, but he would give him the expressions that couldn't be stifled.

Nate took no time in establishing a quick rhythm. He thrust so fast and hard, his forearm taut with power, that Kyle cried out. Quick. Quick. Quick. Nate bared his teeth. His lids narrowed to slits where the ice blue of his eyes had darkened. Pain and pleasure fused in Kyle's nerves as each of those ramming drives stroked his prostate.

The dazzling agony stopped short. Fingers gone in such a rush. Kyle moaned against his shoulder. But Nate wasn't gone, not by any means. His prick took the place of his fingers. No hello this time. A sleek thrust that rocked Kyle's hips against the table and his cheek against the felt. Another gasping cry as his body attempted to compensate for the sudden violation.

"So, rich man." Nate's plunging force accelerated. "You always loved a bit of rough. Slumming it again."

"Yes, sir."

Unprompted. Nothing mattered other than the gritting bliss of being what Nate needed. Kyle would rather hack off his own foot than cry mercy as his lover fucked him with complete abandon.

Nate's breath rasped. His face had contorted around a grimace of need. His fingers pinched the flesh of Kyle's ass. Digging. Holding him in place.

"The windows are open, Kyle. We're right here. Do you think anyone in the hotel across the street can see us? Two bodies humping like animals. Would you like that?"

"No, sir."

Another grim, sharp smack. "Tell the truth. Here, at least. You owe me that."

Kyle closed his eyes. To be that free. To flip the bird to the whole world and let Nate ravish him without shame. Good God, what would that be like? A release more total than the one he'd shot down Nate's throat.

"Yes, sir. I want them to see you fuck me."

Nate groaned as if Kyle had said the right thing. "You always took cock like a goddamn pro. How does my big prick feel? Am I hurting you?"

That wasn't a question of concern. It was gloating. Teasing. Kyle lifted his head from the green felt and angled his gaze back. Nate watched him with an avid intensity that stirred up too many emotions.

"You feel amazing, sir." He grunted at one particular stab of that massive cock. "You're as hard as I'd hoped when you were on your knees. Ready to own me."

"Yes," Nate hissed. "Own you."

The pace picked up until their lower bodies slapped in a sharp, sweaty rhythm that blended with grunts and force. Nate bowed closer, ripped at Kyle's shirt. Buttons flew free. Tense fingers dug into the meat of his pecs. Nate held on as his prick swelled and gathered bursting energy.

Kyle never opened his hands, although he wanted to wrap his arms back around Nate's neck. He wanted another kiss. Not the way of it, though. They were the detonation of a grenade.

But Nate arched him anyway. He pulled Kyle back, bending his spine. "Don't let go," he whispered, breathless now. "I own you, remember. Anything I want . . . as I fuck you. I'll bend you in half if I want to. Are you . . . Shit, Kyle . . . are you hard again?"

"Yes, sir."

Nate swallowed roughly. "Another orgasm and your come will be . . . all over this pool table. You won't be able to look at it without . . . remembering how I rode you. *Me* . . . Oh fuck. Hear me, Kyle?"

"Yes, sir. You. Please, make me come again."

Nate released his grip and twitched Kyle's hips back from the table to get enough room. With both hands he grabbed Kyle's prick and yanked, stroked, slapped that full flesh—in perfect time with his blasting thrusts.

"You first," he rasped. "I want to know I won twice."

"No, sir. I win. Jesus . . . I'm going again." Kyle's mind fizzled as another climax shuddered through his body. Despite its weakness, it was no less amazing. He hadn't been able to come back-to-back like that since he was a teenager.

Nate's grinding intensity bordered on pain now. His face was a mess of need before his lips parted on a strangled gasp. He forced one last unrelenting push, so greedy and merciless that Kyle bit his lower lip to keep from revealing how much it cost him. In the best way, he craved that sharp, searing sting. He'd given his all to scramble Nate's brains, to provide a release he wouldn't be able to forget when their gazes met the next morning.

Nate shuddered and collapsed across Kyle's limp body. Both of them breathed as if they'd run five miles flat out. Sweat soaked the back of Kyle's shirt.

He chuckled. "Can I let go now?"

To his surprise, Nate smiled and nuzzled his neck. "Yes, sir."

Laughter shook from one panting chest into the other. Back and forth. That trade of satisfaction that never got old.

Kyle released the pool table and stretched his fingers. He did what he'd wanted to do in the midst of their wild time. He looped his arm back around Nate's neck and pulled him around for a kiss. Gentler now, spent, but powerful in different ways. They'd always been their most vulnerable in these moments after the passion was sated. That was when they'd made quiet, nighttime promises.

Those promises never quite made it to the light of day.

Before Kyle could travel too far down that dark road, Nate swept damp hair back from his temple. "But now the party's over."

He stood and withdrew, quickly ditching the condom in a covered trash can. At least he had that much consideration for Kyle's life. He zipped up, ran fingers through his hair once again, and grinned. "Nice one, boss. Worth writing home about." His lips curled into a sneer. "Oh, wait. I forgot that's not your thing."

Kyle pushed off the table, making some attempt to neaten his appearance. "You had to fuck up something good, didn't you? Christ, Nate. Some things never change."

Nate flipped him off, then blew a kiss before turning toward the door.

A sharp, impatient knock stopped them both cold.

"Kyle?" came Steph's voice. "Hey, you in here?"

Without so much as a blink, Nate didn't hesitate when he opened the door. "Miss Penn. Great to see you again." He glanced back toward Kyle. "We were finishing up. Have a good time sorting this one out, boss."

With Nate gone, Kyle thought he might be able to exhale. No such luck. Steph's expression was dark and angry, so at odds with her usually sunny personality.

She eyed him from head to toe. Kyle knew exactly what she'd see: a guy who'd been fucked well.

"Tell me that wasn't him," she said. "*The* him. And tell me you didn't know it was him from the start. Because those are the sorts of things a trusted friend and partner would be able to tell me."

"I couldn't. I *can't.*"

Graceful steps were made rigid as she met him face-to-face. "For years I've encouraged you to find guys to hook up with. So yay. I'm glad you got your rocks off. Finally." Her blue eyes narrowed. "But you pick *now*? With the head of a stunt crew everyone already thinks is risky? Don't ruin this for both of us, Kyle. We've worked too hard."

The tightness in his chest had eased briefly in those gasping, laughing moments after his spectacular finish with Nate. It was back now, sharp and clawing.

No one has it all.

"It's done, Steph." His voice was rough, laced with that same tightness. "It's been done for nine years."

"Doesn't look it."

He straightened his tie and smoothed a hand over his hair. "Believe me. This was just the proof I needed."

Chapter Four

During his negotiations with Stephanie Penn, Nate hadn't lied when claiming that his team was the best. He commanded a decent rate for Second Chances based on a track record of impeccable safety and prompt, precise results. He gave the cinematographer and directors what they wanted.

Nate managed it because no tiny detail escaped him. He pored over the plans for weeks. Choosing his people was always the easy part, but every variable coursed through his mind, over and over.

All of it mattered once he was over a hundred feet up, clinging to the side of a mirrored office building with only a single rope between him and the crowded street below.

The adrenaline in his veins became so intense that he tasted bitter copper at the back of his mouth. Way, way below him was the Canary Wharf business district. To one side, Lena Portman and Christiano Rosario were suspended as well. Ethan Raney, his best friend and right hand in managing Second Chances, flanked his left side. Since Nate's first day in prison, he'd depended on Raney. Turned out being first-timers who refused any gang affiliation made for some tight relationships based on pure survival.

Head-on, the man looked nothing like Robert Durant, the film's star, but Raney had the same slim, tall body type. The film editors would be the ones responsible for cutting in close-up shots and making the impossible seem real. That was Hollywood.

Wind scraped across Nate's skin, despite his protective black jumpsuit. The rhythmic *thump-thump-thump* of a helicopter reminded him of the film crew following his every move. Though the actual actors had been given the morning off, everyone else watched his team. *His* team. They focused on Second Chances, depending on Nate to get it right.

The stunt meant working in tandem. Nate and Christiano bounded off the glass windows of the office building. Lena and Raney mimicked their moves, propelling out a good fifteen feet while dropping another twenty in leaping arcs. That was the easy part.

Then they crossed paths.

Lena and Raney bounded up, while Nate and Christiano slid sideways. Crossed back again. They were aerial ballet dancers instead of an ex-car thief, a convicted bank robber, a former prostitute with a conviction for rolling a rich businessman's kid, and Raney, a finance wizard who'd defrauded a hedge fund out of a cool million.

Except, after the second crisscross, he and Christiano lagged ten seconds behind the other pair. Three more attempts—starting from the top each time—didn't result in the exact timing Nate had hoped to achieve. The stunt director called it fantastic, but secretly Nate wondered if he'd said it just because the helicopter's time was up.

Nate hated stunts that didn't go according to the plan he saw so clearly in his mind. He clenched his back teeth together, even after everyone was safe on the ground with the gear packed away. A stunt that was off by a fraction could end in injury or death for someone who depended on him. Slightly less dire was a failed stunt's effect on the reputation of his company, but it was still a consideration he couldn't ignore.

When Stephanie Penn had first contacted Second Chances, he'd known it was a spot of luck—and a track record for psychotically crazy achievements. Maybe it wasn't that simple, or flattering. Maybe too much of his luck had actually been Kyle's maneuverings.

Nate was going to figure out why.

At the back of one of Second Chances' vans, he checked a full-body harness by touch, making sure there were no nicks, tears, or weak spots. The sliding sound of a shoe over concrete was his only hint, yet he knew who would be standing there.

Kyle.

The man sported another expensive suit, this one dark blue. He wore no tie—probably his version of movie-set laid-back cool—but the rounded points of his collar were a style Nate wouldn't have ever thought of. Only Kyle could pull it off and look that damn mouthwatering.

And that damn straight.

Kyle flicked the suit coat back and tucked his hands in his pockets. That wide chest bowed an inch. "Well done up there."

Returning to his task, Nate chuffed a harsh breath. "You don't have to bullshit me."

"I'm not."

"Our timing was off."

Kyle moved close enough that Nate could smell cologne, something rich and expensive. That quickly, in Nate's head, they were sprawled over the pool table again. His hands were filled with Kyle's wide chest. His cock was surrounded by the tight suck of that perfect, willing ass.

The way Kyle had flinched at the sound of Stephanie's voice had been like a splash of ice water.

A one-time event was fine with Nate.

As Kyle soft-pedaled compliments in that smooth producer way, memories blunted some of the rough edges. Nate had fucked Kyle, had wrapped his mouth around that tasty prick. Nothing else had the same bite of satisfaction, not even rappelling down the side of a skyscraper.

That only reminded him of the day's disappointment.

He shook his head, his teeth grinding. Even the feel-good endorphins left over from their pool-table fuck couldn't take the edge off almost a decade of bad emotions. "C'mon. I know it's your thing, that producers make sure everyone's happy. We have more history than that. I can take the truth and you know it."

That had been their thing, or at least part of it. At the prestigious boarding school they'd attended, with Nate on a charity scholarship, most of the students had been incredibly two-faced. Some feared him. Some were just snobs. Not Kyle. He and Nate hooked up after Kyle had told him during English comp that his rap was a sad approximation of poetry, and that while some rappers could be street poets, Nate was certainly not one of them.

The strange thing was he'd been right. Nate's calling certainly wasn't poetry—or rap. Kyle had been truthful from the start. That made how he'd hidden behind Stephanie while negotiating the contract for Second Chances more disappointing.

Not to mention how determined he was to stay in the closet.

Kyle leaned against the open back door of the van, seemingly unconscious of his expensive suit. The tendon along his neck, beneath his ear, was drawn tight. Kyle was nowhere near as chill as he wanted to present himself. "I'm not lying. At all. The stunt looked great on the monitors. I'm not promising parts of it won't have to be reshot from a different vantage, but it looked good to me."

Nate stood, tossed down a harness, and leaned next to Kyle. Their hips pressed side by side, with their shoulders inches apart—almost as if they were friends more than has-beens.

Once upon a time, Nate had believed in the unit they'd become, even after he'd fucked it all up. Even after he'd withstood threats from Kyle's parents. He'd believed Kyle would still be there for him. Until that day Kyle had traveled down from New Haven to visit Nate in prison. Kyle's expression had made it more than clear how much he resented having to enter such a shitty place and that he had better places to be. It hadn't been the first time Nate stole a car. It *had* been the first time he'd been caught with both a car that wasn't his and cocaine that most certainly was.

So what the hell was going on now? Kyle still had better places to be. Nate had no intention of giving him another chance to go slumming.

He forcefully loosened his tight jaw. "Looking good on the dailies isn't the only thing that matters. Any errors, being off by three seconds . . . It's a matter of life and death when you're that far up." Hell, his hands were still shaking as the last dregs of adrenaline eased out of his blood. He'd chalk up his relative niceness to Kyle to the sweet feeling of still being alive.

The sun set so early in London during the winter, which added extra pressure to short filming days. Already, twilight surrounded them. Shadows darkened Kyle's warm-brown hair.

"But you got everyone down without any injuries, and Upton got an amazing shot. The whole crew is impressed. You can't beat yourself up for something that didn't happen."

"I want it done perfectly."

"The only one in charge of that attitude is you." Kyle smiled toward the side of a distant building. The van shielded them from most of the crew, who'd set up for evening shots of Robert Durant and his costar, Jessica Lorrie, walking into a Christmas-light-bedecked office. There, the couple was supposed to be attacked by the bad guy.

To Nate, it was the boring part of movie production. The real meat of production would follow the next day when his crew would work on the hand-to-hand stunts, where Nate doubled for the villain. Raney would again stand in for Robert, and former meth head Sandra Nixon would step in as the imperiled heroine.

That was tomorrow. At that moment, he and Kyle had a relatively quiet shelter to themselves.

"The only thing I can tell you," Kyle continued, "is that this business will chew you up and spit you out if you don't believe in yourself."

Nate couldn't help a little grin. "Oh, don't worry about me. I know I'm the shit."

Kyle's smile bloomed in response. "Is that right?"

"Yup. I had you last night, didn't I?"

The shudder that worked its way down Kyle's spine was exactly what Nate had been looking for. *Digging* for. The rest of it could fade away. He needed that hot jolt of power.

Kyle's eyes went heavy lidded. His tongue slicked across his bottom lip. "Look, Nate." He drew the name into a pleading whisper. "Last night was . . ."

"It was damn good." Nate shrugged, managed to look away. Pedestrians streamed by on the sidewalk, but no one they knew. Office workers and chavs in tracksuits and a few tourists with backpacks and maps, all on the go as night fell. "Or it was fucking amazing. Maybe that's the phrase you're looking for."

"Yeah. That's the one."

The maybes were a painful disease. Every thought was one Nate second-guessed—something he'd been doing for nine years.

The physical though . . .

He lifted his hand. The skin across the back of Kyle's neck was surprisingly soft in a way that blunted the edges of Nate's annoyance.

The ends of Kyle's hair brushed his knuckles. "That's one place where we never had any problems. The sex."

Kyle's grin turned a little wistful. "That's for sure."

Nate kissed him, their lips sliding together. Kyle tasted like sweet coffee and fruit. For a minute he kissed back too. There was no denying the way his lips clung to Nate's, the way his tongue twined and soothed, the way his elegant fingers cupped Nate's jaw. One thumb dug into the underside of Nate's chin—a little spike of hurt to counter the nice.

Then the hiss of brakes squealed from somewhere behind the van. Kyle flinched. His mouth froze, and his neck turned to bone beneath Nate's touch.

Nate should have let him go, stopped kissing him. He should have allowed things to just . . . *be*. He couldn't. Kyle had the same damn hang-ups as always. He was a man comfortable about everything in the world except for his *real* place in it. Nate pointed the blame at Kyle's asshole parents.

Instead of pushing away an intimate, unexpected moment, Nate tucked his free hand in Kyle's expensive collar. He yanked them both up from the edge of the van, into a standing position. He kept his mouth on Kyle's. Kept kissing. Kept *taking*.

If this was all he was going to get from his lover, so be it. He'd make sure it was fantastic for him, at least. Nate would take what he wanted. Right now, he wanted Kyle's mouth.

What he hadn't expected was how Kyle melted under the onslaught. His spine curved. He eased against the door of the van. Even as his hands pushed under the hem of Nate's tight black T-shirt, Kyle was still hiding.

Nate pushed him away. Instead of teaching Kyle a lesson, he was only hurting himself. The spike of pain in his chest was undeniable. He'd thought he was beyond his old self-destructive behavior.

Considering the way he couldn't seem to keep clear of Kyle, maybe not. Nine years ago he'd thrown everything away and still managed to make a noble choice. He could have taken Kyle's parents up on their offer and gotten off with probation, but he hadn't. Instead, he'd refused to promise to stay away from Kyle—only to earn his lover's disgust and disappointment.

Principles hadn't gotten him much, only three years in prison and nine years alone.

This wasn't some magic do-over. This was an ambitious producer from old Virginia money who was using Nate for his own ends. Part of him, the less cynical part, hoped those ends actually meant believing that Nate could do the job he was hired to do. Then again, this was Hollywood on vacation in London. In Tinseltown, everyone was a shark in training.

Nate slammed the van door shut, doing his damnedest not to look at Kyle. He didn't need the other man's snotty arrogance, not when he was barely holding on to his temper.

Kyle straightened his impeccable button-down shirt, simply oozing privilege. "Don't give me your attitude. That can't happen here—not again. We're on the street."

"We are." Nate sneered. "So proud of you to notice. Do you also happen to see there's no one here we know? They're all strangers and people who shouldn't matter for shit. I'm no one's dirty secret, Kyle. I got over settling a decade ago."

"I don't want you to be my dirty secret."

"No? Sure seems like it. Private pool-table fucks? Check. Ducking around the issue with your business partner? Check. Kissing, nope."

"No." Kyle's glittering brown eyes narrowed, and his chin lifted with hauteur. "I meant I don't want you at all."

Damn, that one hurt. Bad. Like the time a missed landing onto a garage roof had broken his femur. Pain settled in his churning stomach, but he couldn't let a scrap of it show. He didn't.

Prison had been useful in that regard.

He turned to Kyle with an expression of fake astonishment. "You know, I'm surprised you can walk today. Must've taken some effort to hide how your ass must burn. Well done."

He climbed into the van as if his limbs weren't made of silly putty, and he drove away.

In his rearview mirror, he saw Kyle standing there, but he wasn't watching Nate leave. His head was bowed, his gaze riveted to the shiny tips of his shoes. Alone.

Good. It wasn't much karma, but Nate would take it. Kyle could stand there all night and still wouldn't come close to knowing what it was to be truly alone.

Chapter Five

From where he stood on the director's raised platform, Kyle lifted a pair of binoculars and looked far down the southern bend of the Thames. Dusk was settling. Various barges and boats were in perfect position. Some were staged, but most were the real deal—the advantage of filming on location. Strings of lights along the Embankment reflected in the calm waters of the Thames. They wouldn't be calm for long.

Across the river, the London Eye was bright with flashing holiday sparkle and the illumination of each slow-moving pod of people. The lighting meant the tourists would get quite a show, but they wouldn't end up in the picture. Rescue divers in black wetsuits were already in the water. Ambulances waited to whisk any injured to the nearest Accident & Emergency. Discreet police partitions made sure the banks and bridges were clear of any unsuspecting civilians.

Their filming permit meant they had only enough time for one take. Then the traffic would flow, real people would take the place of extras, and the day's shooting would end, whether or not they had the footage in the can.

Kyle saw the machinations of moviemaking. There was no mystery left. All he needed was on time and under budget.

In need of something genuine, he panned far to the left where a carousel spun families in colorful circles. Kyle had taken a long walk two nights before, trying to clear his head, and had watched that carousel spin and spin. Almost meditative, for an entire hour. On every horse was painted a different name—the single thing on his midnight walk that had made him smile.

Beside him, Stephanie pressed her smartphone to her ear, fielding some manner of crisis between Jessica Lorrie and a hairdresser who'd scorched the actress's trademark platinum hair. He was impressed that his occasionally sharp-tongued partner didn't remind the caller that said platinum hair was a weave.

Cameras, cables, and the accoutrements of movie magic took up most of the room, but this sequence was crucial to their filming timetable. Despite needing to share the space with Peter Upton, and despite a thousand other fires to put out, Kyle and Stephanie had wanted to be there. Hiring Second Chances would again be proved a wise decision, or he'd need to return to the big question of the week.

Had he done it only to see Nate again?

"Quiet, everybody!" called Upton's assistant.

"You heard him," Upton shouted. "The light's perfect and we have one shot. Bring your A game, people!"

Stephanie gritted out a quick goodbye before silencing her smartphone and tucking it into her goose-down jacket. The winter wind off the Thames was damn cold. "He's right," she said under her breath. "One shot. Your boy up to it?"

Kyle glared. "He's not my boy, Steph. Can it."

She shrugged.

Her silent doubts fed his. Kyle didn't like doubts. Certainty was pretty easy to take for granted with his background. Money and privilege and expectation of greatness. Anything that didn't go his way felt like a personal insult, rather than some natural way of things. If he worked harder, pressed the right people, he could bend the world to his liking.

Only, he knew that was a ball of fresh horseshit. Otherwise he'd have woken up that morning with Nate in his arms. Or, more painful to think about, he would've spent the last nine years with him.

Kyle pushed Steph's blonde hair aside and leaned close. "Yes, he's *the* guy. The one from high school. That night in the pub surprised all of us, but don't doubt him. He's the best."

With an unmistakably sharp tone of voice, she whispered right back, "Then no wonder you can't keep your eyes off him. You've never settled for anything less."

Feeling almost defensive, Kyle fidgeted with the strap of his wristwatch. The multimillionaire stars of *Fast Money* would understand the money he'd spent on the classic timepiece, but most people would've been appalled—Nate being one of them. Yet Steph was right. He enjoyed the best of the best in every venture. Too bad life made no guarantees.

After the scene's mark was called, Upton shouted, "Action!"

In the old days that would've involved a bullhorn. Instead, it meant an elaborate system of headsets and coordinated computers, from the production crew and soundmen, to lighting and each of a dozen cameramen who'd capture the stunt from all across the set. They were in London. A real city. But for a few moments it was simply a movie set.

Kyle adjusted his headset and tried to relax.

Not happening.

At the distant whine of engines picking up speed, he returned his attention to the southerly bend of the river. He lifted the binoculars and spotted a trio of speedboats. They were little more than specks. The lead boat was filled with their intrepid stunt camera crew. The two that followed in triangular formation contained the Second Chances crew.

Kyle only had eyes for one. He knew what the sequence required, and his gut was tight with an emotion he enjoyed less than doubt.

Fear.

Nathan Carnes always had that effect on him. Fear they'd be found out. Fear they'd blow up again. Fear they'd fizzle and walk away.

Now that fear looked something like Nate smashing his blockheaded skull into one of the columns supporting the Westminster Bridge.

The throaty roar of the boats became a rumble under Kyle's skin. Sweat rimmed his eye sockets where the binoculars' rubber pads pressed flush. Soon he didn't need them at all. Those souped-up speedboats were the real deal, fast and dangerous. They hopped over the water with the arrogance of a fighter taking to the ring. The Thames' calm waters became choppy slosh.

Individual silhouettes became clearer. Kyle's chest pinched. The plan was so simple on paper. To see it played out was something else. Nate was dressed in black, and from that distance he really did resemble the Englishman cast as the film's villain. Trading punches, Nate and Ethan Raney fought on the bow of the blazing fast craft. On the boat at its side, a female driver from Second Chances steered close. Closer. The hulls scraped together.

Nate lost his balance.

Kyle's stomach plummeted, though it was all part of the plan. Everyone in the sequence was harnessed nine ways from Sunday, but damn did they make the danger real.

The boats parted to speed around a pylon supporting the Charing Cross Bridge, where even the southbound train was timed perfectly in frame. Gorgeous. The drivers angled their boats back together, harder this time. Kyle heard the sick crunch of fiberglass over the roar of the engines. They were within a quarter mile now.

So close to where it could all go wrong.

Strong and agile, Nate had artfully regained his balance. From this distance it looked like Nate was beating up Robert Durant, the film's star, instead of a fellow stuntman. A few more punches. A few more bursts from a prop machine gun, though sound engineers and foley artists would amp up those details in postproduction. Waves crested with frothy white shot out behind the dueling machines.

"This is it," Stephanie whispered at Kyle's side.

Nate leaped from one boat to the other. For a heartbeat he seemed suspended in midair. The black jumpsuit that covered the body Kyle knew so well was perfectly framed against the Eye's glaring sheen of color.

Then that heartbeat was over. Nate landed on the second boat with a crushing thud, grappling for purchase on the slippery bow. He found it.

All according to plan.

The words became a mantra in Kyle's head, as sweat popped out along his brow. Nate was the best. He wouldn't do anything stupid to screw this up. He was too stubborn.

So when the boats rammed together one last time before exploding into flame . . .

Kyle had to trust.

The cameras still rolled. Burning, shattered remains of hot metal showered the river only a few hundred feet short of Westminster Bridge. Check-ins began to pour through the headsets. Every separate team, all with their own responsibilities, reported success after success.

The rescue divers and the ambulances sounded off, although they'd been unnecessary.

A flawless take.

"Stunt crew accounted for," came the voice of the coordinator. "All hale and hearty."

Taking his first breath in what felt like minutes, Kyle removed his headset and sat heavily onto a folding chair. He steepled his hands, still watching the wreckage burn. Nate was out there in the water somewhere, but he was all right.

Damn. This was getting serious.

"And cut! We got it!" Upton swiveled on his elevated camera pedestal and smirked down at Kyle. "I think you were right about them, Wakefield. Not bad for a bunch of cons and faggots."

Stephanie was there in a flash—but almost without moving. All she did was place a hand on Kyle's shoulder. Granted, the hand felt like an eagle's talons as her red nails dug into his trench coat. "We're glad you're satisfied with our call on this one, Peter," she said smoothly. "But really? Insulting LGBTQ in Hollywood would be like calling every male dancer on Broadway a fairy."

"I wouldn't be far off, would I?"

That smirk made Kyle want to do violence. Burning wreckage and nauseating fear and a gut-deep hatred of bigots made a man think primal things.

Steph's smile was sly. "All I'm saying is that they pulled off a million-dollar stunt that was four months in the planning. Don't think your prick's big enough to start name-calling."

If Upton kept fostering a "Bite me, SJW" attitude, he was going to kill his burgeoning career. Kyle would enjoy every burning, flaming moment. Not the whole industry was like Upton, but enough were that it kept Kyle on edge, assured that he was making the right choice in keeping his life private. Some of America wanted to believe homophobia was gone—then they'd elected a radioactive Cheeto with the morals of an alley cat.

"They're being paid. Well. Doesn't change who they are or where they come from." Upton tipped his baseball cap, which was oh-so-tastefully embroidered with his name in white on red. "While I'm sitting in this chair, I'll say what I like."

"Damn, you're a charmer." Steph batted her sultry lashes—a latter-day Lauren Bacall.

"Have a drink with me and I'll show you how charming I am."

"Nearly too irresistible to pass up. But here I am, passing it up." She waved a little toodle-oo. "Night, Peter. Nice work, everyone."

With that, she hauled Kyle out of the folding chair and hustled him off the platform. Back on solid ground. It didn't feel solid. It felt like he was sinking.

His partner, however, didn't seem ready to let him suffocate. "Breathe. Chill. And get that 'I wanna smack the shit out of you' look off your face."

Kyle only grunted. He was incapable of much else. His brain was made of Play-Doh.

She looped her arm through his and gave him a shove with her shoulder. "Can you deal yet?"

"Hmm?"

"Because it's my turn to give you a ration of shit."

He smiled tightly and found his voice. She was their PR lead for a reason, but that didn't mean she was an angel. "So," he said. "Will the ice-queen silent treatment be over soon?"

"Forget trying to charm me, buttwipe. I'm not surprised Nate's team did their job. My problem is with *you*." They stopped beneath a spray of lights in trees that lined the Embankment. "Don't ever try to hide anything like Nate from me again. I've always trusted your business sense and your cold-ass logic. I don't want to start doubting that. We've invested way too much to risk, okay?"

Nodding, he exhaled heavily and watched the plume of frosty breath slip away on an evening breeze. "Okay." He lifted his eyes to meet hers. "Forgive me?"

"Sure." She was still mad though. Unlike most women in Hollywood, she hadn't succumbed to the temptation of Botox. Knowing her adoration for all things vintage, Kyle thought she never would. That only meant her frown was even easier to interpret. "On one condition."

"That sounds ominous."

"You're right to be nervous," she said.

"Fine, I'll bite. What condition?"

She nodded toward where firefighters on river ferries put out the last of the fires. "Go out tonight. With him. If you keep thinking he's some shining star from your past, your concentration will keep being for shit. I saw how distracted you were today. Focused on him, not on the whole picture."

"Steph . . ."

"Do you want to?" Shadowed eyes watched him carefully. "If the whole world fell away and it was just you and what you wanted, would you?"

"Yes."

The answer was so automatic that his neck jerked.

Steph stood on tiptoe and kissed him on the cheek. "There ya go. See you tomorrow."

Kyle headed toward the staging area where the stunt team gathered and where Nate habitually parked his van. Some burly guys, some pretty chicks, some too ordinary to warrant stereotyping, the cons of Second Chances congratulated themselves on a job well done. Even as the medics looked them over, they were packing up gear. They moved with an aura of Christmas-happy sparkle, all from having kicked serious ass.

Transfixed, at a slight distance, Kyle watched Nate go through similar motions. He checked his equipment, accepted and offered grinned words of praise, and put up with a medic's once-over. The lawyers would have Kyle's head if the insurance company didn't get a full medical report after a shoot like that.

Nate looked . . . happy. Relaxed and at peace in his skin. He didn't need the world to fall away—the hypothesis Steph had offered Kyle. No, Nate made his own world. Owned it. Shaped it. Brought it to heel.

Kyle admitted what he'd been holding back for months, for years. Three years, actually, when he'd read an article in *Variety* about Second Chances and seen a picture of Nate. Waiting for the right opportunity had taken time, but Kyle had been patient.

He'd pushed to hire Second Chances because of Nate. That was the truth.

Standing there, however, he felt only shame at his realization. Nate deserved better than having been handed a break because of an old fuck buddy on a nostalgia trip. He was better, so much better than that.

Decision made, Kyle strode down the paved pathway as the last of Nate's crew dispersed. Back to the hotel. Back to the pub. Kyle only wanted them gone.

Like déjà vu, Nate was sitting at the back of his van, again with some manner of harness in hand. This time, his hair was soaking wet, spiked at odd angles around his face. He'd shed his costume and rigging and pulled the top half of his fire-resistant wetsuit down to his waist.

Bare chest.

Kyle's mind fizzed. The smallest flickers of words made sense. Muscle. Ink. Hair.

Flesh.

Strong, beautiful male flesh.

He swallowed. "Hey."

Looking up, Nate pinned him with his icy-blue gaze. "Here for round two?"

"No. It's going to go differently this time."

The surprise on Nate's face matched the leap behind Kyle's sternum. He'd only meant that moment. There. At the van.

It came out sounding a lot more *epic*.

After smoothing his expression, Nate tossed a balled-up shirt into the back of the van. "Aw, what the hell. Go for it."

"That was . . . perfect."

Suspicion was a hard thing to witness in response to a genuine compliment, but it twisted Nate's brow. "Thanks," he said cautiously.

In the gathering darkness, Kyle knew they were alone. So he stopped thinking. He didn't give a shit beyond the hammering of his heart and the need in his gut. His need for this man.

He bent at the waist, took Nate's face in his hands, and kissed him. It wasn't a friendly kiss, and it wasn't as rough as their usual. He hoped Nate would read it as Kyle intended.

As an invitation.

"Nathan Carnes, will you go dancing with me tonight?"

Chapter Six

Hotel rooms were not exactly made for brooding introspection. Nate's pacing was hampered by the small size. The view from the window was a narrow street. Across it was the dark-walled pub that had been rented out as the movie's base of operations. The skinny windows on the second floor were the ones Nate had looked out while he'd bent Kyle over the pool table.

Round and round he went.

He had a theory that the gravity certain people possessed was able to suck people in. It wasn't controlled by factors anyone could help or explain, just something that grabbed at bones and hearts and dragged them into orbit. He'd thought himself free of Kyle's orbit years ago.

Maybe he was wrong.

When Kyle had kissed him, hands framing Nate's face, then asked him out . . . Resisting hadn't been possible. He'd agreed to a nine-o'clock date with Kyle Wakefield.

Snagging dinner with Raney and the rest of his crew had blown by like a hazy dream. He'd simply shoved world-renowned fish and chips down his gullet while he remembered the specific sleekness of Kyle's lips and the no-holds-barred power suit he'd worn under a trench coat. A trench coat, for fuck's sake. Who wore those except men with Kyle's confidence and means?

Men Nate got a hard-on for.

Kyle had looked like a man who owned the world. Hell if that hadn't been half the problem way back when, but now it rushed cold water under Nate's skin.

This night could go so many ways. Kyle had invited Nate out, but he hadn't been particular about where they were going. Dancing. That could mean anything.

More curious, *who* would Nate be going out with? The pent-up, buttoned-down version of Kyle he was in public? Or the version who'd managed to kiss him on the street, who'd fucked him in front of the open windows of the pub?

He stood by the door for way longer than he'd admit to anyone. Impatiently, he tapped his booted toes across the faded carpet and the fat, blooming roses patterned in it. But he waited. He'd let Kyle fidget for a while—make him wonder if Nate would show.

At seven minutes past the hour, Nate headed for the lobby and out onto the street. Kyle stood a few yards away, leaning against a lamppost.

Which version of Kyle? Nate got his answer in one fell swoop. He was drawn nearer, needing to see every detail up close.

Kyle looked . . . not himself. A dark-brown leather jacket concealed most of the skin-tight T-shirt he'd paired with dark jeans. The shirt was dark purple, and the V-neck displayed skin—lots of skin, including the inside curves of his pecs and a sprinkling of hair.

All of that would've been hot enough—seeing Kyle out of a suit and ready to have a good time was a relief.

But Jesus Christ, the man was wearing a collar. Not leather. Not metal. No, it was a collar made of eight stacked rows of tiny rhinestones. At least Nate hoped they were rhinestones. He hadn't thought Kyle able to imagine such a creation, let alone wear it. In public. Subtly sparkling under the streetlight, and mostly hidden by the jacket, it outlined Kyle's thickly muscled neck like a lover's grip.

The suggestion of sin.

Nate swallowed down the surge of lust that threatened to flip him inside out. "I guess we're going all out."

The other man knew haughty—he *breathed* haughty. His chin lifted and his mouth tilted up on a smile that dripped arrogance. "There's no point in doing something if you're not going to go all out."

Nate wanted to kiss that certainty off his face. "I'm not really surprised by that, coming from the guy who went to Yale."

Kyle zipped up the lined leather jacket. "My point exactly."

The first week of December in London was freezing compared to Southern California, where it had been in the seventies before Nate had left. Nate huddled into his own wool coat. Cold air burned down his lungs and sent shivers over his skin. "Are we taking a taxi or the subway?"

"You mean cab or the Tube." Kyle nudged him toward the street corner, and they started walking.

"Pick one."

"Cab. There's this club in Soho I heard about. It's only about ten minutes away. You'll never guess who's playing."

Nate didn't like second-guessing everything or everyone, but he couldn't help but wonder if part of the reason for a club away from the hotel was privacy. It was another example of down-low behavior that would keep him Kyle's dirty secret, while appeasing their desires at the same time.

"No clue," Nate said, wondering if he really cared.

"Vertigo Dreams."

Okay, that was worth a trip to the outside of hell, let alone a ten-minute cab ride.

Memories flooded his mind—a complete whitewash of long-buried emotion. He'd spent hours wrapped up with Kyle in his dorm room, with their most prevalent soundtrack a dance-tinged indie band. Very glam. Very gay. Good music to fuck to, that was for damn sure. It had also been good music to learn what it was to be part of a community. As uncertain as any other sixteen-year-old, Nate had enjoyed the reassurance that others in the world shared his wants and needs and ideas about love.

He'd shared all of that with Kyle, or at least he'd thought he had. Nate had fucked that up too royally for Kyle to ever forgive.

The ride to Soho was awkward. They sat side by side, occasionally brushing against one another as the black cab turned corners. As kids on a boarding-school campus, they'd never been able to see Vertigo Dreams in person. Now they were fulfilling a youthful wish, and Nate couldn't remember feeling more out of place in his own body.

Once, they would've filled the little silences with ease. Now those unspoken minutes were folded into a blank decade. Nate shifted on the padded seat. He watched the Christmas lights and bright storefronts slide past—in between watching the man sitting next to him. Kyle used to tell long, grand stories that always ended in a brilliant if snarky punch line. Nate missed them. And he wanted to talk about how difficult it had been to found Second Chances, how he'd been so worried the entire venture would fail. That he *still* worried in the face of growing usage of CGI.

Sure as hell, neither of them would unbutton about the end of their relationship or Nate's time in prison. He wasn't going to be the one to bring that up. The failure itself was bad enough. He didn't like remembering how he'd kept Kyle's pictures, even after it had all fallen to shit.

The thrill of having seen Kyle wearing that sexy, unexpected rhinestone collar had worn off. Ten minutes in a cab thinking old, bad things was enough to rub the shine off anything. He'd never been so happy for a drive to end.

"Here we are," Kyle said, voice neutral.

Unreadable. As always.

All grown up now, they were well-matched in that.

Called Ginger Beer of all things, the club was down a half level from the street. The music poured out, tinny and warped through the walls. A line curled up the stairs and halfway down the block, but Nate wasn't surprised when Kyle cruised right by everyone else. He shook hands with the bouncer and whispered in the man's ear. Then they were in, that fast. Nate certainly wasn't going to object. Why have connections if you weren't going to use them?

Tiny but packed. The first impression Nate had of the club was bodies. Lots of them, close together. Sweat and cologne mixed with the bite of alcohol. The lights were low, but flashing spotlights bounced off the crowd, catching hold of Kyle's sparkling collar as he shrugged out of his jacket. Nate handed his to a white-blond twink hovering at their elbows.

Kyle leaned in close. "He'll check them. This place doesn't do reserved tables, so the best I could get us was a little extra attention."

"The best, huh?" Nate shook his head. "Do you even hear yourself sometimes?"

Kyle lifted his eyebrows. "I'm about to tell him to get us two drinks and keep them coming. You going to complain?"

Perks were perks, and money got what it paid for. Nate laughed. "Not at all. When's the band playing?"

"About a half hour," Kyle said. "In the meantime, we have drinking and brain-melting music."

"Bring it."

They staked out a spot near the front of the club, where a small stage was stacked with drums, guitars, and a couple of microphone stands. Three dozen strands of Christmas lights looped down from the ceiling. 'Tis the season for hardcore dancing? Nate liked that. A lot. The entire place pumped with heavy bass that threatened to turn his body into one raunchy hard-on. Especially with Kyle nearby.

After the cute little waiter brought two whiskey gingers, Nate and Kyle edged toward a tall table with no chairs. Kyle made eye contact with another pair of men standing on the other side—all as easy as can be, as if he did this sort of shit all the time. While Nate went out regularly, he doubted whether Kyle sought the same sort of relaxed camaraderie.

They introduced themselves, first names only. The slender brunet was Tim, but the name of his burlier companion escaped Nate completely.

Didn't matter. This place was all hot bodies and pumping music. They tossed back their drinks too quickly. Kyle put his hand on Nate's waist. Not expecting it—not at all—Nate jumped. But he lived for it too. His entire body leaned toward the man who'd once been his friend.

He'd been so much more than a friend.

Kyle nuzzled below Nate's ear. Hot breath sent a shiver down his neck.

"Hear this song?" Kyle asked.

"Of course."

They'd had sex for the first time to this song. Nate's hands had trembled. Kyle had acted as if he knew what he was doing. They both had. In truth they'd been a massive knot of nerves and fear, but turned on enough to make it happen. There'd been no going back after that.

Not that Nate had ever wanted to. Despite the way things had worked out, he'd never regretted their relationship—only that it had remained so hidden. At the time, he'd understood despite his frustration. No one else in their expensive boarding school had come out, and there hadn't been any "It Gets Better" campaigns. He and Kyle had been on their own, but together.

Maybe that's all this was, a run down memory lane at full speed. The contract for Second Chances meant a month in London to finish primary shooting for *Fast Money*. He'd indulge, and then he could put a cap on that part of his life. It had flamed out so quickly and painfully, obscuring the good stuff that went before.

This could be their chance to unearth those lost memories.

"Come dance with me."

No request. The words were infused with every bit of Kyle's arrogant expectancy. He knew Nate would dance with him. His mouth curved into a smile that bordered on smug.

Of course Nate would. The biggest hurdle had been agreeing to go dancing in the first place. No way could he refuse when Kyle stood in front of him with that dark-purple shirt skimming over taut lats and a thick chest. Those pecs—those were all for Nate, at least for tonight.

Nate followed the man out to the small dance floor. The shirt was tight enough to show off the way Kyle's wide shoulders arrowed down to the bold line of his lower back. Nate put his hand there. Couldn't help it.

He needed touch. Something to anchor himself in the moment and make himself believe it. He really was going to dance with his ex. His most incredible ex. This *was* happening.

They started grinding to the song that had once linked them, indelibly—like a scar, but so much sweeter. Everything was sweat and heavy breathing. Moving. Dancing became living flashbacks.

Nate wrapped his hand around the back of Kyle's strong, surprisingly graceful neck. The way Kyle moved was magical. Always had been. The sway of his hips wove spells around Nate's entire being, until they surged together, apart, and always returned. Nate drove his thigh between both of Kyle's, feeling hardness. Heady thrusting. Over and again, as if they'd already wound up in bed instead of grinding together in an underground club in Soho.

It went to Nate's head—along with two more rounds of rail whiskey and ginger ale. The songs melted into one long dance. So much touch was more than Nate could handle.

Except, God, it was good to see Kyle let go. He had never been very good at it, always watching who was watching him. Sure, there was the fear of being caught, but Kyle desperately wanted people to like him. He had a thing for that, developing his charm to an almost compulsive level. That meant locking down any part of his personality that didn't fit with what people expected.

Now, with Nate, *for* Nate, he was a living god. His hips luxuriated in every measure of music. Christ, his chest was practically begging to come out from behind that sexy-ass shirt. Gleaming muscles and smooth, hot skin. Smiles. Laughter. And moans that shook past the bass and into the skin along Nate's damp throat.

When the band was about to take the stage, Nate led them back toward the tiny table. Tim was still there with his companion, and he had a waiter by the elbow. The smaller man's grin spread wide. Drunk. Very, very drunk. "Heya, boys. Want a drink?"

Kyle shrugged. "Why not. We're living it up tonight."

Tim waved his hands in the air. "Fabulous, that's the *only* way to be."

Except when the waiter came back, he held a tray of Jell-O shots—eight of them.

"Expecting anyone else?" Nate asked.

The big guy answered. His accent was also British but . . . mushier, with more rounded vowels and sloppy consonants. Nate didn't think it was all due to alcohol. "Nope. Just like to order double. Drinks get scarce as this place gets busier."

"It gets busier than this?"

Kyle laughed. "I wanna stick around till then."

"You should." Tim waggled carefully plucked brows. "Crazy stuff starts to happen." With little ceremony, Tim snatched one of the long, slender Jell-O shots off the tray and stuck it in the waistband of his jeans so the end stuck out. He crooked a finger at Nate. "Want a drink, tasty boy?"

"No thanks," Nate said past a grin.

The nameless guy put a hand on the table in between them. "I don't think so, mate. Mine."

Kyle narrowed his eyes. "Better get a leash on your boy, then. He's the one tossing out invitations."

Nate leaned in close to Kyle's ear. A tiny rivulet of sweat called to his tongue, so he licked. Slowly. "What about you, college boy?" he asked, reverting to his old nickname for Kyle. "You're the one wearing a collar. Will you wear my leash?"

"You're going to have to give me a little more warm-up than that."

Not denial. *Fuck, yes.*

That sparkling collar called to Nate's fingertips like the bead of sweat had been meant for his tongue. He slid his fingers beneath the rhinestones. Tugged lightly, then again. "Then sit your ass up on that table and spread your knees."

Chapter Seven

Kyle had wanted to let loose. That tight, pained place in his soul had *needed* it. Seeing Nate again . . . Remembering how free he'd once felt in the arms of the young man he'd loved . . .

Kyle was strangling on the precepts that kept his life ordered and successful.

Don't let it show.

Don't let anyone know.

And don't get caught.

That last one was imperative. He hadn't been a monk for the last decade, but that meant Grindr-fueled hookups in the recesses of various cities. A guy had to protect his sanity. He'd stayed safe, got off, went home. Not exactly a stable emotional basis for accepting his homosexuality. Too much of it was cloaked in shadow and shame.

There, however, in a thumping underground club in the heart of Soho, he could let it show, and everyone sure as hell knew he was queer.

As for getting caught, that rule didn't seem to apply when he looked passionately into Nate's eyes. The Christmas lights, disco balls, and strobes didn't dispel the power of his intent gaze.

"You heard me," Nate said, so quietly but so near to Kyle's mouth that the words registered as breath more than sound. "Do it."

Kyle did. He levered up and hitched his ass on the table, then spread his knees. Tim and his partner—was it Mick?—laughed and watched the show. Kyle. The opening act. The center of attention in a gay nightclub. His heart hammered with excitement and anticipation. Although he knew sexual release was a ways off, he felt a very different sort of release when he and Nate locked eyes.

Kyle was right where he'd always longed to be. Being with Nate made him honest and real. Maybe he wanted to be that kind of person more often.

With a knowing, naughty smile, Nate grabbed one of the Jell-O shots. "You know where this goes, don't you?"

"Yes."

"Then show me."

Hands steady despite his gut-clenching arousal, Kyle stripped his purple V-neck T-shirt—an impulse purchase, along with the collar, on a drunken, giddy night out with Steph when they'd first gotten to London. The distance from America, from Virginia in particular, had felt like freedom.

He leaned back on one elbow and hooked a thumb under the waistband of his jeans.

"It goes right here," he said.

The air thickened between them, all teasing gone.

Nate's expression was as intense as when he prepared for a big stunt sequence, all focus and calculation. His mouth was serious, but he never compressed his lips. They rested together with a unique, stern beauty, rimmed above and below with a shade of evening stubble. Blunt nose, rough-hewn cheekbones, and a brow twisted in concentration. But his eyes . . . They were large and soulful, searching for something Kyle couldn't name, couldn't understand.

Kyle expected derisive words. A smirk. Hell, he half expected Nate to walk out at any moment, if only to prove a point: that Kyle was gay, closeted, and a goddamn hypocrite.

Instead, Nate leaned forward and licked the notch at the juncture of Kyle's collarbones. "That's right, college boy. Can you handle it?"

"I'm here waiting."

That serious expression didn't abate. "You have no idea what it is to wait."

Cold skittered over Kyle's bare chest, despite the hot, grinding sweat of the club. That unease needed to go. He didn't have the stamina to contemplate dark roads. This was the time for raunchiness, for forgetting old pains and lingering doubts. He shoved Nate's wrist down his body.

From there, Nate took over. Good. Sometimes the man was a goddamn mule.

Nate slid the plastic shot glass down along Kyle's tensing stomach until it nestled between skin and denim. For a moment he seemed to savor his prize, eyeing Kyle from head to crotch. The attention made Kyle feel worshipped. Stripping half naked, wearing his outrageous collar—the decisions that had made his gut churn in the hotel room were so perfect right now.

Nate glanced at the two men avidly soaking up the show. "Watch and learn, boys."

With that, he slid his tongue and teeth down Kyle's chest, past his abs, until Nate's mouth hovered above the shot glass. Nate dug his blunt fingertips into Kyle's hips. Holding him. Immobilizing him.

Kyle groaned.

Lowering farther still, Nate sucked on the shot glass. The sight of his sandy-blond hair, tinted with every color of the rainbow, was more than Kyle needed. Fantasies and memories and reality merged into a heady cocktail of *want*. He gripped the hair at Nate's crown and twisted. Lifted. Nate straightened, his mouth pursed around a mouthful of Jell-O and shaped into a smile of pure sin.

He swallowed.

So did Kyle.

Ah, fuck.

"Damn that was hot," Tim said almost reverently. His hulking bear of a partner was busy sliding rough hands up and down the smaller man's heaving chest.

Fingers still tangled in Nate's hair, Kyle yanked him close for a swift kiss of vodka and strawberry and man. "Again," he rasped.

Nate was quicker this time. His fingers shook slightly as he reached for another shot. To see how much Kyle visibly affected a man who'd spent three years in prison was almost too much. He was upending the hardest badass he'd ever known. Kyle's cock was swollen. He wanted to fuck. He wanted this torture to go on forever.

No matter how unsteady, Nate managed to unfasten the top button of Kyle's jeans and tug down the zipper.

"Turning you on, college boy?"

"*Turned* on. It's a done deal."

That made Nate grin, cocky and boyishly lopsided. Kyle's heart turned over. But then he couldn't breathe—flat out couldn't—when Nate tucked the next shot inside the waistband of Kyle's boxer briefs. The cool, conical plastic nestled right where the head of his cock was contained by that elastic band. Not that it was concealed. The bulge of his erection was unmistakable where it strained against his fly.

To his left, Kyle heard a moan. The bigger guy, Mick, had found his partner's crotch and was giving it firm, pulsing squeezes. Nate watched them too. All around, the thunder of music created a trance of *here* and *now*.

Kyle's head jerked backward. So dazed, it was only afterward that he realized Nate had yanked on the collar.

"Like that," Nate rasped against Kyle's throat. "They're getting off watching us. You splayed out like some gay pinup, chest arched, shoulders brawny. And that monster cock—they can see it, just like I can. Fucking *fantastic*." He licked along Kyle's jaw and bit his earlobe, giving the collar another jerk. "But you know what?"

Kyle was spinning. "What, sir?"

"Shit," Nate hissed. "You always knew what I liked. And I like your long, fat prick. They can look all they want, but it's mine. Tell me."

"Yours, sir." Kyle regained some semblance of power when he turned and kissed Nate. Quick. Rough. Teeth and tongue and biting force. "Now get down there and suck."

Nate chuckled, their game made playful with a single sentence. He released the collar and found purchase along Kyle's tense thighs. Head down, Nate's mouth so fucking close to what Kyle wanted. The sight was incredible enough. The feel of Nate's tongue dipping beneath the waistband—that was mind-blowing. The wet tip slid against Kyle's throbbing head, darted, teased. Every movement was concealed by Nate's face and the hunched power of his shoulders and burly upper arms.

Then slurp, lift, swallow. The shot was gone.

Tim and his partner were kissing with potent intent, oblivious now, caught up in each other as Vertigo Dreams took to the stage. For a moment, Kyle and Nate stilled. Fingers interlaced. Gazes fixed. Sure, the band had aged. Glam was a little less shiny, a little more weary.

Kyle didn't care, and it didn't seem like Nate did either. Simultaneously, they squeezed each other's hands as the first song began.

Something more unfathomable than desire punched Kyle in the chest. Old years. Old hurts and desires and hopes.

Maybe Nate felt it too because he grabbed Kyle's collar and pulled. It was either stumble or follow, so Kyle found his feet and yanked his jeans back into place. He hooked his discarded shirt and two more shots, slurping both for himself.

It was obvious Nate didn't know where they were going. He simply led. Searching. Hunting for something. Kyle grinned, knowing exactly what his lover sought. He could only imagine how hard Nate was, how ready he was to satisfy this aching want, ready to indulge the best of what they'd been.

Club patrons clapped and shouted like mad. Kyle grasped Nate's powerful wrist where he still held fast to the collar.

"This way."

Again, that suspicious brow appeared. "Where?"

Kyle petted up and down the taut tendons of Nate's bare forearm. Soft, golden hair added a vulnerable counterpoint to their lust, but it was no less powerful. "Trust me."

With a curt nod, some of the tension eased from Nate's features. "Make it good, college boy."

Kyle tugged him toward the back of the club. A quick private word with a grim-faced roadie, followed by two hundred-dollar bills, achieved just what he had in mind. He and Nate slipped backstage. They had the length of the band's set to get each other off. Not a goddamn problem.

Vertigo Dreams was on stage, but they were obscured by a black backdrop. No one from the audience could see Kyle, where he led Nate toward that cloaking velvet. The stage was an elevated platform made of metal grating, about four feet off the floor. Kyle let go of his partner and crouched low, then slid underneath. Flat on his back. The gaps in the grating meant he had a perfect view of the band from the most worm's-eye view ever.

Nate rolled in beside him, over and around, until Kyle was on top. The darkness under the stage was splintered by shards of light and prickles of color. The music was almost too loud for words.

They navigated by looks and touches. Mouth to ear still worked, barely. "You're fucking insane," Nate said.

Kyle reached for Nate's tight-fitting button-down and ripped it open. "We're gonna fuck right underneath our favorite band. It's *perfectly* insane."

Hands over skin over hands over skin. They worked to strip each other amid blaring guitars, thumping drums, and trancelike vocals that never failed to give Kyle goose bumps. Their jeans would have to stay where they were, shoved down to midthigh, because there wasn't room to kick out of them. Didn't matter. Kyle found Nate's ass, then clenched and groaned.

"I want to fuck your mouth," Nate rasped in his ear, even as he stroked Kyle toward the point of exploding.

"Yes, sir."

Kyle rode Nate's full-body shudder all the way down. He belly-crawled until his face hovered right where they both wanted him to be. Braced on his elbows, he pulled Nate's underwear down, baring that glorious prick. Light danced across engorged flesh. Sound fused into a living being, curling around and between them. Kyle's mouth watered. The cocktails and shots were going to his head until he was unable to process anything close to thought.

Music. Rhythm. Sucking off the world's most perfect cock.

The rest could take a leap.

They lay sprawled right beneath the singer's feet. If he looked down, he'd be able to see Kyle's naked ass where he knelt on his elbows and knees, as well as the long, uncovered expanse of Nate's rippling chest. Goddamn, Kyle wanted that. He wanted to put on another show. He felt so fucking *free*.

Nate grabbed the collar with both hands, tightening it around Kyle's neck. The alcohol and a slight restriction to his breathing made Kyle dizzier, needier.

Over the din of their favorite music—the songs of their first love affair—Nate could shout. No one would hear. "Suck me. *Now*."

Kyle's parted lips slid down over the prick he wanted to worship. Male flesh filled his mouth, all the way to the back of his throat. Still on his elbows, he wrapped his hands beneath Nate's exposed ass and snuck questing fingers further, pulling those cheeks apart.

Nate set the pace. He used that collar as collars were meant to be used. To guide. To restrain. To correct. Powerful arms forced Kyle's head up and down. Kyle nearly gagged. He fought the reflex. He focused on gripping Nate's ass, finding the tight pucker he sought. His lover's expression became strained and needy.

Nate was simply . . . erotic. Potent. The position of his arms— shaped in a triangle that ended at Kyle's neck—served to bunch his pectorals and flex his abs. His tattoo was a permanent shadow dancing on the world's most perfect male torso. He lifted his head off the shiny floor beneath the stage, eyes avid as he watched Kyle take him throat-deep. Those eyes flared wide when Kyle slipped his forefingers into Nate's anus.

Kyle played with that sweet, tensed rosebud. He stretched and probed as Nate's fierce thrusts blurred his mind into streaks of color, pleasure, and stinging, choking pain.

He only wanted more.

"Suck me. Fuck, Kyle. Give it to me."

More words followed but were devoured by amplified music. The sound of Nate's curses and grunts reverberated through his body, twining with the bass drum and rocketing down to Kyle's throbbing, needy cock. So he fucked harder. Faster. Sucked and tongued and *craved*. He wanted that splash of release against the back of his throat.

Nate arched his neck. His grip on the collar cut off Kyle's air, making a tighter fuck. Nate kept pulsing with long, fast strokes.

With one last burst of awareness as the world darkened at the edges, Kyle shoved both his fingers into Nate's ass. Pumped. Stretched. Abused him there the way Nate abused Kyle's mouth.

That did it. Hardcore. Nate spewed curses as his powerful body snapped taut. Come exploded from his dick and filled Kyle's mouth. He ground deep, forcing Kyle to feel each shuddering pulse and swallow every last drop. Kyle managed, though the collar was so tight that he saw spots—spots that didn't originate with the blazing disco ball overhead.

Nate released him. Flipped him. Oxygen washed back into Kyle's brain on a rush so powerful that he cried out.

Nate retrieved a condom out of nowhere and slid it onto the most painfully greedy erection Kyle ever had.

"You like shoving things in my ass," he growled against Kyle's neck.

"You like it too."

"Love it. Want more."

Nate's words were breathless grunts now. Kyle felt just as primal, just as entranced. "More," he echoed.

"Tongue first. Then that monster cock."

Without waiting for a reply, Nate shifted them again. He assumed a similar position: braced on his elbows, kneeling, ass in the air. In the enclosed space beneath the stage, Kyle needed to duck low to find his prize. He licked from balls to taint to asshole with loving, slurping enthusiasm. So greedy, so fucking lost.

But he wasn't lost. Nate's body, scent, taste, and his growled curses slinking around and between the music—all of it belonged to Kyle.

That sense of ownership wouldn't end with just one night. Kyle refused to let go of that heady satisfaction. He would have Nate, again and again, and he would be taken by Nate. Weeks remained on the London shoot, and he intended to make the most of every second.

Chapter Eight

The post Nate wrapped his hands around was cool and sharp edged. He needed something to keep him grounded—if that was possible. Nothing compared to the blooming pleasure taking him over. His limbs tingled with warmth, and his chest flipped with each probing stroke of Kyle's tongue. Good. So fucking good.

Nate let his head bow, let his shoulders curl down. Part of him wanted to keep these feelings all to himself. Gather them close, hoarding each tremble of pleasure. Because even the way Kyle's blunt fingers fondled his ass was fleeting.

Kyle pulled away. Licked again.

Latex slid between Nate's cheeks. Kyle nudged his throbbing, wickedly hot prick against Nate's opening while pinching and kneading the globes of Nate's ass. Then . . . pushing. Filling. His body stretched to accommodate Kyle's fat cock with so much gratification and, fuck it all, a strange sort of joy. This was right. Kyle's body was meant for Nate, filling him exactly as it should.

Kyle pulsed. Insistent. A little mean, a little jerky. His fingertips dug into Nate's hips. He didn't stay patient for long.

The fucking was hardly nice. Nate liked it that way. Kyle bent low and pressed his chest along Nate's back. Sweaty. Nails digging. Cock thrusting short and fast. Burning pleasure snatched Nate by surprise with every inward thrust. Kyle's strokes reaped the fast, throbbing rhythm of the music that was around them, in them, taking over their lungs and blood.

Owned.

They were owned. By the moment, by the music. By each other.

All of it wrapped together and turned Nate's hold on the strut into an unbreakable grip. Kyle fucked him forward with every thrust.

Nate wanted more. He wanted to flip Kyle again, watch the other man's face when his impending orgasm took away the arrogance and left him wiped. Left him without his act. But Kyle's quick strokes were turning frantic. His face tucked against Nate's shoulder. Mouth over skin, with just enough teeth. Shudders worked through them both as Kyle shot his load.

Nate blew out a shaky, rough breath as he held back his own arousal. He'd come, but his cock was already stirring. So much temptation. The pleasure wasn't going anywhere. He would have Kyle again. But not there. Not then.

After catching their breaths, they shoved their clothing back into place under the rolling wave of applause as the band finished. As he buttoned his shirt, Nate grinned and leaned toward Kyle's ear. "That's for us. Great fucks get great applause."

"You're a dork." Kyle laughed. He tilted his neck to the side, adjusting his sparkling collar. "But fuck yeah, it's for us. We're that good."

Kyle grabbed Nate's hand as they wove through the crowds. They sent the cute waiter to bring back their coats, then wound up on the sidewalk.

Nate didn't want the night to end. It was stupid of him, but he didn't. He pulled on his wool coat slowly despite the biting cold. A streetlight glowed white overhead. Their table partners, Tim and his big boy, spilled out of the door and waved goodbye as they jaywalked across the street.

Nate nodded and Kyle waved in return.

After digging in his pocket for gloves, Nate drew them on. "Now what?"

Kyle zipped up his leather jacket and wrapped a scarf around his neck. Completely casual and yet dripping a level of style few people could manage. "We could walk."

"In thirty-degree weather, at one in the morning."

"Yup. Exactly what I mean." The arrogance was back, tingeing every word. His wide smile took over his mouth. "Don't tell me the big, mean stuntman is afraid of the London streets at night?"

He snorted. "You wish. More like I'm afraid your pampered ass will freeze."

Kyle's hair was still styled in an artfully mussed way that made Nate want to wrap his fingers in the strands. They gravitated closer to each other as they walked down the street—so different from their tense cab ride over. Nate wasn't precisely drunk, but the world took on a shaky aspect that blurred his edges. Made everything easier to handle. It all flowed by.

Kyle bumped his shoulder. "Would that upset you? For my ass to be damaged?"

"It'd be harder for you to take my dick again."

"Keep talking and we'll see how soon that happens."

"Promises, promises."

Nate grinned. More nostalgia. They'd been like this before. Not so much in front of other people, though it had sometimes been fun to flirt in plain sight. Bromance amplified.

They'd been good together, no denying. In many ways, Kyle was good with lots of people. He made friends everywhere he went, like he had with Tim and his partner. Even Raney had said as much, after meeting Kyle in the pub one evening. Kyle made everyone feel special, as if his attention was a gift. It came from his relationship with his mother and father, and the way they'd made him fight for their attention. That was his true talent. No one else came close.

Nate had been looking for that in the years since, someone who made him feel half as good as Kyle always had. At the same time, he knew better than to give in to those feelings with Kyle. He'd nearly lost his mind the first time they'd fucked it up. A second time around, there'd be farther to fall.

Golden light spilled out of a cathedral's grand double doorway, all the way down to the shadowed curb where they walked.

Nate pulled to a stop and looked up. An illuminated church wasn't a big deal—except when he'd prefer any distraction from too-tempting thoughts about Kyle. "What the hell?"

"I'm pretty sure that's sacrilege."

"Sue me. I cuss."

Kyle laughed. "Sure, but do you really want to do it standing in front of a church? Practically on the doorstep?"

What a church it was. Huge, it soared far above the street, up to a spire that was practically out of sight in the dark but for the way it blotted out the stars. Grand double doors were open despite the cold and flanked with stained-glass windows.

And music. Music drifted outside in complete contrast to the pop classics they'd danced to at the club.

He wrapped his grip around Kyle's wrist and tugged him up the stairs. "Come on."

Kyle drew his brows together. "Midnight mass? Wouldn't think it your scene."

"Why not?" Nate faked some happy. With anyone but Kyle, he'd have been ecstatic at the night they'd had—not wondering what else could or would come next. "Think of it as expanding your horizons."

"*My* horizons? Then tell me, who wrote this?"

"John Lennon?"

"Try Handel, dork." Despite token protests, Kyle followed him in, sharing Nate's grinning humor. The front rows were filled with a surprising number of people, considering the hour. There were plenty of the little old ladies Nate might have expected, as well as young families with children. Most craned their necks to see the new arrivals.

Still, he and Kyle didn't sit. He had the feeling this was a temporary sort of moment, something he didn't want to fully commit to. But the singing was too beautiful to pass up.

"Midnight on a Saturday seems kind of random for a choral performance," he whispered with his mouth near Kyle's ear. The scarf tickled the underside of his chin.

"Holiday season, probably."

Voices soared, high and pure, to rise above everything else. Beauty swelled beneath the arched ceiling and swirled around the room. Occupying a choral box behind the altar, every singer wore white robes trimmed with gold. They seemed too ethereal to be true.

All of it was amazing.

He tucked closer toward Kyle. Their shoulders pressed together, as did their hips, but nothing too outrageous. Circumspect. This was how gay men often had to duck and be . . . *less*. At such a moment, Nate could almost understand Kyle's reluctance, until he remembered this was a church. It was a matter of respecting others' space rather than hiding.

Still, he didn't take Kyle's hand like he was tempted to. He folded his arms over his chest and tucked his fingertips under his biceps, the better to hold himself in. "Spill it."

Kyle shook his head and whispered in response. "Spill what?"

"I know you. You've got a wealth of knowledge tucked away in that brain of yours." That was one of the hottest things about Kyle, the way he gathered information and made astute decisions and wanted to know everything about everyone. Nate's cynical side said it was about Kyle's need to protect himself—getting a jump on the world he had no right to be afraid of. But the result was the same. Made him incredibly smart. "It's not John Lennon. So tell me something amazing."

Kyle flashed his cheeky grin, the one that always looked a little embarrassed. He touched his scarf as if to unwind it, but he let it be—maybe second thoughts about revealing his collar in a cathedral. "George Frideric Handel's *Messiah* was first performed in 1742."

Man, he could spill facts like gumballs from a candy machine.

"Lemme guess," Nate said. "Here in London."

"Actually, no. Dublin."

"You mean London wasn't always the center of the world?"

Kyle chuckled, which made a ginger-haired little girl turn. Her mother tugged on the sleeve of her green velvet dress and promptly turned her around. "Not something I'd ask anyone from England."

This time, it was the little girl's father who turned around and tossed a stern expression. The music built to a grand crescendo, signaling the end. Timing was sometimes a hint from the universe. Nate stood and urged Kyle back out onto the street.

He couldn't help but shake his head. "That's pretty damn fancy."

They started walking in silent accord, in the general direction of the hotel. He didn't know about Kyle, but Nate's buzz was starting to wear off. Thoughts of sucking those shots out of Kyle's waistband, and the salty-sweetness he'd tasted of Kyle's wet cockhead, were enough to energize him all over again.

Kyle stuffed his hands back in his pockets, making his shoulders wider. Bigger. Bulkier. "Don't you like a little fancy now and then?"

Nate liked the sound of his own laugh. Nothing cynical there. Just easy. "Did you mean that to sound like it did?"

"Not initially," Kyle said, joining him in laughter. "But gimme a variety of answers."

The cheeky bastard was practically begging for it when Nate grabbed his ass. Firm and tight, just right in his hand.

"You. I like you, fancy gentleman. Now and then, at least."

"Maybe we should make it a thing. Meet up every decade or so for another round."

Nate didn't reply, but he knew those words were a natural barrier, the way Kyle meant them. Whatever was going on, it had an unavoidable stopping point. When production ended, they would too.

A ticking timer was a good thing. Nate would have enough time to wash away the bitter taste of their breakup without being sucked into more hurt. He'd have something better to remember. They might finish as friends who'd shared a few special moments.

Maybe Kyle saw the discomfort that ran down Nate's spine. Sympathy chased his expression into something softer. "And? What, if anything, is the right kind of fancy for Mr. Carnes?"

Nate shrugged, knowing he was stalling. He'd grown up just this side of dirty poor—as in he'd never gone hungry, but there had been plenty of times when there wasn't enough to go around. When his clothes were clean but worn through at the knees, two inches too short. Yet he didn't gravitate toward possessions.

A black cab almost zipped by, but Nate stuck an arm in the air and waved it down. It was way too late, and he didn't want to spend the rest of the night walking. He held the door open for Kyle, who slid in first.

Kyle looked like sex personified. Long legs encased in dark jeans, that dark-brown leather jacket worn exactly so. He was so perfectly shined that Nate could hardly believe the man had been on his knees in a cramped hiding spot, swallowing Nate's come with a choked moan.

Nate slid into the cab and grabbed Kyle's thigh, dragged him a little nearer. The cabbie caught Nate's gaze in the mirror. "Where to, mate?" he asked in a lilting accent.

Nate gave the name of the hotel as they pulled away.

Kyle edged in close. Shoulder to shoulder again. "You owe me an answer."

"The fanciest thing I have is my sound system."

"No iPod in a dock?"

"Nope." He took Kyle's hand. Couldn't hold off anymore. "I've got a full setup at home. Speakers, receiver, the works. I can run an iPod through it if I want."

"Tell me you've got a record player so I can call you an emo hipster."

Nate grinned. "I have a record player."

"That's worse than fancy. That's snobby."

He lifted Kyle's hand to his mouth. Kissed it softly. Then he added the tiniest bite and a lick. "You would know, college boy."

Chapter Nine

London was beautiful and busy and chock-full of people. The teeming streets made Kyle's native northern Virginia look like a collection of villages connected by deserted country roads. Here it was lights. Everywhere. Streetlights and blinking traffic signals, sure, but bright Christmas kitsch was layered over even the most modest shops. Neon signs adorned newsagents and little cubbies selling takeaway curry, kebabs, and late-night off-license liquor.

The scenery, however, was a backdrop to the action. Kyle knew all about that, how the prop department and his own production scouts found the right locations for ensuring the perfect atmosphere.

Cue action.

Only, in the cab sitting beside Nate, there was no genuine *action*. Nothing a screenwriter would waste time with. As if a cab ride back to the hotel was nothing special.

Bullshit.

His hand was twined with Nate's, where their jumble of fingers rested at the inside of Kyle's thigh. They were close. Closer in this moment than they had been when writhing together beneath the club's stage. There, they'd been hot. Desperate. Delicious decisions hadn't really been decisions at all—more like gut impulse. Primal and dark.

Tucked together, pressed body to body as the black cab wound its long, lazy, traffic-packed way through London, Kyle found a piece of himself he never thought he'd find again.

He'd found Nate.

"I need to tell you something," he said quietly. His voice sounded rough and husky. Perhaps it was some combination of a night spent shouting over the music, swallowing cock like a porn star, and admitting what he needed to admit.

Because Kyle couldn't, wouldn't, sleep with Nate again without telling the truth first.

Nate shifted so that their legs touched from hip to knee. He tucked his mouth beneath Kyle's ear. No kissing or licking. Simple lips to skin as he breathed. That he was breathing the sweaty, raunched-up scent of Kyle's skin was almost as erotic as how Nate had inched their hands up, up, up. Kyle flinched and huffed out a little laugh when their interlaced fingers brushed and then settled on his cock.

"Dare you," Nate whispered.

"You're daring me to tell you something I already meant to?"

"Dare you to while we get you hard again."

No. Not yet. He couldn't. Nate's blatant reminder of the sexual possibilities awaiting them had an effect opposite to the one he likely intended. It cooled Kyle down.

"I need to tell you why I hired Second Chances."

The fact it was *that* difficult to broach the topic told him something incredibly real. Jagged and dangerous. He cared what Nate thought of him, and he cared *very much* whether Nate would think himself used or manipulated to the point of walking away—from the film, from Kyle.

Nate had stilled. He didn't stiffen or pull away, but tension invaded his muscles and tightened the breaths huffing against Kyle's neck. He was like a predator. Waiting. In such a moment, who could say whether he was the hunter or the prey? Was he apprehensive about the words to come, or ready to rip Kyle's throat out for being so manipulative?

After a calming breath, Kyle said what he needed to.

"You remember the article that ran in *Variety* about Second Chances? About . . . three years ago?"

No answer. No movement.

"I'd been flipping through the magazine, waiting at LAX to board for Tokyo. And there you were. Your picture. I was surprised how easily I could recognize you after the time that'd passed, but I literally dropped the damn thing."

He squeezed Nate's fingers, hoping for a hint. Nothing happened. He had no choice but to keep talking. "I must've looked like an idiot, scrambling to pick it up, spilling my coffee over my coat. I wanted to find that page again. Must've read the article a dozen times on the flight."

"Spit it out, Kyle."

"I could've pushed to hire any stunt crew. I pushed for yours."

"Why?"

"The answers I gave everyone else, or the one you want to hear?"

Rather than pull away as Kyle feared, Nate twisted their fingers into a painful grip. With his free hand he reached across their bodies and caught Kyle's chin. They had nowhere else to look but at one another.

"*My* answer," he rasped.

"I wanted to see you again."

"You fucking asshole." The words weren't spat or hissed but whispered with a quiet sort of disappointment.

"I've been trying to make it happen for three years. Back then, Second Chances was as new as Pennfield. We didn't have the clout to command a damn thing. Here, now, this was the right time."

"The right time to orchestrate a reunion you could've made happen by picking up the phone?"

Kyle jerked his chin out of Nate's hold and peeled their hands apart. "That's not how it would've gone and you know it. Yes, I wanted to see you again. It's taken me a few days to admit what I've wanted for years—"

"Always takes a while for you and your real self to see eye to eye."

"—but I *sure as hell* wouldn't have hired an inexperienced, sloppy, unprofessional crew so I could get my rocks off with its owner." He couldn't have risked it, not with the way he needed Pennfield to work. Not with the way he felt like he'd never be *free* if he wasn't massively successful. It wasn't enough to not keep his trust fund out of sight and out of mind. For good. He had to be secure in knowing he was beyond the influential sphere of the great and infallible Wakefields. His own damn parents.

He grabbed the front of Nate's jacket and hauled him close. Face to face. Nose to nose. Mouth to gorgeous mouth. "I hired *your* people, who made the Petronas Towers jump that everyone said couldn't be done. Who exploded a semi in the middle of an Arctic ice field. Who just happened to set a free-diving record during a film shoot."

They were both breathing heavily now. The dare wasn't in telling Nate what he had to say, but in kissing him. Kyle nipped and licked and teased, then took Nate's lower lip between his teeth. Nate hissed softly, his eyes rolling shut. His hands found the tendons along Kyle's inner thighs and kneaded.

"I wanted to see you," Kyle said tightly. "But I also needed the best. No way was I going to risk my company and push for Second Chances before I could have both. Besides, I knew you'd have hated the thought of some pity contract because we used to trade fucks."

"Then why all the cloak-and-dagger shit? Why'd you send Stephanie instead of making the offer yourself?"

"Because I didn't think you'd take the job."

Still wrapped tight in a challenge of male aggression, bound together in doubt, they both started to laugh. Spontaneously. Pressing his forehead against Nate's, Kyle chanced looking into those fierce blue eyes. He found Nate looking right back, his expression both mirthful and self-deprecating.

"Admit it," Kyle said before kissing him again.

"Let's say it would've been a close call."

"Good enough."

Nate pulled away slightly, but his hands still clutched Kyle's thighs. They were connected by touch as they sparred and laughed and tried to navigate deep, dark waters. "You meant it though, didn't you? About Second Chances."

"Can you believe me already so we can get back to the good stuff?"

"Which would be . . .?"

Kyle brushed his lips against Nate's ear. He licked along that shell, up and down. "Fucking. Making each other breathless and crazy before we come. You turn me inside out until I can't think of anything else. I know how much you love stripping away the veneer. Exposing me for what I really am under my suits and posturing. You want me to be an animal. For you."

"Jesus," Nate breathed.

"But I have one more thing to admit."

"Oh?"

With his hands trailing down to Nate's broad, hard chest, Kyle smiled with sexual potency. Not the raw physical appeal Nate brought to bear, or the man's sexy-as-fuck profession, but the arrogance of power. Old money power. Influential power. The power of knowing Nate was as needy as he was.

"Our rooms at the hotel are side by side."

Nate lifted his brows. "Your doing?"

"Of course."

"That's why you wanted to meet me downstairs."

"Why ruin the surprise?"

Taut fingers trailed up to cup Kyle's crotch once again. Nate's odd sort of sweetness and humor remained—so much lighter now than the tense moments before—but his expression and the clasp of his hand said he meant business. Very soon.

"You are a devious, brilliant man."

Kyle tilted his head, but there was no sarcasm to be found. His words were lost.

"Here we are, gents," the cabbie said.

Both Kyle and Nate had to shake free of the spell they'd woven. It took a few seconds. Kyle's every thought and sense had been trained on Nate, relieved that the worst hadn't happened. He paid the cabbie, and they bundled out onto pavement slick with the lightest dusting of snow. A giant illuminated wreath adorned the arch above the hotel's double doors.

Kyle checked his jacket zipper and scarf. All the way up. Nate flicked a glance his way, shook his head a little, but said nothing.

They rode the elevator in silence, but because they were alone, Kyle took the chance of reaching for Nate's hand, holding him palm to palm. Although his head was bowed, Nate smiled softly. That Kyle could affect him with such a simple gesture was humbling and terrifying. Deep down, he knew what a guy like Nate wanted. No, he knew what *Nate* wanted.

He wanted Kyle to step out of the closet.

That wasn't something Kyle could imagine doing, not even for the man he'd once loved—the man he still adored. Gay clubs and taxis and empty elevators were one thing. The whole world? Whereas Nate charged ahead, flaunting his sexuality like a challenge, Kyle couldn't live like that.

That didn't mean he had to give up their evening together, or any of the tenuous weeks that awaited them before Christmas—the last day of filming.

The elevator bell dinged. If Kyle had his way, he'd have let go. No telling who'd be on the other side of that door. Nate, however, bound their hands together in a rock-hard grip.

No one stood there when the doors parted. Kyle was relieved as they stepped into the corridor, but Nate stopped him.

His expression was distant, unreadable, born of years of poverty and honed to cruel perfection in prison. "Don't dick around with me, Kyle. Do it or don't."

Familiar anxiety burned in Kyle's veins. Fear. Wanting. An important part of him was slowly dying, leaving him to strangle and suffocate.

He swallowed tightly. "If I can't?"

"You start something like this," Nate said, nodding toward their interlaced fingers, "then you see it through. I won't stand for you jumping scared when *you* took the lead."

Kyle let go and walked toward where their rooms waited side by side. Standing before his, shoulders slumped with sudden fatigue, he pulled the key from his wallet. Nate joined him, hands in pockets. "I took the lead when I asked you out," Kyle said softly. "I'm . . . Jesus, Nate, I'm trying."

"Why? Because you know I won't blow your cover? Convenient."

"Fuck off. I'm trying for the same reason I followed Second Chances' progress for the last few years. Because of you." He unlocked the door, turned, stood leaning against the jamb. "How about you think for half a second that something I do is at least an attempt? That goddamn chip on your shoulder is too big to fit through this door."

"And you're the same egotistical prick you were in high school."

"You loved it then," Kyle said with his back straight, his mind made up. "I'm betting you love it now. But I'm not going to be the only one taking risks here. It's not all about Kyle crawling back to Nate, with you setting the damn-them-all terms."

Nate still hadn't removed his hands from his pockets. If anything, he hunched further into himself and darted a glare from under his brows. "So this is good night. Fine. I had a good time fucking your face, college boy."

He turned toward his own room, but Kyle caught his upper arm. Holy hell, the man was made of granite. His muscles bunched as if ready to land an uppercut. Shit, maybe he was.

"I didn't say good night," Kyle said roughly. "So listen a goddamn minute. Our rooms are connected. I'm leaving my door unlocked tonight. You want me, you know where to find me."

Nate shrugged away. He unzipped the leather jacket down to Kyle's navel. With both hands he grabbed the shimmering collar. Face-to-face again. All confrontation and power and the potential for so much more—better or worse. Both.

"*I* won't crawl either, you self-righteous bastard."

Kyle's smile felt slow and decadent. "Then barge through and *take* what you want. The choice is yours."

Nate's hands fell away. His nostrils flared. The fists he balled against either thigh made Kyle's breath pick up speed. Pushing him was like waving a red cape in front of a bull. All of the rushing, exciting danger. All of the *really* bad judgment.

"Screw secret doors." He shoved Kyle's chest, backing him into the room, and threw the dead bolt. "I'm using this one."

Chapter Ten

Nate knew good things when he had them in his hands. Something about not having so many opportunities in life had made him more attuned to the excellent moments. Folding his hands around the side of Kyle's face, thumbs on the other man's sharp jaw, definitely counted.

He kissed Kyle. Primitive and sure, but keeping back the meanness that could take him over. Kyle still didn't understand what Nate meant. Kyle *was* trying, and hard. Although the little things counted, he shouldn't take Nate's hand if he didn't mean to hold on. It was easier to do without than live by halves.

Hell, that had been part of why he'd acted out all those years ago, screwing up their tidy plans. He'd realized how painful it would be to stay Kyle's secret sidepiece, the inexplicable roommate, while his college boy took his place among the elite—as Kyle was still meant to. What would that leave Nate other than desperately loving and making do? He'd wake up every morning to go work in some shitty garage, while Kyle became the all-American wet dream he was.

Pulling away from Nate.

Yeah, no thanks.

So maybe he hadn't made the best choice—an understatement considering how he'd lost three years of his life to a prison cell. At least things had worked out. At least he'd carved a life for himself that he was damn proud of.

That Kyle seemed to honestly appreciate his skills was a happy bonus.

Nate pulled back, letting the last touch of lips linger. He kissed Kyle's chin, the strength of his jaw. His teeth dragged over skin, which was only now prickling with evening stubble, whereas Nate rubbed his rougher cheek down Kyle's neck.

The man shuddered. His head dropped back, and he looked up at the hotel room ceiling. "Oh, that's nice." Wonder tinged his voice.

"You sound surprised."

"I am." His hands closed around the back of Nate's head. Not caging in, just . . . encouraging. "Haven't had this sort of thing much."

Nate dug his fingertips in the flesh above Kyle's expensive leather belt and the waistband of his jeans. His T-shirt was thin enough that heat seeped through. Nate traced the plunging V-neck with his tongue. "You miss out on the bonuses when you stick to trolling, don't you?"

Kyle laughed. "Yeah, guess so. But you mean to tell me you've exclusively been in meaningful relationships?" The question sounded like a joke, but his voice strained beneath the attempt at humor.

Did he really care? Did he wonder what Nate had been doing for nine years? Nate hid his smile against the inside curve of Kyle's pecs. Then he bit for good measure. "I'm not going to pretend I never have. But I've had my share of relationships too."

Kyle's fingers spasmed on the back of Nate's head before winding in his hair and tugging. The sharp spike urged Nate to lift his head.

Kyle's eyes were dark. "You did?"

He nodded as he sent his hands exploring underneath Kyle's shirt to the ridges of his ribs, the scoop of his lats down his side. All stuff that attested to Kyle's intensity. A body like his didn't happen by accident. "One that got pretty serious."

Dark eyes went darker. He didn't seem to like that. "I see."

Nate felt his lips curve. A smile seemed cruel, but he couldn't help it. The universe was absurd.

"Actually, if you had picked up the phone and called me when you saw that article, it wouldn't have done you much good. I had a guy. Jaime."

"Is that right?"

"Yup. We were living together."

Kyle's mouth went slack, his eyes cloudy as he looked into the distance. Maybe imagining what that would be like? Envying that Nate was free enough to enjoy that?

"What happened?"

"Not entirely sure. We grew apart." Nate let his mouth resume his exploration of Kyle's skin. No sense telling him all of what had driven Jaime away. "He started talking about a place in the valley and wanting a Chihuahua."

"Seriously?"

"Yup. Can you think of a more clichéd dog for a pair of queers?" He flashed a smile. They'd gotten entirely off track. "But doesn't really matter now, does it? I'm more concerned with the fact that I have yet to see you fully naked."

Kyle shuddered on a long, slow breath. His jaw tightened and his eyes drifted half shut. "You have a point."

Wrapping his arms close around Kyle's wide shoulders, Nate kissed him again. Not rushing it. Taking his time with every soft stroke and forceful nip. Then he stepped back, blindly, until the backs of his knees hit the end of the bed. The mattress would be firm but not uncomfortable—an exact duplicate of the one in Nate's room. The room on the other side of the wall.

There were a few noticeable differences. Kyle had carefully unpacked his belongings, storing the closed suitcases in the corner. Nate had his open and dripping with unfolded clothes.

Nate sat on the bed. Watching. He unfurled a slow smile. "Strip for me, college boy."

Kyle cocked his head with his usual arrogance as he peeled out of the leather jacket. The sheer purple shirt clung to him like a gorgeous, colorful second skin. "You're a college boy now too," he said.

"Patched together with correspondence courses, sure. But I like fucking around with your head. And 'Yale boy' doesn't have the same ring." He watched while Kyle lifted the hem of his shirt. Hunger was rising again, along with the need to fill his hands with the ghost from his past. This would end, but not before Nate got his fill. "Maybe I should call you Ivy."

Kyle laughed. His abs compressed into a tight grid as he skinned the shirt over his head and tossed it away. "Hell no."

"Then stop bitching about what I call you and show me your cock."

"You've seen it before."

Nate didn't say a word. Leaning back on his palms, he lifted his eyebrows and waited. He had his own arrogance now and then.

Shaking his head on another laugh, Kyle toed off his loafers, then his socks. His belt snapped and slid next. Such a particular sound in the quiet room. Nate's breathing was turning rough, rushing in his ears. The answering upward pop of Kyle's chest was the only thing keeping him centered as the jeans dropped. Kyle kicked them to the side.

The man looked so fucking good. Strong. So very strong and bold. He stood with his feet slightly apart. His thighs were dense with muscle and covered with sparse dark hair. More close-cropped hair circled the prick that was already filling and swelling toward Nate.

Silently, Nate held out his hand.

Kyle walked forward, near enough that Nate was able to close his hand around that gorgeous prick and worship satiny-soft skin. Kyle looked up toward the ceiling, his throat working past a swallow. "I haven't been this horny since I was a teenager. It . . . doesn't stop."

The head of Kyle's cock was damp. Nate swirled his thumb through the slightly sticky moisture, rubbing it down toward the line between cap and shaft. He loved how thick Kyle was. Some dicks were long, but Kyle had heft and girth too. Meant to fill a man's mouth and stretch a man's ass.

Nate stroked, yanked, pulled, then switched his grip to the soft sacs beneath. "It's the newness. Makes everything seem extra special."

"Maybe." Kyle's tone sounded skeptical. "Maybe not. I'm sure as hell not passing it up."

Nate grinned up at him. "Does it seem like I am either?"

"Hell no." His hand spread across the back of Nate's head. That heavy weight was more than a hint. Practically an unspoken order. He backed it up with a rough command. "Now suck me."

"When you put it that way, how can I resist?"

But he did. His lips parted over the tip of Kyle's prick. The salty tang zipped through him like a rocket. The slightest hint of latex from their earlier round was quickly washed away by wet laves. Nate let the moisture build in his mouth then used it to coat Kyle, the better to suck and stroke.

His tongue caressing the underside of the shaft, Nate looked up past the long expanse of Kyle's abs, the stretch of shoulders to his face.

Kyle wasn't a classically handsome man, with his wide mouth and blunt nose. But he was *right*. It was right, to see him from this angle, to watch his strained expression when Nate pinched low and mean up the inside of his thighs.

He took the cock and let the broad head press the back of his throat, closed his eyes for a long moment. The better to feel fullness. There was something particularly lovely about this act. He didn't get direct physical pleasure off having his mouth full of dick, but he sure as hell loved the rush of power he felt at the sound of Kyle's grunts and moans. Nate got off on making men feel good.

And it was only going to get better.

The dark haze in Kyle's eyes was exactly what Nate was after, but he didn't mean to let him come. Ringing his fingers tight around the bottom of Kyle's shaft, he pushed inward to hold back the feel-good. "We're not done here. Not by half."

The grin Kyle flashed was a doozy. "You always did know how to make it last."

That wasn't exactly true. They'd learned together. But this wasn't the moment to disabuse him of that notion or get distracted by the old days. The here and now was mind-blowing enough. "And you like it that way."

"Damn right."

He pushed Kyle down to the bed, trading positions so that Nate could strip off his clothes. The way Kyle ate him up with his eyes was everything sexy. Once naked, he didn't return to the wide bed. He snagged another condom and a miniature packet of lube from his jeans and looked carefully around the room.

The chair by the window was what he needed. Softly upholstered, it had a low back and arms. He sat and patted his thighs. "Come here."

Obvious trepidation scored Kyle's brow, but he obeyed. His footfalls were almost silent. The light from the floor lamp by the front door was weakest here, at the far end of the room. Bright silver glimmers from outside worked through cracked blinds, glancing off Kyle's ligaments and the big cock that led the way.

Kyle eased into Nate's lap, stretching his knees wide. Nate helped him hitch his legs over the arms of the chair. They were face-to-face, their cocks pressing up together. Kyle's balls rested on his. Nate couldn't help but thrust. Friction and warmth.

He grabbed the condom he'd set on the side table and quickly rolled it over his length. The whole time, Kyle's hands coasted over Nate's skin. Tiny shocking jolts of pleasure threatened to take him down at any moment.

He reached around Kyle's ass with both hands, delving into the sensitive split and glorying in those crisp hairs there. Kyle shuddered and pressed his forehead against Nate's. They couldn't get close enough.

Nate could help that—because they could get closer. Needed to. Flipping open the cap, he spread lube over his cock, over Kyle's tight ring, then stroked his fingers inside.

Kyle's eyes rolled shut.

With his free hand, Nate lifted the man's chin. "No, look at me."

It took him obvious effort, but he finally managed. His tongue slicked over his bottom lip, and he shook on a particularly forceful thrust of Nate's two fingers. "Why?"

"What?" He didn't know where the question had come from. Nate was quickly losing his grip.

Kyle's hips twitched backward, toward the small invasion. He folded his hand around their dicks, wrapping them together. "Why do you want me to look at you? You didn't before. Not on the pool table. You didn't under the stage."

"Circumstances?" He could barely gather his thoughts, not with the way Kyle stroked their dicks together. Not with the hot clench on his fingers combined with the knowledge he'd thrust into his lover soon.

"I think it's more than that." Kyle kissed him, as if purposely cutting off any opportunity to respond.

Nate didn't feel like making sense of the tangled thoughts in his head. This wasn't the time for talk. This was the time for taking.

He positioned the head of his cock against the tight knot of Kyle's ass, then wrapped his arm low around the other man's hips.

It was impossible to tell who took whom. Kyle ground his hips down as Nate surged up into that scalding heat.

Only when he was fully seated in Kyle, completely surrounded by that tight, intoxicating heat, did he blow out the breath he'd been holding.

Then he did the hardest thing of all.

He looked into Kyle's eyes.

Chapter Eleven

K yle gasped.

Nate's beautiful invasion was part of his unconscious sound of pleasure, but at that moment, their joining was so much more than the physical. Eyes the color of a frozen lake stared up at him with more bravery and defiance than Nate ever displayed—not even at work, when he prepared to execute an incredible stunt. Kyle soaked up that clear, icy blue as they began to move, enjoying the vibrant power they both craved.

Yet he couldn't keep his attention solely on Nate's face. He was too busy devouring the unbelievable hunk of man sprawled beneath him. The tattoo was a revelation, one he hadn't been able to fully appreciate in the dark and sparkle beneath the stage. The finger licks of black that crept up his throat—the tiny part visible when Nate wore a shirt—were only the beginning. Marvelous swaths of jet ink swirled in four crisscrossing, interlaced bands down his neck, his traps, his left shoulder, until it curled along his muscular upper arm. One of the four trails stretched longer than the rest.

Kyle traced the paths, following each with a hesitant finger. The pleasure radiating out from where they joined was undeniable, but so was his curiosity.

"It's gorgeous," he whispered. "Does it mean anything?"

"Some paths are dead ends. Brambles. Some make it out."

A tight place in Kyle's chest, already filled with hunger and emotion, squeezed to something near to pain. He wasn't used to feeling this much connection with another man. He'd never allowed himself such a luxury. In fact, learning that Nate had lived with a guy still stuck under his skin like a festering splinter.

Kyle wanted what he'd never had. Could never have.

That Nate had experienced that sort of daily intimacy with other men . . . Damn, Kyle had no right to be jealous, but he was. So jealous that he dropped his hips in a savage, possessive thrust. Right now, in a hotel room in London, Nate was his.

He gripped the back of the chair for leverage and caught Nate's gaze again. Locked together, mind and body, they fucked without reserve. Pelvis to ass. Balls slapping. Panting, quickening breath swelled Nate's chest. His pecs stretched, while the skin around his ribs and abs tightened to outline each perfect ridge of flesh and power.

Kyle groaned. "God, you're amazing."

Nate drove up and in, harder, almost a response in itself. "Don't shit me, college boy."

"My name is Kyle."

"Oh, believe me. I know that."

Despite the power that pistoned his lower body, Nate spread his arms to each side. They negligently lay on the armrests, as if he could fuck just fine without needing to touch. He simply watched Kyle with heavy-lidded eyes and a twist to his lips that was nearly vicious. Kyle had experienced encounters that felt a lot like this—hookups where he and another man wanted only to get off.

To be on the receiving end of that dismissive distance from Nate was too much.

No, it was *not enough*. Not even close.

He crossed his arms behind Nate's ribs. There, with their chests pressed flush, he found the right angle to flex his thighs and to kiss Nate at the same time. He deliberately slowed the pace. Nate was a bigger man, honed by tough work, but Kyle had the advantage of position. He wanted both: the connection and the mind-blowing pleasure he already knew was so easy for them to find.

He touched his lips to Nate's face, all over—little kisses over his nose, his eyelids, his mouth, then up his cheek to one tempting earlobe. No teeth yet, but a purring sort of noise as Nate finally, eventually responded to Kyle's unspoken need to slow down.

"Oh, Christ," Kyle said on a low groan. "Like that. Right there."

"You're *such* a cock slut. And you hide this? Unbelievable."

Now, yes, the teeth. The smartass deserved it. Kyle bit Nate's ear with force enough to make the man grunt out a curse.

He was plain pissed.

Kyle stopped altogether. Slid up and off. He yanked Nate's jaw and forced those magnetic blue eyes back up. "Can we leave the baiting aside for one goddamn minute?"

"What?"

"I get it, okay? I want to keep it private, and that bugs the shit out of you. But do you need to hit me over the head with it *all* the time? You were ramming my ass, I was loving it, and Jesus, Nate, I don't need to be schooled on how to be a proper homo all the fucking time."

"Habit," he said with a shrug. "Cuz you haven't learned yet."

"While you won't look in my eyes without effort, and now you won't touch me. Fine. I'll get down on my knees, you can ride me like a pony while you call me a hypocrite or college boy or whatever you like. Then we can both get some sleep." Kyle's body shook on a rough exhale. He was shuddering with anger, with unsatisfied need. "I know you don't approve of how I live, but it takes a lot out of me to keep this a secret. Do I have to stay on the defensive with you too?"

The room was filled with aroused sweat and the sound of their heavy respiration. Kyle still held Nate's jaw. His cock ached, and nestled between his ass cheeks was Nate's rigid, hot prick. Neither had found the release they craved, but Kyle was willing to walk away if Nate didn't give him some reason to stay—to take the chance that staying required.

Not that he held out much hope. Nate hadn't given him a damn thing nine years earlier. Their argument in the prison visitors' room, separated by bulletproof Plexiglas, shouting face-to-face but having to listen to Nate's bitter, angry voice warped by institutional black telephones . . .

Part of Kyle had died that day.

"Forget it," he said. "Dirty fuck, right?"

Nate took Kyle's hand in both of his and pulled it from his jaw, then kissed each knuckle. A chagrined expression turned down the corners of his lips. If anything, his eyes became more intense, more irresistible.

"Kyle?"

Breathe. Don't forget to breathe. But that was damn near impossible. He swallowed. "What?"

"I'm going to ask something of you, and I hope you'll be able to comply. Can you try?"

A curt nod. It was all Kyle could manage.

"The next time I call you a cock slut, can we agree that I mean it as a compliment?" Nate's grin quirked. He took Kyle's forefinger in his mouth, sucking, swirling his tongue. He licked the sensitive pad, this time with a smile that was full-on playful. "Because you totally are."

Kyle wasn't quite ready to smile, but the god-awful tension beneath his breastbone was easing. "And when you don't touch me?"

With long, smooth strokes, Nate began to worship Kyle's naked skin. Blunt, calloused hands caressed from shoulders to chest to abs, then around to Kyle's thighs and ass. Again and again. Nate's breathing became labored. His prick was harder now. Kyle couldn't help but grind down, where the crack of his ass clenched and teased.

"When I don't touch you," Nate rasped, "it's because I want it to last. Doing this . . ." He gripped Kyle's ass so fiercely that they both gasped. "And doing this . . ." He dug taut fingers all the way up Kyle's back, then cupped his face and dragged him down close. The kiss was soft, lingering, everything honey sweet and slow-burn arousal. Nate pulled away. The tops of his cheekbones were flushed, and his parted lips glistened. He smiled softly. "Doing all that tests a man's self-control."

"It was always difficult to get you to lose control."

"Says the pot to the kettle."

Kyle grinned this time. He trailed his hands up Nate's arms, indulging in the luscious strength he couldn't get enough of. "Are you suggesting we're *both* stubborn bastards?"

"You know it." But Nate's expression sobered. He cupped Kyle's face, his eyes rolling to half-mast when Kyle leaned into that tender touch. "So remember you brought this on yourself . . ."

The taunting tone was the same. The sarcastic-ass expression was too. But he didn't say "college boy."

Nate did, however, laugh. "Don't look so relieved, Kyle. Just get back on my dick where you belong. Cock slut."

Shaking his head, Kyle chuckled. He *was* relieved. He'd never talked about this stuff to anyone but Nate, and now every exchange was minefield dangerous. So much lust, but so little faith in one another.

Slow moves. They had a lot of ground to make up, if that was what they wanted. Right now, Kyle only wanted to come. Hard.

He shifted to reposition himself. Nate's hands met him where they both encircled the man's pulsing cock and guided it home. They slid together on mutual groans. Rejoining was more intense because neither held anything back. Nate looked up at him with something near to wonder in his pale, pale baby blues. His hands continued their rough exploration of Kyle's body, leaving no inch of flesh unmarked by hot palms and taut fingertips.

Kyle pressed forward until their chests united once again. He dug between skin and upholstery until he claimed two handfuls of Nate's perfect, muscular ass. He felt every powerful thrust where Nate pounded out a mind-bending rhythm.

"Talk," Kyle groaned. Temple to sweaty temple, he pushed as if physical force would be enough to break into Nate's shuttered thoughts. "Tell me what a cock slut needs to hear."

"Needs to hear? No way." Nate planted his feet in a wide stance and fucked up. God, so rough now. So determined. "You mean, what a cock slut *wants* to hear. You want to hear how good it feels to ram my prick into your tight hole."

"Yes, sir," Kyle grunted. Answering him that way was so easy, and he'd never known why. Maybe because when Nate and his power owned him so completely, Kyle wanted someone to be in charge. He certainly wasn't. "Yes. Please tell me."

Nate's voice was always low and rough, but now it was guttural. "You make me crazy. I called your hole tight, but it's not. Not really. You're a fucking whore, wide open for me. I could put all my strength behind it and you'd only groan and beg for more. Tell me it's a lie."

"Not a lie."

As if to prove his point, Nate grasped Kyle's shoulders and pushed. Down. Down savagely. At the same time, he bucked off the chair. The tendons on his neck became taut and his forearms shook from the effort. His expression took on a bestial quality—eyes narrowed, nostrils flaring, lips curled back over bared teeth.

Kyle had nowhere to go. Trapped between implacable hands and a huge, unrelenting cock that slid against his prostate. He wanted to grab his own aching prick, to end the gathering torture, but he only held on tighter to Nate's ass. And holy shit did he groan.

A look of triumph swept over Nate's face. "Now beg."

"More. Please."

"More of what?" Sweat slicked between Nate's pecs and made his tattoo gleam. "Tell me, Kyle."

"I want you to come. Please. I want to feel you come up my ass, and I want—" The world began to dim at the edges. Only twin ice-blue beacons kept him centered. "And I want to shoot my load on your fucking gorgeous abs."

"I'll take care of that. Lean back."

Kyle dragged his hands out from under his lover's ass and arched his spine. He braced his weight on Nate's thighs, finding his balance there. The pose lifted his cock like an offering. Nate took it as one.

Kyle ground and circled his hips, trying to take it deeper—never enough. Nate growled low in his throat. He clasped both hands around Kyle's dick and began to stroke in time. Their bodies jerked with the same needy, spiraling cadence.

"Look at this monster." Nate's Adam's apple bobbed on a gulp. "Goddamn perfect. Harder now, Kyle. Fast and crazy like horny, stupid teens who didn't know the meaning of the word control. Let me see you be *wild*."

Something tripped over in Kyle's mind. Yes. He'd been that kid once. He'd fucked Nate because it felt good, because they needed one another, because they always laughed about it in a sweaty tangle afterward. They'd been innocent. And damn it if innocent didn't look a lot like wild.

He gripped Nate's thighs, hooked his toes behind Nate's knees, and let himself go. Their bodies slapped in perfect time. The pleasure of being stroked so completely was stealing everything but the need to explode. Good.

"Aw, damn, Kyle. Look at you." Nate's words were gasps now. "Look at your prick when you come on me."

"I'm close."

"Shit, I've been close for an hour. Give me what I want. Now."

Nate jerked harder, until the quick, relentless flick of his wrist and his fingers squeezing Kyle's head was too much to hold back. His orgasm hit him like a brick between the eyes. He cried out, pumping into clenched hands. Hot streams of come streaked across Nate's chest.

"Fuck, yes." Nate's curses became a mantra until he threw his head back, neck straining, and shoved his prick one last time. Ground up. Tensed. Groaned. "Yes, Kyle. Oh, shit—*yes*."

A minute later Kyle bowed low and slid off Nate's softening dick. He'd be sore in the morning, but it was worth what they'd shared. They gathered each other into an embrace that was almost apologetic. That word didn't sound right, but it felt right—as if apologizing for the violence and the mean feelings.

But then, same as when they'd been kids, they started to laugh. First a low chuckle from Nate, and then a grin from Kyle, while he licked rivulets of sweat from Nate's throat. The laughter had been as much a part of them as the passion and the secrets. It felt unbelievably good to have that back.

"Cock slut," Nate whispered.

"You know it." Chest to chest, they were plastered together by sweat and Kyle's release. "But, Nathan, my dear boy, I'm afraid something's come between us."

"Oh, you did not just say that."

Kyle laughed, full-bodied and freeing. "I did."

The look of exhausted amazement on Nate's face was a surprise. Not an unpleasant one. "See? Wild. We were always good like that."

"Seems we still are."

The air between them grew thicker once again, only this time with all that remained unspoken. The old hurts. The old fears. Kyle didn't want that night ruined. They'd skated too near ruin already.

"So," he said, awkwardly standing as his blood rushed back to his feet and his brain. He pulled Nate up to join him, where they wound their arms together automatically—kissing, holding, quietly thanking. "Your bed or mine?"

Chapter Twelve

Nate wasn't unfamiliar with the feeling of waking up tangled with another man, but this was different. Normally, he was the one sprawled all over his partner. It had always been that way with Jaime, his ex. This time, Kyle held him in a death grip, with one arm around his waist and a leg hooked around his ankle.

It was all Nate could do to wiggle out of bed and hit the bathroom. After he was done, he paused in the doorway and leaned one shoulder against the jamb. He gazed at Kyle.

With the bed to himself, he'd rolled onto his front, legs splayed. His taut, round ass barely thrust into the air. His face pressed flat into the pillows. One arm curled around his head, as if even in sleep he couldn't completely open up.

Which was fine with Nate. This thing they had going was temporary. He knew that. Even more, he was somewhat relieved. Last night had been . . . intense. Certainly more intense than a fling. Kyle had asked things of him that Nate wasn't ready to keep repeating.

Besides, taking risks to maintain a relationship with Kyle would verge on suicidal. Kyle made friends everywhere he went. He knew the names of every hotel clerk, the bartenders at the pub and most of the busboys, as well as the names of their family and where they grew up. He'd been in perfect form the night before, making friends with that couple. Maybe if he worked hard enough, it seemed, he'd eventually earn a welcoming smile from every single person he passed.

That wasn't the same thing as making connections—knowing people beyond superficial levels. Nate needed something more, something big enough to wipe away the pain of their youthful go-round.

He could return to bed. Run his hand over the small ligaments up the side of Kyle's spine and maybe put his teeth to Kyle's shoulder. Lick the peach-fuzzed cleft of his ass. Wake him with wetness and heat and need. Self-preservation told him to back away.

He ducked into the bathroom and turned on the shower. Water pattered down, filling the small room with white noise. Steam rolled out as the water heated.

Being near Kyle was like mainlining heroin. That potency drove straight to Nate's veins. He'd get a wild shock, followed by drowsy afterglow. The pain came with the withdrawal. How much worse would it be this time? Even if he wanted an affair with Kyle to last beyond London, Nate couldn't trust who they'd be together. The golden boy in the closet and the ex-con in the shadows, waiting, never really knowing which life Kyle would choose.

Nate couldn't live that way.

He stepped into the shower, drawing shut the curtain. Hell, the fact that he was about to shower in Kyle's room instead of his own made no fucking sense—except that fear of withdrawal. He might not be ready to crawl back into bed with the man, but he didn't seem ready to leave either.

Scrubbing both hands down his face, he ducked his head under the stream. Near-scalding water stung his skin.

Still, there was no mistaking the sound of the door opening, nor the quiet sounds of Kyle getting cleaned up.

The curtain moved aside. Kyle's mouth was curved in a smile, but his dark eyes were shadowed. Maybe hesitant.

"Room for two?"

Nate tugged him in by the wrist. "Of course."

"Kind of cramped."

It was, in the best kind of way. The shower wasn't built for two grown men, but that meant plenty of slipping and sliding against each other. Nate's dick brushed over the rough texture of Kyle's outer thigh as they traded positions. Kyle ducked under the water with a sound of pleasure that went straight to Nate's head. Then way lower.

On a ledge was a small glass bottle of expensive-looking body wash. Only the best for Kyle, but the scent alone seemed worth it. Lively and clean, the gel smelled like woods and crisp leaves.

He lathered up, letting his hands run slowly over his stomach and chest. Kyle watched, and Nate liked that too much to say. His cock stirred lazily. He was surprised they both weren't rubbed raw considering how hard they'd gone.

"Got any plans for the day?"

Kyle briskly washed his own body. "Paperwork. I've got to go through a giant stack Steph left for me."

"So fun. And on a Sunday, no less."

His grin was sudden but bright. "It is, kind of. It's all about making my production company the best on the block."

Nate shook his head and traded places to rinse. "I never, ever would have guessed you'd end up in Hollywood."

"No?" Kyle rinsed off fast, then bracketed Nate with hands on the tile walls. "Not even a clue?"

His hands found a resting place on Kyle's firm waist. His thumbs made tiny strokes over the sharp V-line that arrowed downward. "I thought you were going into finance like your dad."

"Running hedge funds? No way." Kyle chuckled. "I always said that was the last thing I'd do. You didn't believe me?"

Nate didn't answer. He couldn't. Yeah, Kyle had always *said* that, but he'd also talked about coming out. Eventually. Once he was free of his parents. And look how well that went.

"You were always damn good with numbers," Nate said, sidestepping the issue. "You got me through pre-calc."

"Nah, once you got stubborn, you had it made." Kyle nuzzled his shoulder, wet on wet. "But all those hours we spent watching movies. Everything. Every kind of movie. All the genres. It was practically training."

Nate remembered those hours. Thousands of them, spent in Kyle's larger dorm room at the boarding school. They'd always gone to Kyle's room because his rich parents paid to make sure he didn't have a roommate. Most times, they'd spent their hours wrapped up on the couch, free to get as grabby as they liked.

Nate had lived for lying with his head in Kyle's lap. Nothing in his life had been easy, starting with growing up without a mom. First she'd been an alcoholic, then she'd been . . . gone. His dad had done the best he could, filling out a hundred grant applications so Nate would have a better option than the slums of DC. But ultimately he was a trucker on the road more than three hundred days a year. Nothing had been easy for Nate, except for curling into Kyle and hoping for more—more than a kid like him could ever have.

Being with Kyle had made that sort of dreaming possible.

But all he said was, "I remember."

Kyle's grin spread with endearing enthusiasm. "We practically went to film school together."

"If you wanna put it that way." He ran his hands up Kyle's firm sides, let his thumbs slide over flat nipples that quickly beaded. "But if we're talking percentage of time used in those days, you and I ought to be porn stars."

"We watched plenty of that too. Another education in itself." The heat woke between them. Kyle's neck thickened on a heavy swallow. He wrapped a hand around Nate's prick in a tight grip. "Want to practice for our next close-up?"

He kissed Nate. His mouth, warm and soft, tasted of mint. Nate framed the sides of that strong jaw, feeling it shift under his touch. He pushed back and liked that Kyle subtly strained forward to keep the kiss going. Small challenges. Neither giving ground. Neither wanting it any other way.

"Let's get out of the shower first," Nate said.

They managed to dry off between a few more kisses and made it to the bed. Where they'd slept together. Slept. Dreams and coziness. Nate couldn't think about that anymore.

He'd always liked morning sex. A little lazy, a little indulgent. He wrapped his hands around both of their cocks, lining them up so that heads knocked and shafts stroked. Pressure and softness was enough, and he wanted to be able to watch Kyle's eyes, to see the lovely drugging haze that enveloped him in no time.

Nate switched his grip, taking only Kyle's prick in hand. With strong tugs from the base to the head, he moved faster and faster. Kyle's expression strained. The skin over his cheeks tightened and the tips of his ears turned red—the moment when he gave up everything. His hands clawed Nate's back, his grip tough and rock steady.

Nate handled him firmly enough that the bed jerked. The headboard made a knocking noise against the wall, once, twice.

He slammed out a hand and pressed flat against the cool wooden headboard. No distractions.

He couldn't help but grin. "I want you to come for me, like last night. All over me, Kyle. You're going to make a mess and it's going to feel damn good."

Three wanks later, he did. One long groan accompanied a spurt across Nate's stomach. Lovely, taut hips twitched with the last jerks of pleasure. Kyle's words were mostly gibberish with a "fuck yeah" or two thrown in for good measure.

Nate rocked back on his knees, feet tucked under his ass. His own dick was pulsing with hunger. He framed it in a solid grip, held it out. "You know how to thank me, don't you?"

"Hell yes," Kyle said, scrambling for his prize.

He sucked with pure enthusiasm. His mouth was a slippery, sleek furnace that burned up to Nate's skull and vacuumed his brains. Not that he was trying to hold back. He cradled Kyle's face in both hands and added gentle pressure.

He wanted to flat-out *take*. Jam Kyle downward and fuck and growl and bite. But he wasn't going to last, not when Kyle scooped bold fingers beneath Nate's balls and tugged and pushed with a rhythm that matched the way he mouth-fucked.

Kyle slid his lips off with a gentle plop and looked up. His hands kept working. "It's your turn now. You're going to come in my mouth, and you'll feel me swallow every last drop. And then we'll go again later."

Returning to his task, Kyle swallowed Nate's head beneath the nudge of his tongue.

"Later," Nate said, trancelike.

That was it. That was enough. The thought that they'd be able to have another round. Something *more*.

Pleasure rocked him from head to heel. At the first twitch, Kyle snatched Nate's hand and pressed it to his throat. The man's lovely neck shifted and tightened with swallows Nate could actually feel happening, adding another layer of amazing to his release.

Kyle always did know exactly what he needed.

They fell into a sweat-sheened heap on the bed. Kyle rested his head on Nate's heaving stomach but didn't seem to mind the slight bounce.

"Morning quickie for the win." Nate's voice was still rough. Not that he was complaining in the least.

Kyle stretched, one arm over Nate's chest. "Great. Now give me coffee."

"I'm fresh out."

"Phone by your elbow."

Ordering room service was the work of a moment. He passed the phone to Kyle after he'd made his own selections, but he needn't have bothered.

Nate smirked as Kyle hung the phone back on the receiver. "Two eggs, an English muffin, and coffee? Really?"

Kyle watched him, wary and amused at the same time. "Yeah?"

Pouncing, Nate pushed his lover flat to the bed and tickled up his ribs and down the inside of his thighs. "You're so fucking predictable."

"I am not. And that's just mean," he said through helpless laughs.

"You eat the same breakfast you did ten goddamn years ago." He wrenched Kyle's wrists overhead, pressing them into the pillows. "I bet you still drink your coffee the same."

Kyle sighed. He rolled his eyes, his usual attitude sneaking back in. "One sugar, two creams."

"See? Same."

"I like what I like. Absolutely nothing wrong with that."

Nate kissed him because he couldn't help it. Because he wanted to taste that self-assurance. It was part of what made Kyle's reluctance to come out so damn strange. In everything else he was assured and confident. Why not this?

Why not the parts that involved Nate?

At least that question didn't have the same sting it used to. Their original blowup had revolved around that very problem. Afterward, alone in prison, Nate had assumed some of Kyle's reluctance was because he'd be forced to claim a street-rat ex car thief as his lover. It was reassuring that a decade hadn't been time enough for Kyle to creep out of his cramped closet. The problem had been his, with nothing to do with Nate.

That didn't change the fact that Nate wouldn't settle for a man who hid.

But he did sure as hell like the way Kyle kissed, as if they were the only people in the world.

Good enough for now.

Nate reluctantly dragged the kiss down, pulling away with slow licks. He took Kyle's bottom lip between both of his, then offered a smaller, softer kiss to the side. "No, nothing's wrong with having preferences. But I bet you haven't done anything silly and stupid and pointless in years. *Years*," he echoed, drawing the word out into a complete tease.

"Last night wasn't proof enough for you?"

"That wasn't silly." Nate smirked. "That was fucking hot. So spill it. Silliness. I don't think you have it in you."

"You think so?" Kyle's expression was painted with disdain. His brow furrowed, and his wide mouth quirked. "You know what? It is *on*."

A trace of alarm made Nate's heartbeat pick up. "What does that mean?"

"You'll see." At last Kyle grinned. Wide and pure. "You're so going to regret your dare. That, Nathan, is a promise."

Chapter Thirteen

"**W**hat do you mean you won't have the Taggart proposal done by tomorrow?"

Steph's voice was sharp with displeasure. She was very, quite, *much* displeased, though she was doing a great job of speaking calmly.

"You obviously heard what I said." Kyle smiled at Nate as their minicab stopped to let pedestrians cross. He'd thought the rail stations were packed, but traffic was thicker in Woking where so many had congregated for shopping and holiday activities. "So, why don't you ask what's really on your mind?"

"Are you with Nate?"

"Yes."

There was a long silence, then a sigh loud enough to carry over cell phones. "Okay. I got Taggart. Might work better this way," she said with a wry-sounding laugh. "He's a lecherous old man who thinks I'm a total babe."

"You *are* a total babe. See you tomorrow."

"Riiight. I'll believe that when I see you both on set." She paused for a heartbeat. "Have a good time, Kyle. You deserve it. Just . . . be careful."

He couldn't answer that one, so he grunted something and thumbed off his phone. The issue of whether he deserved another shot with Nate—not the makings of the best afternoon. Not to mention Steph's general dislike of the situation, and Kyle's resulting flakiness. He'd never been someone she had to doubt. It wasn't a new habit he wanted to cultivate.

So he turned the phone on vibrate, stuffed it in his trench coat's inner pocket, and took Nate's hand. "Figured it out yet?"

"Hell no. At the moment it looks like you're taking me to a mall."

"But it's a *really big* mall."

"Because we don't have those in America," Nate said dryly.

"No, because they don't have them here. Not like this. So technically this is a British novelty."

Nate's skepticism was amusing. He was so damn avaricious when it came to control. "Worth an hour on the train?"

The trip had been something out of a dream, leaving the fantasy of London for a place where no one knew them. Maybe it was cowardly of Kyle, but he craved that anonymity. More than that, he craved having Nate all to himself—no work, no pressure, no arguments looming with each new sentence.

Curled together, they'd watched the sunset and the lights flick on across countless little London boroughs before reaching the southwestern suburbs. Quiet conversation. Comfortable silence. And touching. Always touching. The train had taken them out of one fantasy into another, where it was all right for Kyle to kiss a man in public.

He wanted to do it again, so he leaned near. Lips on the gently salty skin of Nate's throat. "Tell me you didn't enjoy it."

"Shut up and tell me what we're doing here." But he said it with the barest smile.

"We're going inside." Kyle gave his best nonchalant shrug. "Stuff to do."

"Good, college boy. Let's shop for another collar for you."

"What's wrong with the one I have?"

"Nothing. But there's something to be said for variety."

Kyle warmed in ways that had nothing to do with their shared passion. The buzzing undercurrent of desire was always there, but he was beginning to seek more of their renewed camaraderie and fun. He hadn't realized how much he simply wanted a male friend. He'd always kept men at arm's length, knowing that nothing more meaningful could ever come of an accidental mutual attraction.

The cabbie dropped them off outside the soaring, massive front entrance of the Peacock Shopping Centre, where people hustled in and out. Little kids. Shopping bags. Couples, arm in arm.

Kyle caught Nate looking at one such couple as the man and woman passed. No, it wasn't even a look. Just a glance, ending with a shift of his blue eyes. The heartbreaking part was how he let those beautiful eyes drift toward the pavement, which was slick with a sheen of ice and rock salt.

It wasn't silly or stupid, but it was spontaneous when Kyle took Nate's hand. This time the blue glance was meant for Kyle, with words of protest already shaping Nate's firm lips.

"I'm not dicking around," Kyle said quietly. "This is a date and I'm treating it like one."

"You'll see it through?"

God, the suspicion in his rough voice was enough to shred Kyle's guts into bloody strips. He'd never had any faith they could face the tough stuff together, that maybe, with enough time and trust, Kyle could be the man he needed. Instead they spiraled on this nauseating twist of doubt and self-doubt.

Kyle reined in his frustrations. Nate didn't understand how much safer they were here. It was an entire ocean away from his family's cronies and political influence. They didn't just participate in key circles of wealth and understated power; they guided them.

Keep it light. Keep it a good time. That was becoming more and more difficult. Truthfully, he didn't *want* to keep it light anymore. Nate, however, had made his expectations clear. All or nothing. In or out. That meant a casual, "really, it's nothing" evening was the most he could have. If he had to live on that knife's edge, he wouldn't be sane for long.

December, though. He could enjoy December if he curtailed any expectations of more.

"I did on the train, didn't I? No flinching or pulling away there. You going to poke at me that it wasn't enough?"

Nate only shook his head.

"All right, then. But the deal is, you've got to see *this* through."

"The mall? Christ, I have yet to see anything other than collar-shopping potential."

"Probably some at Ann Summers, but it's BDSM for the vanilla crowd. And not much for guys."

Nate arched his brows. He tucked away his surprise just as fast. "Too bad. But you should know I'm getting impatient."

They stepped into the shopping center where a huge banner proclaimed the seasonal production of *Puss 'n' Boots*.

Kyle nodded toward it. "There."

"There, what?"

"We have tickets to a pantomime."

At least his doubt was aimed at the giant, light-festooned banner, with some pretty young man as the hero and a faded British television star as the so-called headliner.

"You're kidding," Nate said.

"Not in the least." He glanced toward where they still held hands. "A deal's a deal. Come on. We'll be late."

Nate shook his head again, but this time he did so with a bright and beautiful grin.

Walkways crisscrossed the mall over multiple stories. People surged and pushed and laughed—the general atmosphere of the season in a rush to corral the kids and grab the right gift. Or a good enough gift, if it came to that.

Nate laughed. "Santa barfed all over this place. I mean, *damn*. So this is how the Brits do overblown commercialism?"

"Yup."

"I'm liking them more and more."

They found the walkway toward the New Victoria Theatre entrance. A plush red runner led them past poster after poster for future productions.

"Look," Nate said. "We're walking the red carpet."

"One day."

"What was that?"

Kyle swallowed, glad the whimsical comment was drowned out by the tighter corridor where a hundred conversations between a hundred families bounced off the walls and the low ceiling. After handing over the tickets, an usher showed Kyle and Nate to their seats. It had cost him a pretty penny and a few favors to get good seats at such short notice, but Kyle was pleased by the results. Fifth row. Center stage.

Nate let go of Kyle's hand so he could look through the playbill. "What's *Coronation Street*?"

"A soap that's been on for something like fifty years."

"So the headliner is a soap opera has-been? What the hell *is* this? And how do you know so much about all this crap?"

"You're rather surly for wanting something stupid and silly."

Nate shrugged, his shoulders tense. "Prison makes a guy leery of surprises."

Despite the sharp reminder of Nate's past—it was so easy to forget when they were mindless and wrapped inside one another—Kyle was determined to keep the afternoon lighthearted. He didn't know what he deserved, like what Stephanie had suggested, but he and Nate really needed to unwind.

"Look, I was here at Christmas last year to scout locations. My guide was a local, showed me all the goofy traditions. I was a skeptic too, but you'll have to trust me that it's a good time."

The lights flickered to indicate the show was about to start. Kyle set the handbill on the floor and took Nate's hand once again. Damn, he liked how that looked, so openly entwined. He leaned in close and whispered as if what he described was the most erotic story he could ever imagine—though having Nate so close was erotic enough.

"Pantos are held all over the country every Christmas. Anyone who's ever been on television and on the West End spreads out over the country, with practically every town and village putting on its own show. They're always based on fairy tales."

"Like our *Puss 'n' Boots*."

"Exactly. *Cinderella*, *Aladdin*, whatever. There's always one star—"

"So-called."

"—a couple young actors and actresses to fill the leads, and, well, one guy in drag."

Nate snort-laughed. "Seriously?"

"Not kidding. Now shut up, enjoy the show, and hiss at the villain."

"Hiss . . .?"

Kyle only grinned as the lights lowered and the curtain opened. The pratfalls made a hundred kids giggle, while the double entendres flew right over their heads. Within minutes, Nate was hiding a smile behind his free hand. Kyle laughed outright.

After a particularly ribald exchange between mother and son, complete with the inference that mama dearest supplemented her laundry business through prostitution, Nate finally cracked up. His laugh was *gorgeous*. He was wiping tears from his eyes by the end of the opening scene.

Kyle leaned close again, breathing Nate's clean, crisp scent. He was slightly musky and incredibly delicious. "I like the hero, don't you?"

"Too pretty for my taste," Nate said with a mean grin. "Give me rough and ready any day."

Kyle hadn't realized he was still capable of blushing, if he'd ever been, but heat burned his cheeks. "You do mean me, right?"

Nate gave his hand a squeeze. "Course."

The villain walked on stage—well, *slunk*—and those same hundred kids hissed and warned the hero with calls of "Look behind you!" So did their parents. So did Kyle. Nate looked ready to sink into his seat.

Kyle grinned at him. "You wanted silly and stupid. I'm fairly sure this counts as buckets of it."

"Yes. You win the dare. Kyle Wakefield can be stupid."

"What was that?" Kyle tucked two fingers behind his ear and leaned toward Nate. "All I heard was something about me winning."

"You're damn lucky you're cute when you're a brat."

"And that you're having a good time."

The easy, relaxed grin he got in return was absolutely worth it. "Yes. That too."

At intermission, he led Nate around a spiraling ramp to the concession area. That Nate stood shoulder to shoulder with him, their hips near enough to flirt, was making Kyle feel younger and more relaxed than he'd felt in years. Steph had always said he was the oldest twenty-eight-year-old on the planet, but he hadn't realized how right she was until right then. Nate breathed life into him.

"What, popcorn or something?" Nate asked.

"Better." Just then, his cell phone buzzed in his pocket. He pulled it out to see the display. His stomach took a sickly flip, but he pressed the red button to reject the call.

"Who is it?" Nate asked.

"My mother." Two swipes later and his phone was on airplane mode. Once she got it in her head that it was time to talk to Kyle, she would call six times in a row. Literally and exactly. Then she'd do it at the same time the next day, then the next, unceasing, until she got a response. No distance seemed far enough. He pushed away thoughts of them and made himself smile. "Come on. We're going to miss our snacks."

Ten minutes later, barely in time to make the purchase before the lights dimmed again, Kyle came away with his prizes.

"You are insane." Nate tossed his gaze around the massive concession area as people filed back around the ramp toward the body of the theater. "No, these people are insane." He took one of the small white containers Kyle handed him. "I mean, *ice cream*? Are you serious?"

"And tea."

Nate trod behind Kyle, still wearing his mixed expression of confusion and amusement.

They settled back in their seats and proceeded to hiss and boo and laugh with the rest of the crowd. It was damn difficult to eat ice cream off a little wooden spoonlike paddle while in a darkened theater, but they managed. Then came tea with milk and sugar. It was all so British that Kyle grinned in wonder. Two countries separated by a common language . . . and a few weird-ass traditions.

"You missed some," Nate whispered.

"Hmm?"

There was no mistaking what he meant when Nate licked a dribble of ice cream off Kyle's lower lip. They kissed softly, almost hesitantly, even as the raucous story amped toward its conclusion. Kyle no longer thought to resist that public display. The dark helped. The distraction helped too. But mostly he *wanted* Nate to kiss him. There was nothing better. Not even the sex compared to giving and taking on such a heartfelt level.

A remembered stab of jealousy and want nearly ruined the moment for Kyle. Since being released from prison, Nate had lived with men, had kept up long relationships with men. That meant he'd shared mundane routines and taken-for-granted moments, such as exchanging quiet kisses that had nothing to do with amping up for a good fuck.

The part of Kyle's soul he'd thought closed off—kept busily distracted with work and silenced by fear—was pushing free. He wanted mundane and taken-for-granted and quiet. He'd never let himself experience that level of closeness.

Nate licked his lips, his voice hushed. "You taste good."

"You smell good."

"I want to feel you up."

Kyle glanced to his right where a sandy-haired boy of six laughed and pointed at the man in drag. "Some other time." He caught Nate's chin, forcing their gazes to lock. The spotlights were aimed at the stage, but enough light remained to see one another clearly. "But it's not because I don't want you to."

It's because I want you too much.

Lost in that unexpected limbo, he looped his arm through Nate's and nestled as close as he could manage. Heat and breathing and heartbeats. Nate, Kyle, and the whole audience continued to play along with the panto as the hero and heroine came together for a melodramatic hug.

Kyle knew it wouldn't last forever. Eventually the curtain would fall, the lights would come up, and he and Nate would lose each other in the crowd. That thought pinched genuine pain under his ribs. The clock was ticking. Christmas Day was the last day of shooting.

Maybe it didn't have to be that way. Neither of them had said that the final day of shooting *Fast Money* meant the end of them. They both lived and worked in Hollywood, after all. Yet dark subjects still lurked between them. Kyle could keep ignoring it all for the sake of a casual reunion, but anything of substance would mean ripping through old scars. How much of them would remain? Raw, vulnerable pain and unforgiveable mistakes?

Kyle couldn't even guess. Just like he couldn't guess what it would feel like to come out. *Finally*. It was probably some mix of terrifying and freeing, powerful enough that his hands began to shake.

But the pantomime was good. Right. Fun. Their sexual chemistry was nuclear. He would have Nate. And have him again. He could depend on that. The rest was the mental ramblings of an eighteen-year-old boy who'd staked everything on a future with Nathan Carnes. They'd both lost.

The cast returned to the stage for individual acknowledgments before taking a group bow.

Then the music started up. "Jingle Bells," to be precise.

Kyle glanced sidelong at Nate, who again wore a startled, mystified expression. "What the hell?"

"What, I didn't mention that pantos are followed by an audience singalong?"

"No. No, you didn't."

"Shut up and sing, stuntman."

"I do *not* sing Christmas carols."

"Fine." Kyle sat up and disentangled their arms. "Have it your way. Wuss."

Nate laughed and grabbed Kyle's arm back. Held tight. And proved to have a fairly decent baritone voice when he finally joined in. Kyle wanted to memorize every single breath. It was a moment out of time, one he would cherish for the rest of his life, when he and the man who'd haunted most of his life sang Christmas carols in a theater full of people bursting with holiday cheer.

It was too saccharine sweet to admit how much he adored each second.

After the music ended and the crowd began to thin, Nate flicked him a mock-wary look. "Dare I even ask what's next?"

"Dinner, of course."

"Oh good. I'm starving."

"Then it's off to the food court with us."

Nate chuckled. "Suuure, Kyle. You and food courts and that fucking gorgeous watch of yours are a natural fit."

"Hater. You won't be complaining after you're stuffed full of a tikka masala jacket potato."

"I don't wanna know."

But he was smiling. And they were still arm in arm as they walked out of the theater.

Chapter Fourteen

Nate knew he occasionally verged on anal retentive, but with regard to his job, he didn't think it was a bad thing. This was serious business after all. Four days following the evening panto, his solo assignment was complicated. Just because he was on his own didn't mean he could relax. Even minor risks could go badly, and today wasn't minor.

Every stuntman in the business could name a colleague who'd broken bones—including skulls—over drops less than twenty feet. So zooming a motorcycle over a bridge, making a less-than-ninety-degree turn onto an embankment, then ditching it and landing on a boat . . . Nate had every obligation to quadruple-check the whole operation.

As he had throughout *Fast Money*, he was playing the part of the bad guy, this time trying desperately to evade and escape. Raney, standing in for Durant, would give chase in a sequence filmed later that afternoon. The set piece would be tied in with the boat chase they'd filmed last week. For all the thought he put into his obsession, Nate might be on screen for about two minutes.

He choked down a grin. Such a sacrifice. Sure.

He fucking *loved* his job. When else would he have the chance to ride a motorcycle into a watery abyss for fun and profit? Didn't hurt that it was a very sweet Ducati sport bike too.

He checked the track along the Embankment one last time, then found Raney waiting at the far end. The man already wore his fire-resistant suit.

Raney's expression was grim. He smacked a pair of gloves in one palm. "I don't like the wind."

Nate had checked and rechecked the weather reports. The gusts were occasionally approaching ten miles an hour, but most of the time they were barely more than a breeze. Still, he couldn't help a measure of concern. "It's the launch that will be the greatest concern. If I'm off by a couple degrees..."

Raney nodded. He was a tall guy with carefully styled golden-blond hair. Very few people would have guessed he'd done almost five years for fraud. Nor would they guess he could drive anything with wheels. "You won't land where you're supposed to."

"If that means the water, it'll be fine."

"And if means anywhere else?"

"I'll break something." He said it casually, but he knew the hazards all too well.

There had been a time when he wouldn't have given a shit. He'd been fresh out of prison, still reporting to a parole officer, when very little had mattered. He'd been determined never to go back, but plans didn't progress much beyond that. Staying alive hadn't been a priority.

That he'd managed to make it through those first months on the outside had been a happy accident.

"We have some room to delay," Raney said. "If we need to."

"Not much." Nate glanced back toward the far end of the bridge, where he'd start his run.

Kyle stood there. Not alone, of course. Stephanie was at his side and they were facing Peter Upton, who sprawled in his personalized director's chair. Even from that distance, Nate read the body language. Peter's chin was angled high in the air, yet he wasn't looking at either Stephanie or Kyle. The smile on Kyle's face was conciliatory, and to most it would have seemed quite friendly.

Nate couldn't possibly be the only one who saw how pissed Kyle was. Stephanie shot him a wary look before matching his eat-shit-and-die smile at Upton.

Stuffing down a grin, Nate rechecked his clipboard.

He should have known better. There was no hiding from Raney. They'd known each other inside the joint. Become friends. Allies. Forged together by an environment only ex-cons could understand. That made it a little hard to run the same tricks Nate used on everyone else.

"So." Raney crossed his arms over his chest, drawing out the word.

"So," Nate intentionally echoed. If his friend had a question, he could go ahead and ask it.

"How's Jaime?"

Nate jerked up on his toes. "What?"

Raney's smile was rather . . . pointed. Smug. He had a too-pretty face and was certainly handsome enough to be a star rather than a stuntman. Good for Nate that he couldn't act for shit. "Heard from him lately?"

"No."

Nate was friends with a couple of his exes, but not Jaime. That one fell under the category of *spectacular blowout*. Which Raney very well knew. He'd been there through it all.

Nate scowled. "Do you have a point?"

"Why did he dump you, again?"

"Man, you're heartless. I lived with the guy for almost two years. You don't think you should be more tactful than 'why did he dump you'?"

Raney started walking toward the start point of the stunt. "You tell me. That was a year ago. You still all crushed and sad feeling?"

"No. Fucker." Nate grinned. "But you could at least try to wrangle a few manners."

"Just because you're gay and I'm bi doesn't mean we have to hold hands and talk about *feelings*."

Nate handed his clipboard to Raney and hitched up his jumpsuit as he walked, zipping the front placket and patting down the Velcro. "You try to hold my hand and I'll think you're hitting on me."

"I have a feeling that would put someone else's nose out of joint."

Nate came to a jerky, sudden stop in the middle of the bridge. Hot, spiking fear turned his stomach into a burning coal. "What?"

"That's him, isn't it?" Raney had finally found his damn point. He angled his head toward Kyle with a tiny nod. "That's the one Jaime had a problem with."

"Jaime had a lot of problems. I think the final straw was when I forgot to buy soy milk."

But really, his head was spinning. Kyle would freak the fuck out if he had an inkling of this conversation. Nate trusted Raney implicitly and knew he'd never talk, but that was beside the point.

"Do me a favor, Carnes, and don't bullshit me."

"I'm not."

"Uh-huh." Raney's blue eyes were filled with doubt. "You want to tell me why we haven't been out for a beer since we got here? Why you've ditched on me twice?"

"Ale. They drink ale here. Or lager."

"Shut the hell up, asshole." He slugged Nate's shoulder.

Nate was pretty sure Raney had guessed only because he had inside knowledge. Jaime hadn't been the most discreet person in the world, and he'd bitched about their relationship problems far and wide. His complaints included everything from Nate's "cruel punishments," like forgetting the soy milk, to his "unrequited love" for Kyle. The extreme level of drama had made it complicated to sort out which complaints had merit and which were complete crap.

As they drew to a halt in front of a knot of people that included Kyle, the ember of worry in Nate's gut turned into a flame. He didn't like that Kyle kept everything secret. That was for damn sure. Since the panto, they hadn't spent intimate time together. They'd both been too busy to spend whole nights fucking, but Kyle's rules meant even dinner together was out of the question.

So he did his damnedest not to think about having Kyle's mouth wrapped around his cock. That was actually the easiest to ignore. If he set his mind right, Nate could convince himself that Kyle was just another fuck. The real torture came when he remembered the silky texture of Kyle's hair under his palm, or sleeping together, curled in a place of contentment he'd never known with anyone else.

He shoved his hands in his pockets and stared at Stephanie. She was the safer half of Pennfield. "We're ready to go."

Upton shifted in his chair, chest puffing up slightly. "I think I'm the one who determines that."

Nate ignored the tension that turned his spine into a soldered line. He needed to be relaxed and in control—not letting the taunts of a bona fide asshole turn him inside out.

"Of course you are, Peter," Kyle said, his voice pitched toward soothing. But behind the director's line of sight, Kyle's glimmering brown eyes telegraphed amusement. "And I know you were about to ask about the possible impact of the wind."

Upton fiddled with the back strap of his baseball cap. "If anyone would give me half a second, yeah, I was."

Nate was sure glad Upton made blockbuster flicks. Somehow. Otherwise working on *Fast Money* wouldn't be worth the hassle of dealing with his condescending attitude. Nate proceeded to explain the possible repercussions of the wind and what they'd done to prepare. As he did, he assessed the path down which he would maneuver the Ducati. More particularly, he eyed the ramp at the end of the route.

"In the end, it might be easier to make it two shots. The bridge portion, then cut away before the embankment and ramp."

"You'll kill the artistic tension," Upton said with a scowl.

Artistic tension? Nate couldn't control the way he chuffed a laugh. The assmunch had to be kidding. Unlike a lot of action flicks, *Fast Money* had plenty going for it—actors with realistic chemistry, a script with a surprising turn and snappy dialogue.

But artistry? This wasn't Fellini.

Kyle shot the director an unreadable look—part professional tact, part arrogant attitude. "Sometimes we have to sacrifice artistic integrity in favor of safety. You wouldn't want your name attached to injuries or recklessness. I know you value your ethics too much for that."

Damn, he was good at that. So charming. The golden boy everyone wanted to know and everyone wanted to be near—even Nate, when he was one of the few who realized what magic Kyle conjured.

Did anyone understand the whole of Kyle? Probably not even Steph, who by all accounts was his closest friend. No one was privileged enough to witness each aspect of him, or what he was really like in all possible situations.

Nate probably came closest. He'd seen Kyle doubtful and furious and sad—plus turned on to the point of losing control, that rare state of being. He'd seen him as a fantastic student, an obnoxiously good athlete, and a proper society boy.

But never as the good son. Nate hadn't been welcomed into Kyle's family life, not as a friend and certainly not as a lover.

Maybe that was fine. No one got to see all the shine of a golden boy. That would ruin the charm and mystery. At least Nate had a leg up on the rest of the world. Maybe he didn't get everything, but he got the *most*. It was barely enough to make all the sneaking and hiding palatable—to make up for the fact that he couldn't ask for a kiss for luck.

For now.

Unlike Kyle, Nate couldn't keep his feelings under wraps forever. Prison had taught him about confinement. He'd never volunteer for that trapped, airless existence again. Staying with Kyle beyond this pleasant rendezvous would mean sacrifices Nate wasn't prepared to make. Would *never* make. Not even for Kyle.

Once Kyle finished talking Upton down from his snit, he turned to Nate. "Ultimately, this portion is your call. Delaying to another day is impossible with our permits, but if the wind means you need to break it up differently, we can shift the cameras."

Nate's eyes narrowed. Part of him wondered what Kyle was getting at. Did he doubt Nate's ability to make the stunt work? He'd thought that was a matter in the past. There were so many reasons for Kyle to waver at that moment, but Nate didn't know which were legit and which were his old doubts creeping back.

Upton seemed to pick up on the tension. His embroidered baseball cap jutted forward. A wide, fake smile spread over his face, showing off blinding white caps. "Just remember. If I see one single review that says 'subpar stunt work,' you'll be the one who never works on a big-budget picture again. I'm totally on the books as being against hiring your asses. Wouldn't have happened if it weren't for these two," he added, hitching a thumb over his shoulder at Kyle and Steph.

It wasn't the threat that did it. Nope. Nate wasn't exactly the type to cave to pressure. Otherwise, he'd have shaken the hand of Kyle's father, agreed to the man's terms and settled for only six months in jail with a year of parole. Even as a dumbass eighteen-year-old punk, he'd had the guts to resist that cop-out.

No, he made up his mind at the reminder that Kyle had argued on his behalf to secure this gig for Second Chances. He wasn't letting anyone down. Not his crew. Not Kyle.

"One shot," he ground out. "Like we planned."

Everything started like clockwork. He revved the bike up to top speed in no time. The extras were placed for safety, with his personally selected stuntmen and women jumping dramatically out of the way.

Nate counter-steered into the sharp left turn, leaning until the tires screamed.

Adrenaline tingled in his veins as he dropped to one padded knee. The back of the motorcycle sprayed out in a carefully planned fishtail. Down the embankment, past more extras.

He leaned forward, into the sharp angle of the ramp that would be edited out in postproduction. A shimmer of triumph distracted him in a way no stuntman could allow. He was two steps ahead in his mind, landing in a crouch on the boat where padding waited for him.

Instead, it went wrong. Just wrong enough.

One gust. One fucking gust of wind swirled over the Thames at the same moment the bike's front wheel launched into open air.

Chapter Fifteen

K yle had seen stunts go right. Since taking his first assistant producer's position straight out of college, he'd watched as various crews from around the world, from Chinese acrobats to trick helicopter pilots, did the impossible. Despite the world of CGI, sometimes the real thing was too valuable to forego.

That meant he knew exactly when Nate's stunt went wrong.

He could see the storyboard in his mind, and the computer animation Nate had used to figure angles and velocities. He could see how Nate and the stunt director had placed a discreet ramp along the Embankment, and how the speedboat was supposed to ride close enough for Nate to leap.

Literally leap from a motorcycle.

The leap happened. Nate was suspended for what felt like an eternity between the bike and the boat. This was the sort of insane feat of daring Nathan Carnes was known for. No rigging. No backup plan beyond a leap of faith.

The unmanned motorcycle careened into the nearest pylon, which was wired with explosives for a dynamic finish. Perfect. But Kyle's heart had crammed in his throat as he peered through the flying sparks and billowing flames.

Nate missed the padded landing platform on the speedboat's hull, concealed inches beneath the water. He should've landed there, then pretended to scramble for a hold. Except he wasn't pretending. He'd saved himself by snagging one hand on the boat's slippery stern deck fitting.

His feet flew backward. Dragged at forty miles an hour, his body trailed nearly horizontal behind the craft.

"Shit," Stephanie whispered.

Kyle couldn't look at her. Couldn't look away.

Propellers churned the water.

One hand.

Jesus.

Among the chatter in Kyle's headset came one terse exchange—one he actually registered.

"Abort shoot?" That from the stunt director.

"No! Keep rolling!" That from Upton.

Kyle would've argued and, hell, knocked the man unconscious for keeping Nate at risk, but his feet had become the roots of a tree. He was paralyzed by the truth: aborting the shoot wouldn't save Nate. The boat's driver couldn't risk letting go of the wheel. Any turn, or even slowing the boat, could shake Nate's grip and fling him back into the churning blender of propellers. He needed steadiness—even at a thousand miles an hour—to work *with* momentum, not against it. It was man versus physics.

Kyle had to watch the entire fiasco play out, if only with the childish hope that by watching and hoping and cussing in his mind, he could keep the worst from happening.

Goddamn it, Nate, don't you fucking fall.

With an expression hewn of agony, Nate flailed with his free hand. He kept stretching and reaching, even as the boat's powerful engines rocked his body above the flowing river.

Only a lucky bounce over a wave threw his right foot forward. A boot specially designed with a gripping sole caught on the transom. Anchoring his foot, he was able to catch the deck fitting with both hands.

Kyle knew that expression, even at the distance of a few hundred yards. Nate was wearing his dangerously stubborn face. But now he had the grip necessary to save his dogged, idiotic ass. He caught his second boot in place, then launched forward to tackle the boat's driver. A half second later, Nate shoved the driver overboard, took control of the craft, and turned it in a sharp arc that sprayed a wall of water across the base of the nearest bridge pylons.

A goddamn perfect piece of cinema.

But the shot had run long by about twenty seconds. No telling whether the computer-controlled cameras—placed strategically down the river and along the Embankment—had been able to catch the stunt as Nate practically redesigned it on the fly.

"Cut!" Upton shouted, sounding furious.

Kyle added his own terse command. "EMTs on to the point of debarkation. Fire crews on the motorcycle wreckage. Divers, status?"

"That's the stunt coordinator's job and you know it," Steph said. Yet the tense lines around her eyes and the way she held her ubiquitous clipboard with white knuckles revealed her shared anxiety.

A report came in that the boat's driver had been successfully recovered by divers, unharmed, but no news yet on Nate. Pungent smoke lingered from where the motorcycle cooled beneath a layer of fire-retardant foam. Gasoline and exhaust tainted the afternoon air. Kyle felt like he was going to throw up.

They'd almost lost the shot. Kyle didn't give a fuck. The fists at his side had nothing to do with business or film. He wanted to know whether Nate was okay, and he wanted Nate to be any other man. *Any* other.

Because Kyle would have to watch his lover accomplish insane tricks like that for the next fourteen days.

It was no longer a matter of whether he'd hired Nate for professional or personal reasons. It was about escaping this goddamn December with his sanity intact.

Looked unlikely.

"That fucking useless douchebag."

Kyle whirled to find Upton striding forth with his headset down around his neck. Bundled in a giant parka, the punk asshole looked better outfitted for the North Pole, not London. Kyle only noticed because he'd quickly determined that hitting the man would mean aiming for the face. Upton wouldn't feel it painfully enough if Kyle struck his padded gut.

Steph's slender, cold fingers curled over Kyle's fist. "I got this."

"No." Kyle shrugged away from her cautioning touch and met Upton halfway. "What was that?"

"Your boy Carnes." Upton poked a finger toward Kyle's chest. "This is your production, but it's *my* movie. You said these jailbird dickheads were pros. *That* was not professional. That was a fuckup."

"Bullshit," Kyle spat. "He saved the whole damn thing, and our insurers will be happy to know he saved his ass too."

"Stuntmen are replaceable."

A low growl clawed up from Kyle's throat. Nate. Replaceable. The two words didn't belong in the same vicinity. Yet he had both of their careers to salvage, no matter how satisfying it would be to see Upton bleed. Kyle hadn't hit a guy since high school, and that had been over Nate as well.

Nate had been pissed as hell. "I can fight my own battles," he'd said.

Of course he could. But Kyle was in the mood for combat. No one had the right to call Nate charity trash or homo or *replaceable*.

He snatched off both of their headsets and threw them to the ground. Then he grabbed the placket of Upton's parka, hauling him close. No one else needed to hear this.

Upton's eyes went gratifyingly wide. "Get your hands off me, Wakefield."

"Not until I've told you exactly what I think of you right now. First, you were irresponsible. The stunt director asked to abort. *You* wanted to keep going. You knew it was off course and dangerous, but it was your call."

He gave the man a vehement shake—a poor substitute for the violence he really wanted to do. That Upton had intentionally left Nate at risk . . .

"But then," he growled, "you shot off that raunchy, bigoted mouth of yours, saying the shot was ruined. You can't have it both ways, Upton."

"Funny way of running a business." Upton's sneer was defiant. "See if behavior like this gets you another gig. Ever."

"Oh, don't worry about me. Worry about what will happen the next time I hear you treating *any* of my professionals like the piece of shit we know you are." Kyle shoved Upton away as if ridding himself of a rotten piece of meat. He wiped his hands along his trench coat to get rid of the feel.

Upton narrowed his eyes, stupidly arrogant to the end. "I'm gonna have you strung up by your balls."

"I'd only need to call the people with enough money to cut me down. You, however . . ." Kyle shrugged. "An up-and-coming director with a half-finished film starring two incredibly furious superstars. Agents. Lawyers. And yes, insurance men. I hope your sneer is strong enough to stare each of them down."

"The dailies," Steph called. She approached them cautiously, perhaps Kyle most of all. "Let's look at the dailies and get Tony in here to see how it'll affect the pacing."

Tony Manolo was the film's editor. The man was brilliant and gruff as fuck. Forty years in the business would do that to any man. Kyle hoped that wasn't his future, but after a day like today, he couldn't imagine otherwise.

He looked at Steph. Her chignon had come undone along her temples, where blonde hair flipped and twisted in the gathering breeze. The warning on her face was perfectly clear. Kyle could make all the threats he wanted against one man, and yes, most would understand losing one's temper around Peter Upton.

But they were a team.

Pennfield had been their dream for seven years, and their triumph for only the last two. It was still new, tenuous, in the proving stages. Kyle's name would buy a limited number of opportunities before the whole enterprise failed, buried under a reputation for volatility.

Producers could not be volatile. They were the lynchpins holding an entire project together. *Kyle* couldn't afford to be volatile, not in a way that would make itself known in Virginia. After the lengths his mother and father had gone to through the years to try to determine his every decision—and after as many years fighting back—he was tired of the war. He was tired of it even being a thing.

At the same time, he knew they played dirty. He's seen successful political and financial careers vanish in a whirlwind of scandalous tabloid stories, when people dared stand up his father's strong-arm "lobbying" and "negotiations." It wouldn't take more than a few calls over afternoon drinks for him to destroy anyone on set. Upton had no idea. Kyle did, and it left him feeling both powerless and furious—an absolutely toxic mix.

He wasn't stable. Not then. So he let Steph balance the gray edges of his temper. He gave her the barest nod.

He didn't like that he'd forced her into looking so relieved. But damn, he'd been close to losing it altogether.

"Here, let me get Tony on the line," she said, already dialing.

Kyle stalked away and grabbed a headset to inquire after Nate. Still no news. His heart constricted, making a complete joke of his attempt to breathe calmly. He stared at the ramp where the stunt had first gone wrong.

What the fuck was happening to him? He'd felt the same sense of panic back in high school. First he'd joked around with Nate about that so-called rap poetry for English class. Then they'd been paired for a science project about burning magnesium strips. Terror had taken over his life throughout the two-week science project, because he'd felt things, wanted things, dreamed of things that had no place in his life. Back then, he'd been plain terrified. To his family, being gay was the equivalent of being a leper.

Or a convict.

Now . . . Kyle knew exactly what was happening. All over again.

"Kyle, c'mon." He turned to find Steph waving him forward. "Tony's on his way."

Cameramen would assemble in the room above the pub, each downloading their footage and presenting it for a rough viewing. Tony, Peter, and the CGI specialists would be there too, able to determine whether the shot could be used.

If not, they'd be pretty well screwed.

Fuck.

He strode after Steph, only to be stopped by a familiar voice calling his name. Nate trudged up the inclined sidewalk leading from the Embankment. He wore a dry set of clothes, a coat, and a wool stocking cap, as well as a sling around the arm he'd used to save himself from becoming human chum. He looked exhausted, pained, and so damn tempting, like a warrior having returned from battle—worse for wear, but triumphant.

Overcome by relief, Kyle stopped short of hugging him. Barely. The temptation was strong. He could envision folding Nate into an embrace of gratefulness and comfort.

Instead Kyle settled. Settling was the half-life he'd forced on himself for years. This was the price he was paying for aiming to be the biggest producer in Hollywood—and for keeping the peace with his family.

"You made it."

"Yup. Did our fearless leader stop the shoot?"

"No," Kyle said tightly. "He ignored Johnny's request and kept rolling."

"And I bet you bitched him out for it."

The darkness in his eyes didn't seem fair, not when Kyle had been ready to fight for something much more important—for Nate's safety.

"I did."

"You should've saved your breath. I didn't tweak my shoulder for shits and giggles."

"Tweak? What does that mean?"

Nate shrugged, then winced. "Somewhere just shy of a sprain, says the doc. I'm lucky I didn't dislocate it."

"Dislocate . . .? Damn it, I knew you'd play Superman about this. You know what could've happened."

"Better than you." Nate shrugged with his good arm. "Forget it. I have ibuprofen for now. Percocet for after we watch the dailies. That is where you're going, yes?"

Kyle nodded.

"I'm coming too. No way am I letting that asshole rip apart what I managed to save."

"Would it help to know I'm with you?"

Wow. That hadn't come out right. Kyle almost dropped his eyes, but he held steady.

Completely committed to surly pissed-at-himself mode, Nate only scowled. "Drop it."

Side by side, not touching—not touching in a way that made Kyle want to claw out of the emotional pit that was his life—they bundled into a crew van. Luckily Peter Upton wasn't in it, but there was no avoiding the man when everyone assembled in the pub. Kyle caught sight of Steph, who was smoothing things over with the director and a few bigwigs. Damn he felt guilty about that. Steph didn't deserve having to mop up his anger spill.

Nate stiffened. At least his scowl had changed targets, practically boring a hole in Upton's skull. He didn't say a word, just kept up that steady, scornful blue stare and went to sit next to Ethan Raney like delinquents at the back of the class.

The room was packed with insurance men, the CGI techs, and whatever curious hangers-on could sneak in the door. Kyle didn't want to deal with any of them, but he managed. Smile in place. Handshakes all around. Yes, he'd lost his temper.

He wouldn't lose his business.

"This should've been routine," he heard a suit mutter.

"Every stunt comes with inherent risk." Kyle offered his sleekest expression. "We should be thankful to have a group of professionals able to salvage the worst and still make it work."

"I'm not convinced," said a man Kyle knew to be one of their financier's representatives. "Can we really trust this crew with the Maserati sequence?"

"I'll ask you a question in return. Who would you trust instead?"

The rep only shook his head. "We'll see."

Finally, as the lights dimmed, Kyle felt free to join Nate at the back of the room. He stood next to Nate's chair, arms crossed. Yes, he'd be forced to watch the footage, but Nate's body heat next to his thigh was a grounding potency.

As were the dailies. Nate didn't have to *play* Superman when he looked superhuman enough in real life, wrestling back from the edge of disaster. Sure, the camera positioning wasn't as they'd planned. Tony Manolo, however, was smiling as he scribbled notes the whole time. It was impressive, breathtaking work.

"Best I've ever seen you do," Raney said to Nate under his breath.

Kyle glanced down, sure of what he'd find. Nate was furious at himself. Whether or not the footage was ever used, it would always be a mistake to Nate, even if the mistake made the movie better. He stood to leave while the lights were still low.

"Nate—"

"I don't want to hear it," he said, face-to-face. "I saved it. They'll use it. Whatever. I'm going back to my room."

Kyle would stay and help Stephanie salvage the whole mess. It was his job. He was very, very good at it—Peter Upton aside. At that moment, however, as Nate stalked out of the room where they'd reignited their sexual relationship, he wanted nothing more than to follow.

Nate could've been killed.

And Kyle hadn't touched him in four days.

Chapter Sixteen

Percocet was Nate's friend.

The on-set doctor had given him an entire bottle, which he found slightly ridiculous for a strained shoulder. He certainly wasn't going to be able to take any of the white pills in the daytime, not when he had work to do and safety inspections to pass.

But being alone in his hotel room meant he could crack the thin red seal and down two with a bottle of water.

He didn't want to admit how much it hurt. That he didn't seem to have full range of motion worried him. Badly. As the cloudy haze of the drugs crept over him, Nate planted his hand flat on a wall and gently stretched his arm. When he pushed too far, his ligaments jerked on a sharp spike of pain.

Fuck.

He tucked his arm back in the sling and flopped on the couch. There wasn't shit on the television, so he clicked absently through the channels.

Until the connecting door opened.

Something pleasant and good eased his mind. He hadn't realized how much he'd been waiting for Kyle until he appeared. Leaving the door unlocked had been . . . hopeful.

Kyle had ditched most of his suit. The coat was gone, as well as the skinny tie he'd worn throughout the day's shoot. He'd rolled up pale-white shirtsleeves, displaying forearms wound with prominent veins and a dusting of dark hair.

The part that really got to Nate was the bare feet with long, slender bones and surprisingly graceful toes. Mostly, it was the intimacy implied. Who got to see the golden boy go barefoot?

Something heavy stuck in Nate's throat. He forced his gaze up. Smiled. Thoughts were becoming difficult to string together. "Hello, you."

Kyle's dark-brown eyes were completely at odds with the smile he wore. Ah, so somebody was faking it. Better now than when Nate had him riding dick. Later though.

"Hello yourself." Kyle tilted his head. "Have you had anything to eat?"

Nate shook the little brown pill bottle. "Not in the least hungry."

"Which means even more that you need to eat."

Kyle didn't consult Nate to find out what he wanted. He picked up the phone and hitched his hip on the edge of a small desk. With one hand in his pocket, gaze fixed out the window, he was the very picture of moneyed assurance. He ordered half a dozen different things that Nate barely heard. He'd know soon enough, and he didn't really think Kyle would order an injured man pickled calves' feet.

Nate chuckled. Calves' feet. They'd be slimy.

"You're stoned, aren't you?"

He blinked. "Maybe. A little."

Shaking his head, Kyle ducked back into his own room and emerged with a small stack of DVDs and a laptop. "That means I'm not going to bother asking what you want to watch."

"Got *Wizard of Oz*?" He grinned. "I hear it's awesome if you put it to a Lynyrd Skynyrd soundtrack."

"You mean Pink Floyd."

"That was a good night."

Smiling gently, Kyle popped in a DVD and snagged the remote out of Nate's hand. "But no, I don't have *The Wizard of Oz*."

The blue upholstered couch wasn't particularly big, but Kyle still managed to sit down with distance between them. Nate watched him instead of the movie, which was one of last year's nominees for best picture.

Nate wanted to ask Kyle to come closer, so he could hold a warm, strong hand as they had at the panto. Except his brain could barely put two words together.

He must have faded gray for a moment because the next thing he knew, an on-screen girl in a yellow dress was spinning with the

LA skyline behind her and someone was knocking at the hotel room door.

Nate stayed put while Kyle let the busboy wheel in a cart bearing two covered plates. The white-uniformed busboy accepted Kyle's tip with a wide-eyed expression and a nod, then ducked back out into the hallway.

Kyle put a plate of shepherd's pie into Nate's lap, along with a napkin. "Here. Another British thing, though not exactly in the silly category."

"There's nothing silly about food with meat in it. There is meat, right?"

"Probably hamburger. It's underneath the mashed potatoes."

"Good enough. Manna of the gods."

Kyle rolled his eyes as he staked a place on the couch and set his own plate on the coffee table. "Good to know some things never change. You always did love shitty food. I have no idea how you stay fit."

"It's the job." Nate aimed what he hoped was an endearing grin at Kyle. "I don't suppose you got me a beer too."

"On those pills? Dream on."

Instead Kyle hopped up to grab a soda from the mini fridge. His wide shoulders bent along with the *crack hiss* of an opening can. He froze for a moment. "Am I . . . Am I overstepping?"

"No." Nate grimaced to himself. It was his fault that Kyle would worry about that—walls a mile high, and he knew it. "I left the door unlocked, didn't I?"

When Kyle returned to the couch, he seemed pleased. Nate put out a hand to tug him closer.

"Yeah, but . . ." Kyle jabbed a fork into his own serving of shepherd's pie. "Maybe that didn't mean anything."

"Maybe it did."

Nate carefully concentrated on his food. The movie on the laptop was flowing by in whole minutes of missed footage. He was way too hazy to pay attention to more than one thing at a time, and Kyle took precedence.

"You said you wanted to be alone," Kyle said quietly.

He had. But Nate realized now that he hadn't meant from Kyle. He'd wanted away from Upton and Steph, who'd watched him with worry shaping her lipsticked mouth. Even Raney, despite his appreciative comment, had projected an air of worry. His best friend. Doubting him. It made Nate's skin go cold.

He'd wanted to be alone *with* Kyle, because he only got this sort of closeness—the peaceful support—when they were alone.

This was the good stuff. This was the part that might make the inevitable fallout worthwhile.

They finished the rest of their food in relative quiet, watching the movie. It was a little too complicated for Nate's state of mind, so after he put his practically licked-clean plate on the coffee table, he let the images slide by without concentrating. The girl in the yellow dress was quite sad now. Likely going to die, in the hallmark of intellectual cinema.

Nate was tired. Exhausted. So he lay down, abruptly and probably awkwardly.

Damn if his head didn't fit as perfectly in Kyle's lap as it always had. He was cushioned with more muscle—none of those gawky teenaged hip bones jamming into Nate's skull—which made it better. Kyle's hands hovered for a second before one came to rest in the center of Nate's chest, and one combed through his hair, blunt nails barely scraping. Such a rush of warmth swept through him.

Tomorrow, he could blame this vulnerability on the drugs. If he needed to. If he wanted to.

Kyle turned the sound down. "This director's gone downhill."

"I don't think I know him."

"His best picture was *Sand and Blood*. It came out when you were in—" The hand in Nate's hair stopped moving.

"It's okay." Nate's jaws creaked on a giant yawn. "I'm not going to bite your head off if you say it came out while I was inside."

"It did."

"Prison sucked, but I know the world didn't stop. Everything kept rolling. The sun kept rising and setting." He knew it did. Honestly, he'd *hoped* that it would all continue. That there'd be new and exciting stuff to return to. A world that would still have a place for him. Somewhere. "And hell, I had some good things while I was in there."

"Tell me something that was nice." Kyle resumed petting Nate's head, his hair. The soothing, soft touches were going to melt his bones into the couch. "I used to think of you in that shitty place and wonder . . . I didn't understand at all. And I could only picture misery."

"You were still with me."

Nate hadn't meant to say that. Not really. The words were more of that same melting, the barrier between his thoughts and his mouth completely dissolved.

Tonight, there was only the way Kyle's eyes turned so very dark and the way lines carved down his cheeks with a sudden flush of emotion.

"Tell me." Not a question. In times of stress, Kyle Wakefield didn't question. He demanded.

"Picture." He yawned again. "A handful of them. Took them with me. Kept them."

"You silly, stupid idiot."

"Don't be mean."

Kyle's chuckle passed from his chest to Nate in a rumble. His hand stroked all the way up to Nate's neck, his fingers assured and comforting.

"I don't mean to be."

Nate lost the thread of their conversation. The moment turned sticky slow, and he slid helplessly into sleep. It was too much, being surrounded like that. Being held.

He jerked awake some time later. Kyle had that computer on the arm of the couch, flipping through what looked like some sort of document. He'd turned the TV back on, muted.

Nate scrubbed his eyes. "What time is it?"

"Almost eleven."

"I was out three hours?"

Kyle shut the computer's cover. "You were. How do you feel?"

Gingerly, Nate rotated his shoulder. The faintest twinges of pain lanced down to his elbow, but it wasn't anything he couldn't deal with. "Not too bad, actually."

He only hoped he'd feel the same reassurance when the drugs faded completely.

"Good."

He sat up. "Is that *Parks and Recreation*?"

"The real deal, American and everything." Kyle smiled. So contained. So perfect. This late at night and after a crazy day, his white shirt was spotless.

"I wouldn't have thought you were in the *Parks and Rec* demographic."

"Because I don't have a sense of humor?"

Nate chuckled. He scraped the heels of his hands across his eyes. "More like Chris Pratt doesn't seem like your type."

"I've been watching for years. It made me think of you. The comedies you always picked."

Nate shouldn't have been so pleased by how good that felt. How those quiet words, said at his side, made him feel like a fucking god—like he was completely in charge of the world. For a man as impressive as Kyle to need contact with him, however small, was such an ego rush.

But Jesus Christ, he could not believe what he'd said before falling asleep. Did he trust his foggy memory? Had he really confessed that he kept Kyle's pictures in the joint? *Really?*

At least he hadn't admitted that he'd slept with one under his pillow.

He liked sucking cock. That didn't mean he was lacking balls. He wouldn't ever admit something like that, too personal and sentimental.

Complications. He could do without them. Totally.

The way Kyle watched him, however, was considerably complicated. The weight in his expression threatened to drown Nate under the hot wash of the Percocet again, slipping toward emotions so much more dangerous than any stunt.

He reached out and traced his knuckles across Kyle's cheek. They shared these moments, when it was perfectly acceptable to say nothing at all.

He kissed Kyle, softly, and swept his lips over the other man's firm ones. He found purchase along Kyle's shoulder. So much strength there. Kyle's brightness was the thing that saved him. If Kyle had been the one to go to prison—though he never would've been so goddamned stupid—he wouldn't have let it dog his heels for years.

Nate kissed him harder, the better to get outside his own head. He wanted Kyle. Wanted him again and again, and he was starting to worry that this month wasn't going to be enough.

Too damn bad. This was all there could be.

Considering how devastated Nate had been the last time they'd crashed and burned, this was all there *should* be.

Chapter Seventeen

They were living in the past, but they hadn't talked about the past—not in any meaningful way that would wipe away the hurt.

Kyle's heart had crunched tight like a fist upon hearing Nate's slurred admission, that he'd taken pictures with him to prison. It didn't make sense. Before their nine-year hiatus, during that last, awful argument, Nate had worn institutional orange and an expression that said seeing Kyle's face was the last thing he wanted. All Kyle had wanted was one tiny fucking admission that Nate had fucked up, or maybe an explanation. Why had he decided to try cocaine *that* night? Why steal that car? All he'd gotten was a close-mouthed sneer.

So the past could stay the fuck away. They were kissing. They were winding closer and closer on the couch. And at least for Kyle, they were celebrating the success of what could've been a devastating day. No more than two weeks remained in this brief, blissful reprieve. He intended to keep the history buried, even if opening that old grave would finally answer decades-old questions.

Why did you do it?

Why did you send me away?

Why didn't I come find you when you were free?

Kyle pushed his tongue into Nate's mouth—anything to keep from speaking those words. He shoved them back down into the pit of his stomach, where he kept all the secrets that had the power to eat him alive.

Only a quick hiss snapped Kyle out of those dark places. "Shit," he said. "Did I hurt you?"

"It's okay." Nate's eyes still held the glassy sheen of painkillers, but he was coming back into himself. That meant the return of his pain.

"No, it's not."

Desire and fatigue and caring fueled a bubbling burn in Kyle's lungs. He wanted to breathe. Maybe breathe for the first time. He'd felt like that once with Nate—chest expanding with pride and hope and love—but he'd been holding his breath ever since.

Would it be so terrible? What if coming out meant keeping Nate? Kyle could be the man he'd always wanted to be. Pennfield was almost strong enough to withstand any outside attempts to crush it. Maybe his father wouldn't even try. He would be free to express himself in newer, more honest ways. Then, with that freedom giving him strength, he would hold on to Nate for longer than the next few brief days. Maybe all Nate needed was a show of faith. Then they could sort through the past, put it away and start fresh.

That show of faith, however . . . Coming out would undo everything Kyle had fought to achieve. He'd lost Nate once. All that had remained was school and ambition. Even if he threw all of that away on a chance, he had no guarantee Nate wouldn't self-destruct again. Throw *them* away.

He couldn't take that risk, no matter how much he ached for a different sort of future.

He stood from the couch too quickly, nearly knocking his laptop off the coffee table. God, he could run a marathon with his unspent energy, building and building.

"Come on," he said, holding out his hand. "You need to get cleaned up."

Nate made a face then yawned so wide his eyes scrunched shut. "In the morning. Get back here. We weren't finished."

"Just getting started. And that means hygiene. I'm not going down on you if you smell of swamp balls."

"Classy, man. Seriously classy."

His smile was almost always sharp, as if mistrusting that anything merited true amusement. For two weeks, however, Kyle had been unique. He'd been on the receiving end of so many warm, caught-by-surprise smiles, all of which spun him in circles.

"But you know it's true," Kyle said. "I've already showered. Your turn."

"I'm tired and horny and a little out of it. Handjob and sleep?"

"Sponge bath and rimjob?"

The dim lights in Nate's room hid the bright shimmer of his blue eyes, but the way they narrowed and his lips parted scored Kyle a big win. "Well. When you put it that way."

"So forget what I said. Stay *right* there."

Kyle grabbed the ice bucket on his way to Nate's bathroom, where he heated water and added two drops of complimentary shower gel. His hands were shaking so badly. What he was doing . . .? This was probably the most intimate sexual experience he'd ever proposed with any man.

Two washcloths in his teeth and the bucket of hot water in his hands, he returned to the room. And stopped. Nate had disobeyed, the naughty boy. He was already completely naked. Standing. Waiting.

Kyle angled his brows into what he hoped would be a disapproving expression, but he couldn't help admiring the feast Nate presented. The tattoos looked particularly fierce in the soft lighting, while sandy-blond hair added a glimmer to his skin. Nate's stance was proud—feet apart, chest and chin lifted, prick rock-hard.

Looking away was difficult, but Kyle managed. He had plans.

He set the bucket on one of the nightstands, just in time as Nate's arms wrapped around Kyle's middle. Turned him around. Pulled the washcloths from Kyle's teeth.

"You should've seen your face," Nate said, grinning.

"Shut up and get on the bed, swampy."

As Nate complied, Kyle stripped his shirt and trousers. His own erection was unmistakable, pressing up from his boxer briefs. Nate eyed him with the same blatant interest that made Kyle feel larger than life and completely free.

After arranging a few pillows, they both wiggled Nate into a position that would support his injured arm. He stretched back along the bed, half-propped against the headboard.

"You really should lie all the way down."

"Nope," he said, appearing salacious and so very hungry. "You're going to bathe me, and I'm going to watch."

Shit. Kyle had thought he'd be the one in charge of this little experiment. Yet they'd always shared power in the bedroom. That give-and-take had been born out of mutual, youthful curiosity.

Why stick with giving a blowjob when there remained the possibility of receiving one too? They'd traded knowledge and pleasure.

Now they were grown. They knew every way men could give and accept pleasure. That thought amped Kyle's anticipation as he knelt beside Nate on the bed.

He wrung out the washcloth. The water was nearly too hot, but he didn't mind. The sting kept him grounded, when his nerves were so crazy needy that he felt numb, as if he were short-circuiting.

"Come on, then," Nate said quietly. His voice was so low that it barely registered as sound. Just vibration. "Get on with it."

Kyle took a centered breath and began.

He stroked the washcloth across Nate's soles. After a few jerking reflexes, the man began to relax. Kyle traveled up and up. Beneath his hands were some of the most perfectly formed angles he'd ever seen.

Ankle, calf, knee, thigh—he washed one leg and rinsed the cloth, then started up the other. Only when he reached Nate's hips did he dare glance toward the headboard. Nate had eased considerably. The Percocet was probably helping still, but he appeared in a complete state of bliss. That Kyle could affect such a potent man was beyond comprehending.

When Kyle skipped a particularly tempting area in favor of abs, Nate chuckled. "Missed a spot."

"I'll get to it," Kyle said. As if making a promise, he kissed the head of Nate's prick.

"As bad as you feared?"

"Totally. I'll have to be extra thorough there. But later."

Cleaning became petting as he stroked Nate's stomach and chest. The boxy ridges made his abs mouthwatering. The heavy sweep of his pecs and the little bulges and ripples between each rib made the man a work of art. Each time Kyle refreshed the washcloth, reheating it, Nate sucked in quiet breaths and those beautiful muscles tensed against the hot tingle.

"Fuck, that feels good," he said, sinking into the pillows.

"Don't get too comfy. Turn over, but don't hurt your fool-ass self."

Nate whined like a kid, grinning the whole time, until the wide, glorious stretch of his back was clean, from shoulders to the twin divots at the base of his spine. He returned to his place against the headboard pillows with a satisfied sigh.

Kyle was anything but satisfied, at least not physically. Every touch worked into his mind like an opiate, while his body became more tense, as if he was taking all of Nate's rigid aches into himself. He didn't mind that. Not a bit. Especially when he knew the payoff would be amazing. Only, he needed, *wanted*, to draw it out.

He gingerly washed Nate's sore arm and beneath it, almost chuckling at himself for the heat spreading across his face. Just an armpit. But the intimacy of caressing that masculine hair until it was wet and glistening was more intense than he would've imagined.

Nate reached up with his good arm and traced a fingertip along Kyle's cheek. "This blush is pretty. Something got you heated up?"

"Watch it, smart-mouth. I'll stop."

"Oh no you won't."

Kyle straightened and assumed a straddling position. "No. I won't."

Another refresh of the washcloth and he finished with Nate's neck, collarbones, shoulders, and his tattooed arm, which was like working as an art restorer. He uncovered where true, potent black met flawless tan skin, and returned the vibrancy to that contrast. He was getting dizzy at revelation after revelation.

So much of Nate he wanted. So much of Nate he didn't know.

After a return trip to the bathroom for clean water, he settled into the task they both awaited with hitching breaths. Nate was no longer so easy, so calm looking. He held his body's considerable power in check, but the effort shimmered around him like heat waves on a long desert road. Kyle could relate. He rounded the bed and almost dropped the bucket when Nate trailed his fingers along Kyle's thighs.

"Are you trying to make me spill this?"

"Nah," Nate said with a shrug. "I like ruffling your feathers. Nothing gets under your skin."

You do.

Kyle kissed Nate while trying to disguise how deeply that moment affected him. Simple, see? Limited time only, see? Yet their tongues touched with more hesitancy. This was no greedy fuck. Honeyed power gathered between their bodies.

Slowly, he ended the kiss and sat away enough to wash again, this time Nate's face. He wiped jaw to chin and back to jaw, then up strong cheekbones, across a forehead first furrowed with lines, then smooth as Nate relaxed. He watched Kyle the entire time, that icy-blue gaze more intense than ever. They were bound up in each other's every moment and every matched shiver.

Now this . . .

This was intimacy.

Only when Kyle whispered, "Close your eyes," did Nate look away. Kyle softly, so softly, traced the cloth over lids and brows and lashes that clumped with that faint trace of water. He kissed each spot in the wake of his ministrations. He cleaned his lover of dirt and sweat, but he didn't leave him unmarked. Each kiss was a quiet, decadent claiming.

Kyle wondered why he was torturing himself so badly. Having but not having—that had been the story of his love life, especially when it came to Nate. He needed to come quick or get the hell out.

Neither was an option.

Nate's skin was slightly chilled where the water dried, but beneath it was the burning strength of a furnace. His chest heaved with less control when Kyle kissed his way down and licked pebbled nipples. God, he tasted amazing. The touch of soap had left him clean without masking the richness of the man.

Nate curled his good hand around the back of Kyle's neck. "I'm clean enough," he rasped.

"Hell no."

"I want you to get me off, college boy."

Kyle hoped he was able to hide his flinch.

Wariness deepened the lines fanning out from Nate's pale eyes and pinched his lips into a flat, dead scowl. It was exactly what Kyle had feared seeing—a reminder that when Nate got scared, he did incredibly stupid things.

Kyle could've called him on it, but he didn't. He'd been hard as a pipe for a half hour. His body's needs were more immediate and infinitely less complex than whatever the hell was going on between them.

"We've already talked about this. My name is Kyle. And I'm going to finish what I started."

With one last dip of the washcloth, he tried to spread tense legs. Nate fought him, gripped Kyle's nape with more strength.

Kyle resisted that nearly desperate pull and conjured a ghost of a smile. "And you're going to let me, Nathan."

"Why should I?"

"Because you want me to and because here, at least, we trust each other."

With gut-churning slowness, Nate finally exhaled. He let his legs part as Kyle caressed him with the warm cloth. The tendons of his inner thighs were as tense as piano wire. Touch, pet, soothe. Kyle put as much tenderness as he possessed into each steamy stroke. Neatly trimmed hair darkened when wet. Tender skin took on a pink glow.

He wrapped Nate's shaft in the cloth and started at the head. This was more than cleansing. This was ramping up the most decadent foreplay Kyle had ever known. Again he placed kisses in the wake of hot water. Only now, he added his tongue. He licked and laved and took Nate's head into his mouth.

"*Fuck*," Nate whispered on a sharp exhale.

But as soon as he'd wet that blunt, throbbing head, Kyle moved on. Tasting and teasing. He eased his way down Nate's pulsing cock, with its tracery of veins and furrows. Such impressive proof of the man's potency, so long and thick.

Kyle finished washing the very last stretch of intimate skin, all the way to Nate's tight opening, and tossed the washcloth away. "Hands behind your knees. Keep your legs against your chest and don't move."

"Oh, I plan to move, Kyle. As soon as you get those shorts off and start fucking me."

At least a glimpse of his teasing was back. At least he was using Kyle's name again. At least they knew exactly what to do when perched on the verge of mutual satisfaction.

"I'll get around to that," Kyle said.

"What, you got some other pressing task to attend to?"

Kyle settled between Nate's legs and stroked up the backs of the man's thighs. He gazed down at the only freshly washed place he had to claim with his mouth. He licked his lips and bent low, smiling at Nate with a rich feeling of sin and mischief.

"Yes, I do," he whispered against the hot flesh of Nate's ass. "And I'm going to enjoy it."

Chapter Eighteen

The only one who'd enjoy this more than Kyle was definitely Nate. Keeping his knees lifted, leaving himself so very exposed, was difficult. He trembled under the need to hold back. To be open. Both for Kyle and for himself.

That first wet streak of pleasure made it all worth it.

Nate let a long, low groan go. Too good.

Kyle peeked up at him, his brown eyes bright with amusement. And desire. The firm stroke of his tongue over Nate's pucker sent shocking, electric sensations through his body. His stomach clenched, as if he'd forgotten how to be. How to enjoy.

Firm and soft and slippery—all of it swirled together. Kyle added his thumb, notching his grip under and around Nate's balls. He wrapped his free hand around Nate's cock. Slow pulls said Kyle knew exactly what he was doing to Nate's dick and in probing his ass. Sensation centered and twined until Nate's mind jittered away. He spun. Too many tingles and greedy shots of pleasure.

Then Kyle went farther, ducking low between Nate's thighs. The tip of his tongue pushed at but barely broke that tender seal.

Nate jerked and puffed erratic exhales. He needed to look away from Kyle's dark eyes, which were visible over the vise of his fist gripping Nate's red, flushed cock. The ceiling was plain—the perfect escape from bone-shaking pleasure. He meant for this to last. All of it. Kyle seemed to be enjoying himself, and that's what Nate wanted.

He didn't want to be alone in this.

He coiled his good hand in Kyle's brown hair and tugged. Gently at first, then with more insistence when Kyle didn't stop what he was doing. He enthusiastically licked and sucked at Nate's flesh. His growl created a tingling buzz between Nate's ass cheeks as he intensified his abrupt, fast strokes.

Nate grunted. No words beyond the sounds of need. Fuck all, he was going to lose it if Kyle kept that up. Maybe he should. He should lie back and let the man service him until he came in the college boy's mouth, watch his throat work as he swallowed. Nate would never get tired of that erotic temptation.

But the idea was still second to fucking Kyle.

He grasped Kyle's neck. No more screwing around.

Kyle only grinned at him. "Problem?"

"You're dangerous."

Still, Kyle didn't unwrap his pulsing hand. He ducked his head, fighting Nate's attempt to set the pace. He licked his palm and then the shaft of Nate's cock, adding wetness to the long strokes. Base to crown. His thumb dallied over Nate's slit, dipping and swirling that sleek stickiness.

"You like it when I'm dangerous."

"No doubt." His hips thrust up, into the snug clasp. He closed his eyes on a shaky breath. When he opened them, he found Kyle's intense gaze. "But I'm going to fuck you silly, Kyle. My cock in you, until your mind flips and you're begging me to come because you want to feel that burst of release inside you."

Kyle licked the lower lip of a growing smile. "You seem awfully sure of yourself."

Nate had tweaked his shoulder, but there was no stopping him when he levered up. He wrapped an arm around Kyle's neck. Pulled. Tightened. Holding him and testing him at the same time. Would he rip away? Would he keep up that antagonizing grin?

Nate kissed him. Teeth clicked and lips smashed. The strokes of eager tongues were more than enough and not what he needed. This was out of control.

He flipped their positions on the bed. Kyle released Nate's cock and spread his arms wide. His head rested in the pile of blinding-white pillows. The grin he shot up at Nate wasn't intimidated in the least. "I liked what I was doing."

"I liked what you were doing too." He nuzzled the underside of Kyle's jaw, where the skin was tender. Darting the tip of his tongue, he dragged each caress along the rasp of five-o'clock shadow. A shiver worked from Kyle's skin into his. "But you'll like this more."

"You say that with so much assurance. Like you'd lay money on it."

Nate laughed. "Can you honestly tell me you don't crave the way my cock fills you? The way I fuck you? The way I grind my hips against yours?"

Kyle lifted his mouth to Nate's ear. The wash of his breath was a lush tickle. "I *love* it."

Those kinds of words threatened to undo him. Nate ignored that, ignored how close it was to all that was right and good. This was temporary. He was still the same damaged goods and Kyle was even more perfect and untouchable. This was putting a pretty bow on their connection and hoping the past wouldn't hurt so bad when they parted.

A determined grip on the waistband of Kyle's boxer briefs yanked the soft material down. Kyle wiggled his hips, twisting and helping so that he was naked that much faster. His cock sprang up in a proud, thick exclamation point. He was so stiff that the vein across the underside stood out in stark relief.

Nate dug around in his nightstand for the small bottle of lube and a condom. The blue lid opened with a quiet snap in the almost silent room. He could feel Kyle's gaze on him, a weight like a touch. Or a kiss filled with sweet promise.

He started slowly, opening Kyle's tight pucker. It didn't take long. One finger, two. Then three. But right now, he wanted more. He wanted some response that meant Kyle had given over—that he was fully Nate's, at least for tonight.

He stroked deeper, until his knuckles brushed crisp hairs and firm cheeks. Kyle's body clasped him with every push. Nate nudged with his fourth finger, almost daring Kyle to reject him.

But he didn't. The carefully put-together man was a sweaty wreck. His hair tumbled over his forehead, but he seemed totally oblivious. He only spread his heels wider, dug them into the soft cushion of the comforter. Perfectly open.

Nate couldn't hold back any longer. The condom rolled on in a near-painful snap. He pressed a hand across Kyle's thigh. Holding him down.

He lined up the head of his cock with Kyle's asshole, then nudged inside with tiny, rubbing thrusts. "Ask me."

Kyle's eyes were unfocused. His chest heaved so that his pecs stood out in solid bands. His stomach ridged and released with every breath. "Will you fuck me?"

"Maybe that's not what I want. Maybe what I really want is for you to beg."

"Just ask." Kyle jerked his ass up toward Nate. The motion engulfed the head of Nate's cock. Hot. Tight. But more enticing than that was the desire painted across Kyle's features, the carved lines under his cheeks and the way his color went hectic. "Just say it. I'll beg. Sweet, pretty words."

"And if I want you growling? Screaming? Cussing at me?"

"Fuck me deep and you'll get it. I promise you'll get what you always want. Me. Completely undone."

Then Nate was the one growling. A burr started in his chest and rasped through his throat.

He slid forward, unstoppable now. His prick was surrounded by heat and the unresisting clench of Kyle's body. Nate was lost in him, lost in the moment and in the way his body wasn't his to control.

He'd had good sex, with a certain level attributed purely to mechanics. Friction felt nice. When he got enough of that, the results were great.

This was more—the return to some better version of himself when he'd been so very young and naïve. Scared too, but he'd tried to be better. For Kyle and for the couple they could've been.

The way Kyle looked up at him, the way he wrapped a strong hand around the back of Nate's neck and wouldn't let him look away . . . It was enough to take Nate back there. To those moments when he'd wanted to be someone *more*.

It was a beautiful place, wrapped up in Kyle, taking him over.

Nate stroked slow but mean, with unrelenting digs and angles he changed just to hear his lover gasp again. They pressed flesh to flesh when his torso sat flush against Kyle's cheeks. Bound together.

He wasn't going to last. His strokes were longer, faster. A frantic mantra of *now* echoed into each greedy fuck. He shoved his hand between bed and pillows and skin and wrapped his forearm around

Kyle's shoulders. With his other hand, he spread Kyle's thighs and held the man wide open.

Nate gritted his teeth. Trying to hang on. He wanted this to last. Wanted to make Kyle come—fiercely, brutally. Instead he was the one who groaned again, as Kyle's hot passage clamped down.

Kyle's wide mouth split on a grin that flashed teeth and arrogance and a fuck-ton of challenge. His dark-brown eyes narrowed as he looked up at Nate. "God, that's it. That's what you want to give me. Everything you've got."

"You're giving too," he grunted.

"I am. You like my ass, like my cock. So show me how much. Make me sweat. Make me thrash my head. You want to see me undone, so do it. *Take me.*"

He stretched up to kiss Nate in something that was more challenging than soothing. He dragged teeth down to the edge of Nate's jaw in a menacing promise of threats and sharp edges. They'd be something better if it killed them.

Kyle twisted his leg out from under Nate's grip, then lifted his knees to tuck along Nate's hips. Chest to chest, they slicked back and forth on a tiny sheen of sweat.

After reaching between their bodies, Nate enfolded Kyle's prick with a tight grip. Long strokes matched the relentless length he shoved into the other man's ass. "I'm going to make you come."

"Promises," Kyle said, a breathless rasp.

"I don't make many, do I?" Nate jerked the dick in his grasp as fiercely as he fucked. "You're going to come all over your stomach. Then you'll feel me shoot my load. Condom or not—fuck, you'll feel it."

A full-body shudder surged from Kyle into Nate. His lover's eyes had completely hazed but his jaw was locked firm. Tendons popped along his shoulders and down his strong ribs.

Kyle's prick twitched. Pulsed. Jerked. Come splattered white across taut abs as Kyle shouted, his neck stretched back and his damp hair spiked across the pillow. "Fucking Christ. Just right. Nathan, *just right.*"

Gasping now, Nate spread his hand low across Kyle's stomach, relishing that thin skin and sticky wetness. The quivers pulsing along Kyle's passage were enough to send him over.

Pleasure didn't burst, didn't roll over him in waves. It scalded. It took him down and made his toes curl and made the bottom of his feet prickle. The orgasm didn't just make him feel good—it owned him.

Maybe he'd started this reunion to make Kyle pay, or to wipe out the past. Rewrite something he regretted. That was nothing compared to the here and now, which was exactly perfect. Too damn perfect.

If prison had taught him one thing, it was that beautiful things were crushed—and perfect things didn't exist at all.

Chapter Nineteen

The week before Christmas passed in a haze of work and pleasure. Kyle and Nate no longer denied themselves the release of spending their nights together. One of them would drag in late, either Kyle from a massive stack of paperwork or an around-the-world, time-zone-bending conference call, or Nate from a night shoot. Although Kyle felt a compulsive need to be there for the stunt set pieces, he wasn't always able to. His concentration wasn't ever entirely focused on whatever task kept him away.

At the moment, his task was sitting down to a *Very Serious Chat* with Steph. At a hole-in-the-wall café that served English breakfast all day, he stared absently at his cooling coffee.

"You're not here. Not even now."

He glanced up. Steph had stopped tapping her red lacquered nails on the tabletop, instead crossing her arms. She looked as '40s glam as always, but her bright-red mouth was turned down. Frowns didn't suit his sunny, most loyal friend.

"I'm sorry," he said with a heavy exhale.

"And you're as tight-lipped as always." She leaned forward, although the angered tension in her shoulders didn't ease. "It's *me*, Kyle. Doesn't that mean anything to you? Seriously. It's like I'm working with a stranger. An unpredictable stranger, I might add, which is the last thing I need."

"I've never been the front man."

"And neither have you been a man who misses paperwork deadlines or makes threats against the director! Do you know what alienating him will do to Pennfield? Kaput. End of eight years of planning and investing everything we have into this goddamn company."

Kyle stirred the shitty coffee with a skinny plastic stick. Brits did tea like nobody else in the world, but they were crap at brewing a simple cup of joe. It didn't matter. His stomach was already a mess. "What do you want me to say?"

"Anything!"

At her outburst, they both glanced around. Yup. Curious yet disapproving English disdain. Kyle felt uncomfortably conspicuous. They should've had this little chat in their office above the pub, but thinking of that space as a mere place for work had changed on day one.

Steph rubbed her lips together, eyes narrowed. "You have a fallback plan, Kyle. You have that fat bank account. *Money*. I don't have anything but what I've sunk into Pennfield. If you fuck up, I lose everything. Have you thought about that? Jesus. How is that fair?"

Money from a trust fund that came with thick chains wrapped around his throat. Money that he hadn't done a single thing to earn except to stay in the closet. The shock of shame was quickly smothered by guilt. Damn it. He was acting like a supreme jackass.

He laid his hands, palms up, on the table. Wiggled his fingers. She sighed and shook her head in apparent frustration, but she put her hands in his. They squeezed at the same time.

"I've never seen you like this," she said quietly. "Please. Just tell me. That might make it . . . easier. You know? I can cover a lot if I know you're finally happy."

"Finally? I've been happy."

"That's bullshit and you know it."

Kyle swallowed and briefly glanced toward the bland taupe ceiling. "Thing is, I can't tell you that. It's good but it's probably temporary."

"Christ. Are you really that dumb?" She pulled her hands back and downed the last of her straight black coffee as if it were vodka. She'd never lived in half measures, which was the reason he'd always been so close to her, like the darkness finding a firefly. That made his behavior even less forgivable.

"Look," he said tightly. "Nate and I have history. Serious history. You knew that much. But it didn't end well."

"I could've told you that. You guys spark off one another. Good and bad. I'm surprised the whole damn crew doesn't feel it."

Kyle cringed. "That obvious?"

"No. Chill, okay? It's me, and maybe whoever on Nate's crew might know him best. Maybe that guy, Ethan Raney? But why would you having history mean this is only temporary? Guys talk. I'm assuming." She lifted one eyebrow. "Do you?"

A shrug was his only reply.

She frowned. "What, hot sex and see ya?"

"Not always." He risked a grin. "Sometimes it's room service, a movie, and then the hot sex."

Laughing, she threw up her hands. "And this is a disaster how? Other than your head residing perpetually in your dick these past weeks."

"Look, it's a nostalgia trip. That's all it can be. Something to sort of, I don't know, make the shitty way we broke up seem a little less grim."

All of which was true and none of which managed to turn off the thoughts in his head. A tiny flame in his heart that said if he made it good enough, Nate wouldn't run again.

Yet good enough, by Nate's definition, was being able to hold hands in public. To kiss when they wanted to. To live together without giving a shit what anyone else thought. The fear that stabbed Kyle's guts was enough to make *him* the one who wanted to run.

"And you still can't tell me how that all ended? You've never been able to. I won't pretend that doesn't hurt."

Kyle couldn't meet her eyes. He'd never been able to when he lied. "Not worth telling."

More like too hurtful to think about, let alone speak.

Steph balled up a paper napkin and threw it, hitting him square on the nose. "I hereby dub thee *idiot*. Supreme idiot and possible self-deceiver extraordinaire. You're working toward that lofty title. Obviously breaking up a second time will be way easier to handle things and won't hurt *at all*."

"There's nothing to break up. You and I will leave for the Bangkok project in three weeks, and that'll be the end of it."

"Bull. Shit." She stood and gathered her purse. "Lie to yourself all you want, my dear friend. But when it comes to our company, don't lie to me. Can you handle this?"

He unfurled from a maroon plastic chair and rubbed a pinched place in his low back. Jaw sore, ass sore—he was marked by tension and by the lingering effects of his unrelenting nights with Nate. Maybe if they had a lifetime to indulge, they could take it slower. Breathe. Sleep.

He would like that, to sleep in Nate's arms for reasons other than desperate exhaustion. He'd been mentally referring to it as a mundane routine, something amorphous and comforting. Yet each day added details. They weren't the kind to do crosswords in bed. No, they'd be as ambitious as ever, poring over the trade papers. They'd go to movies every Friday night—critiquing, of course, while tucking close to one another in that otherworldly darkness. Christ, just walking through a grocery store while holding hands sounded like heaven. Ordinary, but so special that Kyle couldn't wrap his head around the possibility.

Because what if it really did end all over again?

Being left behind for *prison* had been the single most painful experience of his life.

He met Steph's vibrant blue-eyed gaze, because he had never failed her. Never failed their dreams. At least in one area of his life, he was confident to the extreme. "I can handle this. You don't have a partner for nothing."

They hugged as if their shared future depended on this moment of contact. In truth, it did.

Kyle loved parties, especially the high-end kind he'd been raised to navigate with the fluidity of water. The drawbacks of his childhood—expectations, repressed emotions—were not all his parents had passed down. He could walk into any room and make sure he came away with what he'd expected of the experience. That was a career-saving skill in the cutthroat bizarro universe of Hollywood.

So with his Savile Row tux immaculate, he stepped into the ballroom at the Savoy. Crystal chandeliers that looked vintage, possibly dating back to the first installation of electricity in the Victorian building, added an elegant glow to what was meant as the ultimate

schmoozing event. This was the Saturday night before Christmas. This was the night to make sweet, sweet love to every single person who'd invested a dime in *Fast Money*.

Kyle accepted a flute of champagne from a passing waiter and took a second one for Stephanie. She looked radiant in a shimmering blue cocktail dress—just enough glitter and sass, just enough hardcore professional bitch. That combo was her trademark.

"Kyle," she said, taking the proffered glass of Cristal. "You remember Mr. James Watson of Opal Communications."

"Of course. How's your daughter adjusting to life at Bryn Mawr?"

Mr. Watson's eyebrow lifted, but he seemed pleased that Kyle remembered that detail. "Very well. She's majoring in astronomy. Well, this week anyway."

Stephanie smiled broadly, then turned to Kyle. "James here was on set yesterday."

Of course she was already on a first-name basis with the man.

Which shoot had that been? Between trying to get his head back in the game and finalizing plans for their next project, the one in Bangkok, he was losing track. But apparently he could still whip out facts about investors' kids. Good to know.

Steph nodded toward where the two leads, Jessica Lorrie and Robert Durant, mingled with fellow actors. "The finale argument between Jess and Robbie," she softly prompted. "It was amazing."

"Yes, sorry I missed that one. I caught the dailies, though. Really impressive work."

She raised a perfectly arched eyebrow and shot him a sly smile. No accusations or disappointment this time. Instead, it felt like she was pleased to have each other's backs again. Whatever one of them missed, the other filled in.

At least in that respect, Kyle knew how to be a partner. But only in business.

Mr. Watson sipped from his tumbler. A screwdriver, by the looks, but a remarkably pale one. The pink flush to his cheeks suggested the man loved a strong drink. "I admit I was surprised by what I saw. Really good work, for a movie like this . . ."

Now the look Kyle exchanged with Steph was very brief and very annoyed. Yes, it was a big-budget action flick. That didn't mean it required shitty acting and a plot like Swiss cheese. But if Kyle's memory served, Mr. Watson had personally invested upward of sixteen million, with an extra bump from his company when it came time to market the film. Whatever shit the short, snobby, heavy drinker spewed was shit made of pure gold.

"That was our thinking," Kyle said smoothly. "We really have to credit the actors and our casting agent. She spotted their chemistry from the first screen test."

That Jess and Robbie happened to be shagging like bunnies probably helped. Kyle didn't care whether their affair lasted forever and ended in gated mansions and haute couture babies. He just wanted their spark to survive through the end of filming.

Cold, but that was the business.

"Now if you'll excuse me." He shook hands with Mr. Watson. "There are so many people I'd love to greet this evening. I'm sure Steph will be happy to keep you company a while longer."

"Certainly." Her smile was business perfect: interested but clearly off-limits. The girl really was a marvel. Kyle was lucky to have her, which made him all the more determined to ensure a successful night.

He strolled through the collection of patrons even more staggeringly wealthy than he was, although "patron" made them sound too beneficent. Everyone was there because of the business. They expected a financial payout, a possible step up the ladder of success, an exclusive scoop, or the chance to play starfucker for a night. They were sharks, and Kyle swam with the best of them.

Only, successful men with gorgeous women on their arms nettled him in a way he'd never experienced. The evening was satisfying, immensely so, from a professional standpoint. But damn it all if he didn't want Nate on *his* arm.

Suit coat and jeans. Tattoo and earring. Eat-shit-and-die smile.

That glitzy ballroom was a million miles away from a sweaty gay nightclub or the mind-blowing fuck he and Nate had shared the night before. The two would never mix. For people in the public eye, coming out remained the stuff of gossip, worthy of blog fodder and magazine covers. Excellent actors and directors could find themselves relegated to niche projects. Even as a producer—not a profession generally hounded by the paparazzi—Kyle's opportunities to work on a big-budget film like *Fast Money* might evaporate. It'd be all indie flicks about troubled gay teens and jokes about when he'd finance a Judy Garland biopic.

He would never be able to mix his two worlds. That fact shook Kyle to his bones.

He was worse than a shark. He was a liar and a fraud. Apparently, that was his fate. No wonder Nate was so quick to think him a hypocrite. He was one.

Nate hadn't even been invited. No place for the hired help at a soirée meant to woo the top tier of Hollywood wealth and luminary hopefuls. No place for an ex-con who made no bones about his homosexuality.

Shit, Kyle needed to get his head together. He'd promised Steph, and he owed it to himself. He didn't want to be one of those trust-fund babies who failed and failed again, only to be bailed out by money they hadn't earned. He was better than that, and a helluva lot more determined.

Which made seeing Nate stroll into the ballroom all the more dizzying.

When Kyle finally thought he'd pulled his scattered pieces into alignment, he was undone by the man who'd given him an exquisite blowjob that morning, edging him three times. Nate was the king of slow, masterful torture, followed by the roughness that made them both crazy.

Yes, crazy. This whole thing was crazy.

Damn. Just . . . *damn*.

He looked as good as Kyle had imagined—dark jeans that hugged his thighs and hips, battered but shined motorcycle boots and a black cambric shirt that appeared as soft as Nate's expression was brutal. He was a man out of place, heedless of the stares. He seemed to soak up the hints of disapproval, and even the outright stares, and magnify them back. Brighter. More aggressive and confident.

That was *his* skill.

Kyle had never been that brave. Blending was so much easier than telling the world to sit and swivel. That is, until blending meant squelching the impulse to meet Nate at the ballroom's entrance and kiss him. There. For everyone to see.

His heart raced, thinking about that impossibility.

Their eyes met. Kyle was glad he hadn't been speaking with anyone at that moment because he would've become completely insensate to anything but Nate's icy, shimmering blue eyes.

That gaze spoke volumes.

I wasn't invited. You didn't invite me. And I don't give a fuck.

No matter the turmoil in his gut and heart, Kyle walked over to greet Nathan Carnes as if they were nothing more than business acquaintances. He offered his hand. "Good to see you here, Nate."

Nate glanced at Kyle's hand and lifted an eyebrow. "Cut the crap and introduce me around."

"These are investors . . ."

Kyle had learned a great deal about how much prison had inoculated Nate against displays of emotion. He could mask almost anything. Probably another skill that had served him well, honed in the roughest of classrooms.

But Kyle's words hurt him.

The flash of outright betrayal darkened the blue of his eyes, turning them a sickly, wan gray. His nostrils flared slightly. "Lord knows we wouldn't want to offend the cash flow," he said under his breath. "Should I take out the earring, Kyle? Button up my shirt in the hopes no one will see the tattoo you licked last night? Would that make me being here okay?"

"That's not what I—"

"Save it. No invitation is fine. I can party crash with the best of 'em. But when I walked in, your expression was the same as it was that day you visited me in prison." He shrugged, but the effort of it showed on his rugged, handsome face. "Forgive me for wanting a little recompense. Introduce me around and help me keep my goddamn company in business."

Kyle quickly assessed the room. Which fat cats brought the most money? Which were fond of stunt-heavy action productions? And yes, which were known to be more accepting? He couldn't afford for Nate's brashness to get either of them in trouble. He wanted Pennfield backing box office smashes, not lost in a sea of tiny, respectable pictures that never paid the bills.

He'd stopped to think with the best of intentions. Maybe that wasn't good enough for Nate, because his taunting sneer was back.

"I promise, Mr. Wakefield, I won't humiliate you."

Chapter Twenty

A man who knew how to wear a tux was flat-out sexy. Nate had never managed it, not with that same level of insouciance. Before spotting Nate in the doorway, Kyle had sported a delicious air of man-about-town. Shoulders loose and easy, with a hipshot posture that said he knew what he was talking about and that any person listening should *want* to hear it. The world revolved around Kyle Wakefield, even if it didn't want to.

Been here. Done this. Got an orange jumpsuit.

A brief moment of near absurdity flipped Nate's brain. He chuckled. There was no fighting it. "Breathe, Kyle. I won't be biting anyone."

"Just me."

"You know," Nate said, drawing the words out slow and long as he skimmed one last appreciative look down Kyle's body. "I do believe this is the first time you've said that without sounding pleased. Normally you like my teeth."

"I know these people, Nate. It's my job to know them. You're going about it all wrong if you want my help."

"Standing too close, am I? Getting you hot under the collar?"

Kyle darted a frantic look to the left. Steph was watching them over a glass of champagne that was so full she couldn't actually be drinking it. Perhaps wetting her lips on occasion, still the professional. The man next to her, with the red nose and hefty paunch, was another story. But he was too busy trying to get a peek down Steph's cleavage to notice the direction of her wary gaze.

"The movie's almost in the can," Kyle said. "I need distribution commitments and financing for our next project."

"I'm not going to hurt your chances." Nate lifted three fingers. "Boy Scout promise."

"You were never a Boy Scout."

Nate shrugged. He made himself look across the crowd as a whole. No one was paying attention to them, not the way Kyle must be assuming. Peter Upton had topped his tux with his customary baseball cap. Maybe he thought it was edgy, but the result was more cheese than cool.

Upton was actually one of the few attendees assessing them. Intently. No surprise. He seemed to have a hard-on for either Nate or Kyle. Not that Nate would blame the director if he wanted to crawl into Kyle's fancy pants. But no one got a shot at that but Nate, at least as long as they were both on British soil.

Come to think of it, though, he'd need to dial down his antagonism if he wanted another of those opportunities. He made himself smile. It was surprisingly difficult. This was entirely too much like his last night in Virginia.

The night it all went to shit.

"Look, I'll behave. I really do need to make a good impression. You *are* good at your job. I'm not gonna make it harder on either of us. Playing nice is in my best interest."

Something eased in Kyle. His mouth tweaked into a hint of a smile. He lifted the glass of champagne to his mouth. "Now that I'll accept."

"Self-interest is a fairly universal concept. Now, come on. Find me some friendly faces."

Kyle was good at that. He introduced him to a cluster of older women. Nate hadn't expected him to stay glued to his side all night, so when Kyle peeled off to chat with a young, handsome dude in a dark-purple cummerbund, he didn't care. At all. He turned back to a middle-aged brunette who had a home in the Maldives and a penchant for expensive wines—and hopefully a love for big-budget action flicks that called for plenty of ridiculously dangerous stunts.

That didn't mean Nate could turn off his awareness of Kyle. It simply wasn't possible. He tracked his lover across the room. Watched him drink three more glasses of champagne. Noticed when he ducked out to the rooftop terrace for air several times.

Through it all, no one else seemed to have the slightest idea that Kyle was stressed. This was a whole other party, and a whole decade later, but Nate was still watching Kyle from afar.

Fate was being a goddamn bitch.

So long ago, Nate had been invited to the college going-away party thrown by Kyle's parents. Why wouldn't he? He'd been sure they considered him simply a school friend who was interested in moving to New Haven, splitting the cost of rent. No biggie.

Despite what he knew would be a pleasant welcome, Nate had found it impossible to enter that big, shining house on the hill. Instead he'd sat in his beat-up hatchback, trying to muster up the guts to belong there, in Kyle's world. The party had been held in the glass-walled pool house, and from inside his car, he'd seen Kyle.

He'd watched Kyle.

A lot like he did right now, but it had hurt even more.

On that night so long ago, Kyle had appeared happy. He'd been fucking *ecstatic*. Nate had seen him dance—with girls—and chat with practically every guest. Not only would Nate have had to fake it, as if he knew those people and was comfortable around them, but he would've been in competition for Kyle's attention. Fine. He could've dealt with that. But he also would've had to tell Kyle that he didn't have the money to move to Connecticut.

So he'd left. He hadn't meant it to be forever. Just for the night. He'd wanted Kyle to have his party with his friends before Nate had to break the news. But then he'd run into a buddy from the old days. First Nate had asked for something to make the feelings go away. Then hanging out in front of a gas station had led to bitching about money, which had led to the dude offering up a solution—a one-time thing, utilizing Nate's specialized skills.

Unfortunately, they hadn't gotten to the fast getaway Nate was so good at. Turned out his ability to pop an ignition was rusty. He'd barely fired up the car he meant to steal before the cops showed up.

To make it worse, he'd been in the jurisdiction of a good friend of Kyle's parents. His name had rung bells and gone up the chain in no time flat. When Kyle had refused to leave town while Nate was still locked up, the shit hit the fan.

"There's no film in today's market," said the bleach blonde standing at Nate's side.

She was gorgeous, if one went for women. Her features were perfectly balanced, but her nose had enough of a crook to it that she didn't blend into anonymity. Words popped out of his mouth before he was able to sort them into something less accusatory. "Does that make any sort of sense?"

Her chin lifted. "Martin Scorsese had plenty to say on the truth of film versus storytelling when I was at his place this summer."

Ah. That explained it. Name-dropping was a nearly fatal disease, to the point that some victims would say any nonsensical thing in order to squeeze in a choice reference. He schooled his features into what he hoped passed for seriousness, but he was no actor. Best to get out of there quickly.

He headed for the terrace. Of course. Cold as fuck outside, with a white dusting over the elevated planting boxes. The balustrade around the edge of the roof was marble, but the wind had swept away all but the barest traces of snow.

Kyle stood with both hands on the railing, looking out at the London cityscape.

Nate shoved his hands in his pockets, the better to avoid reaching for his lover. Kyle would let him do intimate, dirty things later, but right now Nate wasn't even allowed to hold his hand.

"I keep expecting it to be warm tomorrow," he said. "And the next day."

Kyle didn't turn around, but the harsh line of his shoulders relaxed. "A month isn't long enough to get used to things."

Was that a message? Maybe. If anyone knew their month was temporary, it was certainly Nate.

He stood next to Kyle anyway. "Didn't mean to be such an ass earlier. But damn, you should have seen your face."

"I'm sure I was all very amusing." Kyle's voice was dry.

They didn't move. Nothing quite so simple. Instead, it was as if they . . . blended. Each hand shifted on the railing, a little nearer. Their hips slid and moved. Even soft puffs of white breath turned toward one another.

Technically, they only touched in two places. Their smallest fingers aligned, where a tiny streak of warmth edged Nate's hand in contrast to the frozen marble. And the sides of their shoes were nestled together—Kyle's fancy, shiny black ones next to Nate's polished but beat-up boots. No feeling came through, but he gathered a sense that everything was okay. Underneath all the old shit and the drama and the worry and the sex, they were friends.

Fuck, it still wasn't enough, but maybe that was okay for now. For the first time, Nate got the feeling that their potential was waiting. Possible. Something intangible but right there, if only he could reach out—if they both could.

There was no warning, no noise or absence of it. Just a raucous laugh.

"I knew it." The slurred voice was incredibly gleeful. "All those times. Everyone talks about how fucking perfect Kyle Wakefield is and how he hasn't put one wrong foot in Hollywood."

Peter Upton swayed between a dwarf birch tree in a round pot and a bank of snow-swathed bushes. He wore the same damn baseball cap, but it had acquired scribbles of graffiti. Someone had drawn a goofy face with what looked like lip liner.

Kyle all but flew away from Nate. He contained his body into one sharp, upright line. His head shook in automatic denial. "I don't know what you're—"

Upton cut him off. "No matter to me if you're a pole smoker. Shit, the gay mafia runs Hollywood." He slapped a hand flat over his mouth. His drink-reddened eyes went wide. "You gonna report me?"

Kyle froze. Absolutely froze. Nate didn't dare touch him. That much he knew not to do.

Steph appeared in the doorway behind their strange little trio. "Is everything all right out here?"

"No." Kyle didn't say anything else, and Nate wasn't sure who he was talking to—Upton or Steph.

"I discovered something interesting," Upton said on a near giggle.

"You think so, huh?" Nate finally said. He kept himself as calm as possible, but his stomach was a knotted mess. It wouldn't take much to turn his head and hurl off the side of the Savoy. "Two guys working on the same movie, having a talk about the next week's shooting. That's worth snickering about?"

Upton blinked. "No, you were . . ."

"What, exactly?"

It killed Nate to have to do this. Absolutely killed him. Wild animals slashed at his insides. But with Kyle apparently incapable of self-defense, he needed to step up. No way was it his place to force Kyle out, and he sure as fuck wasn't going to let him be attacked by a shithead punk.

Upton's face contorted around obvious confusion.

Nate crossed his arms. Intimidating. He knew, because he had stared down a lot worse than Upton using that same pose. "So where did you get this sudden idea about Kyle? Are you sublimating your own desires toward him? In which case, I'm sorry to tell you that you'll have competition from the blonde standing behind you. They live together."

Upton scratched the back of his head and glanced at Steph. "But . . ."

"Peter," Steph said gently, taking him by the shoulders. "You know everyone has secrets in this business. You just guessed the wrong secret." She blew Kyle a kiss, then returned her attention to the tipsy, bewildered director. "We'll get another drink, okay? Midori on the rocks?"

When she wound her arm through his, Upton had no choice but to follow. Nate and Kyle were alone. Again. This time there was no easy air, no biting chill. Just the hot churning of Nate's loss.

Kyle's neck worked on a swallow. "Thanks."

"Don't mention it."

"No, really. It shouldn't have been a big deal—"

Nate put up a hand. "No. Don't mention it. I cannot fucking believe I just hopped into a closet with you. But why shouldn't I?"

"What are you talking about?"

He shook his head and shoved his hands back in his pockets. He didn't *want* to touch, not when his hands were shaking with anger. Coming down to earth and having to hide *for* Kyle was that much more painful after the ridiculous thoughts he'd just indulged.

"It's the same old shit. Nothing ever changes with you, and that's fine. If I want a friend, I know to go somewhere else. And if you want a fuck, you know where to find me."

Chapter Twenty-One

The rest of Kyle's evening passed in a fog of pain. He and Nate didn't speak again, and Kyle stuck close to Steph. She seemed to know what he needed without having to talk. No looks of pity or concern, simply smiling professionalism that helped drag him through the remaining hours. All of that, even when Nate's quick excuse had thrown her under the bus to protect Kyle's reputation.

God, he owed her. Big-time.

After the initial introductions Kyle had managed, Nate took to the scene with aplomb. Grinning. Shaking hands. Exchanging business cards.

Mostly, he avoided looking at Nate, or tried to. It hurt too much, like touching his hand against a stove's electric burner—then layering his other hand on top, pressing harder.

This had all started as a brief affair and a nostalgia trip. It had built into something much bigger than that, and this pain wasn't going away anytime soon.

Nate left, and the air left with him. Kyle's tuxedo felt too tight. His *skin* felt too tight. Hell, maybe even his whole life.

Taking the next step, though? Trusting the man who'd thrown them away? There were some things that Kyle's money and success couldn't make easy, which included giving him confidence enough to shake up his entire life for such a chancy grab at happiness.

Just after one in the morning, he was exhausted. Steph still looked as fresh as the moment she'd stepped into the ballroom on Kyle's arm—where Nate should've been.

"Go back to the hotel," she said softly. "The walking dead aren't notorious for being the best schmoozing salesmen."

"That bad, huh?"

"I'm amazed you held out this long. After that little near debacle, even I had difficulty catching moments when your mind wasn't in the game. You did great."

"I'm sorry," he said, shaking his head. "About Nate and Upton. If Upton remembers that tomorrow . . ."

Her shrug was elegantly feminine. "You know people have said it about us for years. I'm not going to worry about it now. Just makes Pennfield interesting and worth talking about." She gave him a hug, standing on tiptoes to loop her arms around his neck. "Now get out of here and let it all out before you pop."

Kyle held her, nearly clinging. A lifeboat. A moment of reprieve. He let out a shaky exhale and nodded against her sweet-smelling hair. "Thanks, Steph."

"Make sure my Christmas present is *really* good this year. Think Balenciaga," she said with a wry grin. Damn, her lipstick was still perfect. She was an amazing woman.

They would've been married by now, had Kyle been a different man. Instead, he kissed her cheek and headed out of the ballroom. He had someone to see. Someone he owed an apology.

He trudged back to his room in the hotel. His shoes were filled with lead, and his heart was heavier. Safe within the privacy of his room, he *thunk*ed his head against the closed door and stood there. He took the bow tie off first, then jacket, suspenders, cummerbund. He was peeling off layers of defense that had served him well over the years. He didn't know what to replace them with.

After a quick wash with cold water, he looked himself in the mirror. Same features—the features people only called handsome when he strode through the days filled with confidence. Kyle saw fatigue and a hopelessness he hadn't felt in ten years. He grabbed a scotch at the minibar and drank it down.

No help.

Finally, there was no avoiding the inevitable. *That's not true*, he thought with a grimace. It wasn't inevitable. Technically he could turn away from the connecting door between his room and Nate's. He could finish out the next week as polite strangers and move on.

But they'd already ruined one set of good, precious memories. He wasn't going to be the bastard who ruined these ones too.

He knocked. Instinctually he knew it was necessary. For a week they'd kept the door cracked and sometimes wide open. A blatant invitation for more of what they both wanted. Now it was shut, and Kyle wondered if it was locked. He didn't touch the doorknob. He only knocked again.

The agony of apologizing would be nothing compared to not being given the chance to try.

Again he gave his forehead a good *thunk*ing, but against the doorjamb. There he waited. Hoping.

The door yanked open. Kyle jumped. Rather than some suspicious, narrow-eyed expression, Nate looked *fierce*. He snatched Kyle's shirtfront and pulled. They tumbled into Nate's room, grabbing, fighting, kissing. The shock of that sudden angered press of skin was a thousand times more powerful than the scotch Kyle had downed. Nate, his real drug, was ripping off what remained of Kyle's exquisite tux.

"You really have some nerve, you stuck-up asshole." But his hands were already unzipping Kyle's fly. "Stubborn, stupid—"

Kyle cut him off by biting his lip. Hard enough to draw blood. They both groaned. "Add 'coward' and get it over with."

Shoving taut fingers down Kyle's shorts, Nate kissed him without mercy—roughly, possessively. The same way he gripped Kyle's cock with both hands.

When they came up for air, Nate growled, "Coward. Lying hypocrite. You fucking *love this*."

As if to punctuate words spat like an accusation, Nate jerked and stroked. Kyle tipped his face toward the ceiling. He moaned, unable to conceal how that touch made him mindless.

"Say it." Nate picked up the speed, gripped tighter, then sucked and bit the meat of Kyle's chest. "Say it," he whispered there.

"I fucking love this."

He threaded shaky fingers through Nate's hair and held him to his chest. That silent demand was met with bites from sharp teeth. Kyle relished the sting. He hadn't apologized, but this felt like something close—letting Nate do what he pleased, even if that meant causing pain. So turned on, pain and pleasure fused in Kyle's mind. His body could take anything Nate wanted to inflict.

His arousal jumped a notch with only that thought.

"How much did this tuxedo cost?"

Nate's words took a moment to make sense. "What?"

"How much?"

"Seven thousand dollars."

"Good," Nate said, his voice like gravel. "I'm gonna jerk you off in this seven-thousand-dollar tux. You'll never wear it again without remembering this. Right now."

He bit lower on Kyle's pecs, scoring flesh with unforgiving teeth. One hand stroked from head to base, so damn fast, while he grabbed Kyle's balls with the other and squeezed.

Kyle hissed. "*Fuck.*"

Nate backed him against the nearest wall. "Buck into my hand. Show me how much you want it."

Scraping his hands down Nate's back—Christ, the man was still fully clothed—Kyle did as he was told. He let his hips work the counterpoint to Nate's punishing grip. Each thrust was breathless bliss, so near to agony that he shuddered and throbbed.

"Coming," he gasped. "Nate—"

In the second between orgasm and release, Nate shoved Kyle's throbbing cock back into his tuxedo pants. Come streaked across his shorts, the inside of the trousers, and up past the loose waistband. He felt the hot wash across his bare stomach, where Nate's hands rubbed it into his skin.

Kyle let his head fall back against the wall, needing to catch his breath. The room spun. But Nate wouldn't let him have that reprieve. Damn, the man was *strong*. Thick arms and unmistakable core strength worked together to haul Kyle across the room and practically throw him onto the bed, where he landed on his stomach, supported by his elbows. Nate bared Kyle's ass with one harsh yank.

Fine woolen cloth ripped.

"Damn," Nate said with a mocking tone. "Maybe you won't get to wear it again after all."

"I'll send it to my tailor."

Something primal ground out of Nate's throat. Kyle couldn't decide whether his lover liked that idea or was ready to punish him for it. The former would be possessive. The latter would be more proof that Nate had always been intimidated and resentful of Kyle's money.

But none of it mattered. The sound of Nate's belt unbuckling, that telltale metallic *clink*, made Kyle shiver. Then the zipper.

"You know what comes next, don't you?"

After hiding a tight smile against his forearm, Kyle said, "You. You come next."

"Damn right."

The man wasn't going to undress. He'd ruthlessly torn the clothes off Kyle, but Nate still wore the same jeans, white button-down and battered motorcycle boots. Although part of him craved the closeness of their recent encounters, body to naked body, hands and mouths everywhere, Kyle knew that wasn't in the cards that night. Raw emotions meant a raw fuck.

He didn't know *how* raw.

Condom. Lube. Thrust.

Kyle cried out. He'd had every intention of taking whatever punishment Nate needed to inflict, but that fast, cruel invasion was too much. He dug his fists into the rumpled comforter and tried to pull away.

Nate leaned close and wrapped his arm around Kyle's throat. He thrust again. "You're not going anywhere. You're going to take this and you're gonna love it, like you wind up begging for everything I do to you."

That didn't feel possible with Nate bearing down with so much force. His prick drove hilt-deep into Kyle's ass. One rock-hard arm wrapped low around Kyle's hips, holding him steady to take every inch. Nate's other arm shifted from Kyle's throat to wrap around his shoulders. They were pressed inch to inch, inseparable.

"Bring it," Kyle ground into the mattress. "Bring it."

His vision wavered. The aggressive fuck was nothing like anything he'd ever taken. He felt battered and lost, even as Nate showed his appreciation with grunted curses. Ass burning, Kyle bowed his back and pushed his head into the sheets, which only increased the pressure of Nate's body laying across him.

Nate's temple was sweaty as he aligned his mouth with Kyle's ear. "You gonna cry mercy?"

"No," Kyle panted.

"Because you could. You could call it off right now. I'd jerk off on your back. You'd have two sticky loads of come smeared on this fine body."

Tears gathered at the corners of Kyle's eyes. But there was no goddamn way he was letting Nate win this round. Apology or not, whatever was owed between them—fuck that. Kyle was a man. Pride kept him silent, his fists clenching sweat-damp percale.

"I wonder if you'd sleep like that." His tone was mocking but strained and breathless. Nate was losing control. "Or if you'd chicken the hell out again and go shower."

"Sleep . . . like that."

"Damn you, Kyle."

Something clicked over in Kyle's mind. Maybe it was the pure lust in Nate's curse, or the way he began to grind rather than invade. He relaxed. He opened for his lover and moaned as his prick surged to life.

He reared back to meet Nate's next thrust.

The arm wrapped low around his pelvis dipped lower, between Kyle's body and the firm mattress. Nate growled. "Never knew you could take it so rough and like it," he said against Kyle's nape before claiming a fierce bite.

"No. Never."

"Can you reach your prick? This one?" Nate squeezed with ruthless strength.

"*Yes.*"

"Do it."

Nate lifted until Kyle's lower body was no longer pressed flush against the mattress. Groping down his own body, with every sense and nerve beginning to malfunction, Kyle found his aching cock. Nate had slowed, grinding with more purpose and less mindless violence.

"Do you feel this moment, Kyle?" Throaty and low, Nate's voice didn't sound right. He was feral. His lower hand slipped down until he cupped Kyle's balls. Massaged. Teased. "This moment right now— right now when we're suspended."

"Yes."

"Good. Hold on to that thought, and be ready to keep up with me. Because you might not like what comes next."

He twisted Kyle's balls.

"God*damn*."

Pinned between Nate's fingers, forearm, and massive prick, Kyle's mind hazed. All he could do was stroke his cock as Nate pounded and grasped and tugged. Their bodies slapped together in a sweaty fight. It was a test of wills and physical combat rolled into the hardest fuck of Kyle's life.

"Pain and pleasure," Nate ground out. "Always us."

Kyle began to shake all over. He'd reached his limit. Complete muscle failure. His hold on his cock began to falter into helpless jerks without rhythm or grace.

Without warning, Nate let go. Balls free of that wrenching pain. The counterpoint loosed Kyle's orgasm. He shot like a cannon into his own hand—a weaker stream of come but a climax that left him light-headed and cussing into the sheets. The last shivers of sensation made him arch onto his knees. He looped an arm backward to reach Nate's neck, pulling them close once again.

"Nathan," he said breathlessly, softly. "Come now, love. Please. I know I hurt you. I'm sorry. Do you hear me? Tell me you hear me."

Two more strokes sent Nate over the edge. Kyle could feel the pressure of that powerful release despite the condom. His passage swelled, accommodating, being what Nate needed right now.

It was the least he owed the man.

They collapsed onto the bed. Furious panting filled the room, which was thick with their heat and the scent of sex. Minutes of mindlessness followed. Slow. Dizzy. They'd slammed from a hundred miles an hour to a dead stop.

Finally Nate moved first. He took Kyle's hand and interlaced their fingers. "I heard you," he said, voice rasping. "But that doesn't change anything."

The place inside Kyle that briefly, potently flickered back to life whenever he was with Nate turned dark again.

"No." He stared up at the ceiling because he couldn't face the accusation and hurt he knew he'd find in eyes like ice. "It doesn't."

Fingers unclasped. Nate pushed off the bed. The sound of his condom snapping off was sordid. Shameful. He tossed it into the nearest trash can, then unbuttoned his shirt as he walked toward the shower. "Good night, Kyle. You know your way out."

Chapter Twenty-Two

The Christmas spirit was a fucking myth. Nothing got easier. Happiness didn't automatically fill a guy just because someone hung a long string of green branches over the fireplace in the pub.

Nate sucked back a swallow of his pint. The ale had a better chance at inspiring a happy flush than any piped-in carols pervading the dead space between endless chatter.

One of the chattering people was Raney. He lounged next to Nate, their seat backs pointed toward the wood-paneled corner so they could look out at the crowd.

Well. Maybe Raney was looking at the crowd. Nate was watching for Kyle.

It was starting to feel like he never did anything else. Never *had* done anything else, not for a very long time.

Quite the way to spend Christmas Eve.

Their time in England was drawing to a close. Nate couldn't decide if he was looking forward to getting back to the States.

Of course Raney seemed to know exactly what he was thinking about, in that annoying way friends had. "I don't see Wakefield."

Nate rolled his fingers around the side of his glass. "Why don't you go ahead and say the rest of that sentence."

Raney's head tilted. Golden hair fell onto his forehead in an artful sweep. "Why don't you tell me, since you seem to know what I'm going to say more than I do?"

"Or we could play twenty questions all night."

"Not as much fun as watching you twist," Raney said. "So. Out with it."

"Something like 'Wakefield's not here—thank God.'"

Raney's blue eyes narrowed. "Whatever. Like I give a shit." Except his words were laden with a sharper anger than he was admitting to. They'd known each other long enough to ignore that.

Nate didn't have to wait long. He counted to five silently, listening to David Bowie and Bing Crosby sing "Little Drummer Boy." He picked out the song's words from under the hum of voices swirling through the pub. Everyone was in really high spirits, drinking beer or heavily laced eggnog, with bursts of laughter erupting at random moments.

The English *really* liked partying on Christmas Eve.

"I didn't come all the way to fucking London, leaving Vicki behind on Christmas—and you know how much court drama it took to get visitation on major holidays—only to watch you flush it all away."

There it was. Christ, it was almost a relief to hear. Because it wasn't anything Nate hadn't said to himself. Vicki was Raney's three-year-old girl, the result of a very brief marriage, and she deserved to have her daddy home for Christmas. She also deserved to grow up knowing her father, a reformed embezzler, had worked like crazy to make up for old mistakes, forging a successful, respectable career. That was what made it worthwhile to Raney when Nate dragged him around the world.

"The filming is going fine," Nate said. "And we'll be wrapped up tomorrow. Nothing to worry about after that."

"It won't be fine if this goes up in a spectacular blaze and your producer boyfriend cuts our stunts down to two-minute explosions."

Nate laughed at the thought, which did absolutely nothing to clear the dark shadows on Raney's handsome face. "Kyle wouldn't do that."

"Kyle, huh? You don't even pretend anymore, with the 'Mr. Wakefield' crap. But I wouldn't be so sure. That's the kind of guy he is—rich and fickle."

"Not true." Something dark and unpleasant shifted in Nate's memories.

Raney sneered. "Don't forget, I was there. I was two cells down when you showed up on the block, a street kid who was still only a kid. You were goddamned heartbroken and lost."

"You've always been a poet."

"You've always been oblivious."

Nate clenched his teeth on the words he wanted to say. Any more of this and they'd descend into childish name-calling. "That was a long time ago."

"Yeah? How about Jaime? That wasn't so long ago."

"Not the same thing." But Nate didn't like where this conversation was headed. "For fuck's sake, Jaime organized gay pride parades. He couldn't be any more out."

Raney shook his head. Complete disgust drew his mouth down. He didn't look so much like film star Robert Durant. Instead he looked like a guy who'd seen the shittier side of people and was waiting for it to pop out of his friend. "No, but even then you thought you had everything under control. Did you see it coming when things exploded in your face? Course not."

That struck uncomfortably close to home. Nate shifted on the wooden chair. Kyle's ass must be raw today with how hard Nate had slammed him. How rough they'd been. Together.

Jesus, always so together. He'd bury himself in Kyle's brain if it meant getting closer. They'd already done everything physically possible. That hadn't ever been enough.

Which sure as fuck sounded a lot like things exploding in his face. He swallowed the last of his ale, but it didn't fix anything. Alcohol never did. "We're practically headed home. Only one more stunt."

"The big one, Carnes."

"It'll be fine."

Raney leaned his elbows on the wood table, which had been polished to a patina by decades of men striking the same pose. "I have no worry about the stunt. That's the easy part. I'm worried about what comes after."

Nate ducked his head on a nod, hoping Raney would take it as agreement rather than Nate being simply *done*. He couldn't think, couldn't talk, couldn't feel like this anymore.

He smacked the table. "So. I'm going to get another round. Same for you?"

Raney pulled a face, then gulped down the last few mouthfuls of his pale beer. "I'd kill for a Bud."

"You have no fucking taste." Nate wound his way toward the long bar at the far side of the pub.

The shit-ass problem was that Raney could be right. This could be inches from going very badly. Neither of them had said a word about what would happen next. What *could* happen next? Nate couldn't think straight when it came to Kyle. His every sense was stretching out, waiting, looking for that moment when Kyle would find the strength to reach back.

But when Kyle walked in the front door, bringing in a gust of frozen winter air, Nate knew. That moment sure as hell wasn't going to come in the middle of a busy pub.

He hooked an elbow over the edge of the bar and dragged his gaze away. Didn't matter. In those few seconds, he'd catalogued every detail. Kyle's trench coat opened over a sleek, ultra-mod blue suit, with a paler blue shirt and striped tie. A few flakes of snow dusted his brown hair, but he didn't bother brushing them off. They were beyond his notice.

Much like plenty of other things.

Nate needed to get a grip. He had a red-eye ticket out of town after shooting concluded on Christmas night. The stars did too because Upton had made it glaringly clear that his plans for a trip to the Alps were *not* to be ruined. But for Nate, breaking it off with Kyle at this late juncture was leaving him hollow and disappointed. Skipping out early. He'd felt the same way when he stole that car. No talking. No compromise. Fucking it up on purpose. He'd always known their relationship came with strings. Be better. Be more. And be ready to feel like shit when he didn't measure up.

Prison had made that as permanent as his tattoo.

And there he was, in the same situation again. The bartender pushed the round of drinks across the gleaming wood, but instead of heading back toward Raney, Nate stayed put. He took a long swig of the slightly bitter ale—while trying to do his damnedest to keep his gaze off Kyle.

Total failure.

Meanwhile, Kyle hadn't seemed to notice Nate, but no way was that the case. An electric pull arced between them.

Yet, after how the fundraising party had gone down, Nate didn't feel he had the right to walk straight up to Kyle.

So, fine. He'd make Kyle come to him.

A small cluster of extras mingled to his right. Rough accents and too much hair gel and super-wide eyes as they tried to act like all of this was no big deal. They'd probably been paid a pittance, but that'd be worth it if they could catch a glimpse of Jessica Lorrie or Robert Durant.

Bonus of bonuses, the extra nearest Nate had been checking out his ass. He was young, tall, and well built—and he knew it too. A dark-green T-shirt clung to solid sinews and showed off biceps that had taken plenty of work.

Nate grinned at him. "Haven't seen you around here."

"Nah, mate. Hired on of late. Did a bit of milling in the background."

"Everyone's got to start somewhere, don't they?" He stuck out a hand. "Nate Carnes."

The guy's palm was a little calloused, slightly rough. Nice. A tingle of awareness wasn't necessary, but knowing he wouldn't have to fake this too much was a relief to Nate.

Kyle was at the other side of the room. His turn to do the watching now.

"Mike," the bloke said with an appealingly crooked grin. "You an actor?"

"Fuck no. I do stunts."

Mike's eyebrows lifted. "Do you? That's pretty flash. What kind?"

"All of them." Dragging out a smile became easier when talking about his work. The good stuff. "I drive fast and jump off tall buildings for a living."

"Like Superman."

"Minus the kryptonite."

Bald-faced fucking lie. Because his kryptonite was headed right toward them.

Kyle. He still wore that trench coat, as if he hadn't planned on staying long. He walked up to Nate and Mike as if he owned the joint—exactly the way he *hadn't* been able to respond to Upton.

Truth be known, exactly the way Nate had been hoping he would respond last night in the hotel room. Sure, he'd practically told Kyle to get out and shut that connecting door behind him. A part of Nate, however—a huge part of him—had hoped Kyle would flat out say no. That he'd draw on his natural arrogance and stay precisely where he was. Maybe it would've been enough to let Nate know his lover was in it for their time together.

Because every day seemed to sink Nate a little deeper.

This wasn't about putting a happy, tidy Christmas bow on what they used to have. This was about relearning Kyle and becoming all the more fascinated with such a complicated, brilliant man.

Nate clamped his fingers around the cool mug of beer, but he didn't let his smile waver. "Mr. Wakefield. You in the habit of introducing yourself to the extras?"

Kyle rose to the challenge in Nate's voice. The smile he spun was gorgeous, all perfect white teeth and the knowledge of how well his friendliness would be received. "Only the standout ones. You and your group did well today. At the Tube entrance, yes? Very good job."

"That was us." Mike preened under the attention, his chest puffing up a few inches. His friends had drifted away toward the cluster at the back of the room where the movie's leads held court. Nate shifted to lean back against the bar with Mike at his side. He let his elbows spread. Outward. His arm nestled against Mike's ribs, which were padded by plenty of hard bulk.

Nate's smile felt like danger. "What a conscientious producer you are. We all must be in great hands."

"So grateful to hear that," Kyle said, his voice slicing with the precision of a scalpel. "But if you're not too busy here, I need to borrow you for a minute."

Nate shifted nearer to Mike. Not because he wanted to. Not because there was any huge appeal in the blunt instrument of a man. But because Nate could tell by the way Kyle's shoulders drew together that it bugged the fuck out him. "Can't it wait? I've got a damn big day tomorrow." He inclined his head only a fraction toward Mike. "And who knows how late I'll be up."

"No. Sorry. Can't wait." Except Kyle didn't seem the least bit sorry. He turned to leave.

Feeling dumb as a box of hammers, Nate delivered Raney's beer, grabbed his jacket, and followed in Kyle's wake. He slipped into sleek leather as they stepped outside, but it was little defense against the biting chill. The barest flakes of snow swirled around them both.

"Now what?" He wanted to add some sort of smart-mouthed nickname, but he faltered. This was . . . too close to who they really were. No defensive, demeaning name-calling now.

Kyle sighed. A white puff blew out from his lips. "Now? I have no idea. I don't even know why I did that."

Kyle smelled of expensive cologne and delicious skin. Too tempting. Nate needed to back off, to step away. He sat down on the curb if only for a change of atmosphere.

"Don't feel too bad. It was my fault."

"Oh?" Haughty wasn't even the word for it.

"I wanted to know if I could get you to scoop me up and drag me away. And I won." Nate licked his top lip, trying vainly to hold back a smile. "You mad?"

Chapter Twenty-Three

K yle tucked the tails of his trench coat under his sore-as-hell ass and joined Nate on the curb. The occasional black cab passed, but that area of central London only permitted fee-paying passenger cars. That meant a lot of pedestrians, all hustle and bustle. He and Nate were still, quiet—two stubborn rocks in the sea, refusing to budge as the tide of Christmas Eve surged around them.

"No, I'm not mad." The bracing air made for a nice sting in his lungs. "I'm flattered."

Nate snorted. "Great. Just when I was trying to take you down a peg or two."

"And why are you always trying to do that?"

"Easier to reach you."

Stunned by that flash of honesty, Kyle turned to stare at Nate's profile. Rugged and jagged, he had a heavy brow that gave off unconscious "back off" signals. The end of his nose was blunt, which offset his supple lower lip. From under the collar of Nate's leather jacket crept the licking black of his tattoo. Paths taken. Paths tangled.

"You think I'm a coward who hides behind my money. What's so high that you have to reach so hard?"

"Does it matter right now?"

Kyle looked up where the snow was beginning to fall in swirling gusts. The lights, the sparkling white, and the strains of music and ever-present laughter—they conspired to lighten the heaviness that had settled around his heart since his reunion with Nate.

"No," he said quietly. "Not tonight."

"I've decided to leave for the States on the last plane out tomorrow night, after the final stunt shoot. Upton and the leads won't be here. No sense staying."

"You're not staying the rest of the week?" Damn, that sounded almost . . . pleading. He had a mile-high stack of paperwork to finish before leaving for Bangkok, and he'd been hoping to have company.

"Not staying," Nate said. "Best that I go."

Kyle shivered into his trench coat, then pushed away a gathering feeling of dread.

"So." He shook out a tight exhale and clasped his hands over his knees. His shoes would be ruined from where they sat in a puddle of slush. "This is it."

"Seems like."

He wanted to keep talking. He wanted to ask if they'd really been the excited, eager, hopeful kids he remembered. Yet he didn't need to ask, because memories layered between them every time they spoke. The first time their eyes met . . . and held. The first time they'd touched, almost but not quite accidentally rubbing shoulders as they'd walked back to the dorms after class. The first time they'd kissed, behind an equipment shed near the athletic track—God, like every dream coming true as their lips met.

After that, they'd become one long, mad rush into the best of enthusiasm and youth.

He'd loved Nathan Carnes so much. Too much.

He'd put every ounce of trust into the plans they'd made. None of them had come true, not even the hopes he'd had for this Christmas Eve—apparently the last night they'd spend together. After how badly things had ended in Nate's room, Kyle had decided not to mention the reservations he'd made at Seven Park Place, to try their Michelin-starred cuisine, nor the room he'd booked at Claridge's. Neither had he found the nerve to cancel them.

Then again, four weeks ago, he'd thought an intimate reunion with Nate was an impossible fantasy. They'd work together professionally. That was all.

This was a small, fleeting blessing. Just right for the season.

"I have to shop for Steph," he said, eyes vaguely focused on a bright streetlight. "I owe her something extra after all the shit I've put her through this month."

"I should do the same for Raney. Maybe get his little girl something."

It was the slimmest olive branch in the history of Greek idioms, but Kyle would take it. He stood and dusted the worst of the street grime off his coat. Nate watched silently. In the strange light of Christmas Eve in the city, with the snow feathering over his sandy-blond hair, his eyes were the palest blue Kyle could imagine. One step away from silver. So damn perceptive, and so damn wary.

He wondered if that same wariness was in his eyes too.

He held out his hand. "Come on. Hamleys and a Bulgari retailer are on Regent Street. Toys, then jewelry."

"The gays go shopping?" Nate asked with a smirk.

"Yes. The gays go shopping."

Kyle breathed out when Nate took his hand and stood. Stood very close. "Then let's go."

It was awkward at first. Kyle couldn't shake his nerves. A refrain beat in his mind. *Last night. Last night.*

But why?

Because even on overloaded Regent Street, it took more guts than it should've to loop his arm through Nate's. They were two men amid thousands. To really love him would mean reaching for him without hesitation, no matter who saw.

Love him?

Oh fuck.

But then again . . . He'd never really stopped. Nate had been the rhythm of Kyle's thoughts and the beat of his blood since they were fifteen. Nothing had changed, except now he knew how fragile such emotions could be—how vulnerable a man was left when they shattered. Confirmation of your general unworthiness tended to go that way.

He wanted to stay sane, so he turned away from that nest of rattlesnakes. He tightened his arm around Nate's and leaned in. Shoulders did more than innocently brush together. They were pressing, walking a little more slowly, soaking each other in as they navigated the busy holiday crowds.

Along the Regent Street shopping mecca, fully six stories tall, Hamleys was the toy store to end all toy stores.

"Beats the hell out of Toys 'R' Us," Nate said, looking up. "But it'd be an easy building to scale. Lots of handholds."

Kyle laughed. "Showoff."

With only a shrug, Nate led him into the shop. "Vicki's three," he said. "And a girl. What the hell does a three-year-old girl want at Christmas?"

"Pink things."

"Ponies?"

"Or unicorns."

Nate grinned. "Even better."

Within minutes, amid that glittering and otherworldly plastic chaos, they were laughing and holding hands as they rode an escalator to the third floor, looking for the mass of fluorescent pink that screamed *girl toys*.

"Always so many shades," Kyle said, dazed by the sheer volume of merchandise.

"As if you'd know . . ."

"What does that mean?"

Nate picked up two Hello Kitty purses. "Because knowing magenta from raspberry," he said, indicating each purse in turn, "would light up the neon sign above your head that says 'So Very Queer.'"

"That one's more ruby. Too muted for magenta."

Nate started laughing. And he couldn't stop. He sat heavily on the floor, back bowed as he wiped the corners of his eyes. A store attendant gave them an odd look but must've considered them harmless because she moved on, appearing both exhausted and bored.

"See, now I have to get this," Nate said, still catching his breath. "The ruby one. Because I stand corrected."

For the second time that night, Kyle helped Nate stand. Their mouths were mere inches apart. How could he not kiss the lips he dreamed about? Brief, sweet, playful—because they were still smiling.

"The color doesn't suit you," he said against Nate's cheek.

"No? I'm not a Hello Kitty sort of guy?"

More smiles. Kyle was getting drunk on them. "Not exactly."

"Too bad. It's mine until I absolutely have to give it up." Nate slung the purse onto his shoulder. That he wore it over leather and with his tattoo licking up his neck only made the girly accent he affected more absurd.

"You're not going to," Kyle said. "No way."

"You know I am. Now close your mouth. It's not time for that sort of play yet."

He gave Kyle a tug on the lapel. Kyle would've floated away without that grounding pull.

After a few minutes searching, Nate started muttering to himself. "This place, man. A lot of hype, but damn does it look like a worked-over hooker. Check this out. Every display toy has been stripped and molested." He picked up a mechanized dog that was supposed to walk and bark. "Too late in the season to replace batteries?"

Kyle poked one of the dog's broken legs. "Batteries are the least of this poor guy's problems. But to be fair, it's nearly eight on Christmas Eve."

"But we demand unicorns, damn it!"

Finally they spotted what seemed to be the Holy Grail of all things girly: a pink-and-white stable with all manner of grooming necessities for six fat plastic ponies, two of which were unicorns.

"And the purse," Nate said. "Perfect."

Kyle shook his head at Hello Kitty's vapid expression. "Gimme that thing."

"Only if you're going to wear it."

"Hand it over."

Now it was Nate's turn to drop his jaw as Kyle thumbed the ruby-pink plastic strap onto his shoulder. He held out his hand, which Nate took without hesitation. Damn, that felt good.

"C'mon, I still need to shop for Steph."

"We can't buy two purses and call it good?"

"Not a chance."

As they descended, each floor looked more and more dismal. The last dregs of the shopping frenzy were left everywhere like the aftermath of a battle. The lines were long, but Kyle didn't care. How could he when he was wearing a goddamn purse and Nate kept smirking at him? But the smirk was happier, a little more amazed. Kyle liked being able to do that—to shake up Nate's obviously entrenched expectations.

Expectations he deserved to have because Kyle had done a really good job entrenching.

He stuffed the purse into Nate's shopping bag, and they stepped back out into the night. The snow was coming down now, gathering in swoops and crevices along the buildings and curbs. People ducked into the wind, scarves over their faces.

Nate's levity dimmed. His expression was the one Kyle most often saw on the set, when Nate went over and over the details of a stunt. He was so damn clever. Only now that calculating expression was unwelcome. It was a reminder of real lives waiting to drive a wedge between them.

"What is it?" Kyle asked.

"I want this snow to stop. Soon. The forecast said only a dusting."

"Any more than a dusting means . . .?"

"Added risk."

A chill sank into Kyle's bones that had nothing to do with the strengthening wind. "If it's too bad—"

"Forget it," Nate said with a dismissive wave. "Leave it for tomorrow."

At least that's what he said. But as they walked on toward the exclusive jewelry boutique, Kyle could feel the tension in his hand and see the careful, assessing way he watched the sky.

Every shop was still brimming with people, and every pub was jammed with revelers. Some wore paper crowns from Christmas crackers. Most were smiling. Kyle wanted to be one of them.

"Hey," he said, bumping their bodies together. "Guess what."

"Hmm?"

"It's Christmas Eve."

Nate grinned. "When we were sixteen. That was the best one."

A flush helped warm Kyle's chilled cheeks. "The way that video store clerk snickered at us when we said we were twenty-one."

"It was worth it. I got to see you turn just about as pink—or should I say, as ruby—as you are now. Then we got to watch our first gay porn flick. A very merry Christmas."

"Until you tried a goddamn mentholated blowjob."

Nate's laugh was the best, most wonderful sound on the whole planet. In that, Kyle was not being hyperbolic or a drama queen. It was true. "How was I supposed to know peppermint candy canes would sting?"

"The word *pepper* was a clue. Pepper and my dick shouldn't be in the same thought."

"It didn't stunt your growth in that department," Nate said with a cheeky smile. "And I licked you like that candy cane until it was all better."

Kyle made an appreciative noise in his throat. "Yes, you did. And that was the night we both decided leather chaps would never, ever be our thing."

"Heh. Or tattoos."

"One out of two?"

"Well . . ." Nate licked his lower lip. "Never say never. I'd look amazing in leather chaps and you know it."

They stood at an intersection, ready to cross a street, but Kyle pushed Nate up against a stoplight pole. Their lips were cold at first touch, but they warmed quickly as Kyle took the kiss he wanted. The kiss he needed. Nate's arms stayed slack, holding the shopping bag, apparently too overcome to move. Didn't matter. Kyle thrust his fingers into Nate's hair and deepened what was fast becoming an explosive kiss.

Only when he was swollen and breathless did he pull back.

Nate stared at him, lips slightly puffy. "What was that for?"

"Because, yes, you'd look amazing."

If Nate could do anything better than rappel down buildings and drive every vehicle ever made, it was recover from quick bursts of emotion. He masked shock and a flicker of heartbreaking hope with an arrogant smile. "And that did it for you, huh?"

"Apparently. We didn't know what the fuck we were doing when we were sixteen."

"We managed," Nate said quietly. "And that porno certainly helped."

Snow dusted them both when they reached the jewelry store. Only twenty minutes till closing. Kyle browsed the brightly lit cases full of precious metals and every glittering stone known to man. Yet Nate's distraction was obvious. He kept glancing out toward the snow, until he touched Kyle on the arm.

"You mind if I go call Raney? Gotta get his take on this."

"Sure, go ahead. This won't take long. The girl's a sucker for opals."

Nate made a squished face of disapproval, then shrugged. "Whatever turns her on. I'll be right back. And then you better have dinner plans. I'm starving."

Kyle nodded before returning to the nearest case, which contained nothing but opaque stones—malachite, lapis, carnelian, tiger's-eye. And opals. He waved a short, dark-haired jeweler over and requested one particular piece.

"A lovely choice, sir," the man said.

Kyle held the bracelet beneath a high-intensity table lamp. The gorgeous creation was gold, with twelve fire opal cabochons stations. Each flawless, nearly translucent stone looked like sunset over the red soil of the Outback, but with flashes of blue and green. He didn't blink at the price tag. Steph would love it. She didn't have anything like it in her collection.

"Yes, this is perfect."

As the jeweler rang up the purchase, Kyle's gaze wandered over the store. A very bad, very dangerous idea popped into his head. He tried to push it away, but it wouldn't budge.

After second, third, and fourth thoughts, he finally gave in. "Wait a moment."

He strode over to the case full of men's watches. It took only a few moments to find what he wanted.

"That one," he said to the jeweler. "Box it up too."

Chapter Twenty-Four

S tanding on the sidewalk shouldn't have bought Nate so much quiet, but the swirling snow left the noise of other shoppers oddly muted. Tension slammed knotted fists at the small of his back as he listened to dead air on the other end of his cell.

Finally Raney grumbled, "They're expecting four inches by tomorrow evening."

"Fuck." The word gritted out from between clenched teeth. A sharp spike lanced into an immediate headache. "It's not the snow on the ground."

He was talking to the only person who'd automatically know what he meant. They could clean the roads, lay gravel and salt. Hell, enough people on crew could swarm with microfiber cloths and wipe it up.

"It's what'll be coming down," Raney said, echoing Nate's thoughts.

"Yup. Even with most everything closed for the holiday, we only got the permits for those three takes."

"Big Ben. The actual *plot* calls for Big Ben. There's no way out unless we hand it all over to the CGI geeks."

"And a Maserati worth a couple hundred thousand."

"Waiting to be wrecked," Raney finished.

Nate spun on a heel in lieu of pacing because the packed crowds scrambling for last-minute gifts made that impossible. Kyle was somewhere behind shimmering, frost-tinted windows, but between the weather and the evening streetlights, Nate couldn't see the man. Just his own reflection. His eyes were narrow and his mouth flat. Grim.

"I'm doing this shoot. Hell or high water."

Raney chuckled, a tinny sound. "There's the Nate I know and argue with constantly. Make it happen."

The brass-handled front door of the jewelry store pushed open, revealing Kyle—gorgeous, smiling like a cat with a canary under its paw, and dressed in a suit that made him look like a prince among men.

Enough to make Nate's chest light up with warmth.

"Listen, Raney. I gotta run." He thumbed off the connection, never taking his eyes off Kyle, especially because of how Kyle stared right back.

Kyle wrapped an arm around Nate's waist and kissed him while the world stilled and the snow dusted them. Like a goddamned Gene Kelly movie.

He pulled his mouth away from Kyle's temptation. "What did you find that has you so pleased?"

"The perfect present for Steph."

"How much did you spend on her?" The question didn't have the same sting it might've once had.

Kyle's mouth quirked. "You sure you want me to answer that?"

"Sure, why not." With their arms linked together, they started to walk.

"Five thousand."

Nate only shook his head, chuckling as they went, because the other option was to cringe at further proof that leaving the next day was a damn good thing. "You said a bonus thing. Didn't you already get her something extravagant?"

Kyle shrugged. "I did. I'm sending her to Bora Bora. Maybe she'll hook up with a surfer."

That intrinsic generosity was quite simply a part of Kyle's spirit. For the people who were important to him, he had no limit. Part of it was the need to please, but most of it was . . . Kyle. The goodness of him.

Nate swallowed down a hot rush of emotion and kept his voice steady. "Does she need to get laid that bad?"

"Steph? No way. She just has refined tastes." Kyle pulled them to a stop in front of a tiny storefront. One red bench emblazoned with the Coca-Cola logo and covered in stickers advertising phone-sex numbers faced a small service window. A very busy-looking man in a greasy white apron bustled inside.

"Hungry?"

Nate eyed the chalkboard menu. "I'm not sure. Where the hell are we?"

"Kebab stand. These places are awesome." Kyle looked awfully proud of himself.

Even if Nate had been reluctant to try it, the bright flare in Kyle's brown eyes would've done him in. It did every time. He was a damn sucker when the guy got charged up about anything. "Fine, but I'm not eating on the street."

"But you have to."

He watched the short man in the window use a long knife to scrape meat off a rotating spit directly into a fluffy pita. "Really? Aren't you supposed to be the one into linen napkins and actual forks?"

Kyle silenced him with one soft kiss. "Sit. I'll order."

Nate's shoulders loosened. The air sighed out of his chest, the better to leave room for his swelling heart. Kyle was his for only another twenty-four hours, which made tomorrow terrifying. The days after that looked like a catastrophic wasteland. The fact that he was finally able to admit he wanted more turned it from painful to excruciating. There was no room in Kyle's shining life for Nate, and he refused to skulk in the shadows.

He sat on the bench as Kyle returned with foil-wrapped sandwiches. He was triumphant, like a man who'd shot and slaughtered a mammoth.

Nate made himself smile as he took his sandwich. Kyle sat nice and close next to him. It was damn good, though they were eating on a cold metal bench—or maybe because of it. Nate had the feeling this was a moment that would roll itself into his heart and grab on tight.

"So Steph gets a five-thousand-dollar bracelet, and I get to eat outside in the snow. I see how it is."

Kyle's jaw worked as he chewed and swallowed a bite of kebab. Nate thumbed a tiny dollop of white sauce from the corner of his mouth.

"I had dinner reservations." Kyle said it slowly, poking at a piece of dark-green lettuce sticking out from his sandwich. "Hotel too. But after how we left things last time . . ."

Nate cringed. No other word for it. Just cringed. He tried to hide it with a bite of kebab. "No, I get it." He'd nearly fucked up a good thing. Again. It was one of those bound-to-happen things, but that didn't mean he wanted to hurry up the process. *Again.* "Where would we have gone?"

Kyle slanted him a wary look. *Wary.* Nate didn't like that. "Seven Park Place and Claridge's."

"You always did have class. Even I've heard of those places."

"Don't say it like that."

"Like what?"

Kyle finished his kebab, then wadded the napkin and foil up into a tight ball. He slung it toward a trash can. "'Even I.' You've always done that shit."

Right now, right here, words burned behind Nate's lips. Seared the tip of his tongue. But he didn't know what they'd be: an apology, words of love, or begging to see Kyle again once they were both back in LA. So he held them back. He didn't like uncertainty, didn't like being a supplicant.

He slipped a hand beneath Kyle's warm scarf, holding his nape. Pulled him close. Kissed him. Not too harsh, not too deep. Enough that Kyle's tongue traced the inside of his mouth with velvet rasps, licking away the words that lurked there. When the kiss ended, Nate pressed his forehead to Kyle's, the better to keep his eyes shut. He couldn't look at anything so bright and shiny, or it would burn him from the inside out.

"How far away is that hotel?"

Thank God Kyle ignored how rough and raw Nate's voice sounded. "On Christmas Eve? It'll probably take us about an hour to get there."

"Too long."

Kyle kissed him again. A tease. A promise. Something more than that, but Nate didn't have any room left for hope. Not with his boarding pass to the States already printed and sitting on his hotel room dresser.

Kyle's lips were soft. Smooth. His tongue was exactly greedy enough. "You can make it."

"No." He surged up from the bench and wrapped his hand around Kyle's strong wrist, below that expensive watch. "Come on."

They walked blindly, Nate making turn after turn based solely on sound. What got quieter. Farther away from the bustle.

Eventually, he found the goal he hadn't known he was looking for. A dark alley. The walls were barely more than five feet apart, meant only for walking. A door to one side probably led to a store, because pallets of packing material were piled up.

Nate pushed Kyle back against the cinder block wall. It had to be cold, but layers of coat and suit and an undershirt would protect him. Nate claimed his mouth. Rough. Mean.

Still it wasn't enough.

Their bodies strained together. Nate shoved hands between their stomachs, feeling the press of Kyle's cock against fine wool. Finding him hard was no surprise since Nate was already throbbing. He jerked Kyle's belt buckle open, unzipped his trousers. The occasional whoosh of a car outside the alley was the only competition for their wet mouths and harsh breaths.

Kyle hissed when Nate's hands delved beneath boxer briefs. "Cold," he whispered.

"Doesn't seem to be stopping you." It didn't. Kyle's abundant cock jerked up into Nate's grip as if eager for more.

Kyle's eyes drifted shut, but only for a flicker. He licked his lips. A swallow worked down his throat. He seemed to need an extra effort to gather his thoughts.

Nate let his vicious grin loose. He liked that. Having an effect on Kyle fucking Wakefield had to mean *something*.

Though it took time, Kyle finally spoke. "What do you have in mind?"

Stroking from root to head, Nate watched Kyle's eyes turn hazy and dark. "It's Christmas Eve."

"It is. You're very astute."

"Are you teasing me while I've got your dick in my grip?"

Frantic shaking of his head accompanied a rough chuckle. "No. Well. Maybe. But I'll take it back."

Nate licked up the length of Kyle's neck. A flavor of salt and the wet of snow. "I haven't hung up my stocking. That means I won't get any candy."

"They do pillowcases instead of stockings here. Besides, you'd get coal."

"I want to lick your cock like a candy cane for old times. Could you please stop with the mouthy talk?"

"Fuck yes. Go ahead. Be my guest. Really. I'm—" Kyle's words died when Nate squatted and engulfed the hot prick he held.

No fucking around. No teasing. He sucked Kyle's swollen head, then took the whole, huge beast in his mouth, as far as he could. Again and again. Wet and hard. He popped his mouth off the end. A slender string of pre-come clung to his bottom lip until he slicked it away. Salty and so very good.

"You'd better come fast, Kyle." He shifted his knees out to bracket Kyle's legs, then tucked one hand into soft cotton briefs and cupped Kyle's tender sac. "You're all open here. Public. There's nothing keeping you safe but fifteen feet down a shadowy alley."

Kyle didn't seem to mind because his chest jerked on a harmonic moan that was more feeling than sound. His hands spread on the gray bricks at his hips. Holding himself back. Constrained.

If this was the end, if this was their last night, Nate meant for them to go out in style. He put his full effort into the task of breaking Kyle's control. He leveraged his mouth over that delicious cock, treating it like a candy cane indeed. No peppermint burn this time, only the pure enjoyment of having Kyle in his mouth. Under his grip.

His lover groaned again. Tense hands lifted from the wall and cupped the back of Nate's head. Cold and firm, the way Nate tried to remember Kyle—frigid, unfeeling, the same as every other rich kid. But he'd failed. This heat had always existed between them, a power that could strip any amount of arrogance, any number of defenses.

Two thumbs rubbed softly over Nate's cheeks. "I'm not going to last."

Nate didn't bother stopping to voice his approval or that Kyle's quick come had been his goal. He made his intentions clear with a suck that hollowed cheeks. He pressed his tongue along the sleek ridge beneath Kyle's head. That firm and swollen shaft throbbed with impending release.

When it came, his reward was everything he could have hoped for. Release lashed across his tongue, and he took it all while he pinned his gaze on Kyle's exquisite expression. The way his features crumpled and his lips parted on a sharp moment of bliss was something Nate gathered close to keep forever.

Chapter Twenty-Five

Kyle had barely recovered from his shuddering, explosive orgasm, with Nate's tongue still lapping away the last of his come, when he wanted more. He wanted to make Nate as mindless.

He did up his fly then pulled Nate up by his shoulders. "Your turn."

Nate glanced around the alley, which was barely cover for the chances they were taking. Kyle's heartbeat hadn't returned to normal, and neither had his brain. Logic had fizzled away as soon as Nate dragged him into the shadows.

"You sure? It's awfully . . . risky."

"I had my dick out," Kyle said. "Definitely your turn." He switched their positions so that Nate's back pressed against the wall. "Start. Work your cock."

Nate seemed surprised, but he masked it with a crooked smile. "You want me to do all the work?"

"Oh no. I'll help."

As he spoke, Kyle was unbuttoning his coat, his vest, his shirt—not all the way, but barely enough of an opening. The cold air stung the exposed skin of his stomach. He nestled them together, body pressed against body, while leaving enough room for Nate to get off.

He tucked Nate's swollen shaft between the parted layers of fabric until that hot flesh was flush against Kyle's stomach. Nate groaned. He took his prick in hand as if he couldn't help it, couldn't help beginning to stroke. Kyle liked that. So much.

They had that one simple point of connection, skin against swollen, sensitive skin, but Kyle needed more. He raked his fingers into Nate's hair. Palms curved and taut, he held as much of Nate's skull as he could. He squeezed enough to show his dominance of the situation, then pushed his lover's head against the cinder block wall.

Nate hissed, but his hand picked up speed.

"You're mine. Right now. You're working that gorgeous tool, but I have you."

He used his face to nudge the collar of Nate's jacket to one side and mashed his lips against the tattoo he couldn't see. But it was there, burning like a brand. He latched his teeth on to strong muscle, bit, sucked, licked.

And the words . . . He couldn't stop them.

"You need to come, Nathan," he rasped. "Because you need it too. That trip to the hotel? So long? There's such a thing as too much anticipation. You'd finish before we barely closed the hotel door."

"Nothing wrong with that." Nate's voice was rough and low. Kyle felt the vibrations of the words beneath his tightened palms and how Nate's jaw ground out his protest.

"Nothing wrong with it," Kyle breathed against hot skin. "But I want us on a level playing field. I want us both satisfied when we take a cab across the city, and I want us touching. Soft at first. But it would build again, this fire. You know it would. A whole hour to recover, breathe, start again."

Between their bodies, Nate's arm pulsed faster and faster, his pace becoming jerky, nearly frantic. His quickened respiration was Kyle's aphrodisiac.

Kyle squeezed a little harder, loving the pulse of Nate's temple veins surging beneath his palms. He dug blunt fingertips down to the scalp.

"You know the best part? The part that'll get you right back to this mindless need?"

Nate's answer was a grunt.

Biting again, then licking the sting away, Kyle smiled against a man who . . . *vibrated*. The pace Nate set was shaking through both of their bodies.

"Your come will be on my stomach. You'll love to rub it across my abs, painting me with what your body gives me. Then I'll do up this fancy-ass suit. So when I smile and charm the receptionist at the hotel desk—that's how I'll act, and we both know it—you'll grin the whole time. What we've done here will follow us into classy, upscale Claridge's, smeared across my abs where you've claimed me."

"Yes. Want that." A strangled moaning sound built in Nate's chest and worked its way out, long and low.

Kyle finally released his hands, which made Nate cry out—the sudden freedom to thrash his head against the cinder block. Fingers shaking, Kyle reached between their bodies. He pushed into Nate's shorts and fondled the man's balls, teasing, softly mimicking the rhythm Nate pounded out without mercy.

Kyle whispered, "Claim me, Nate. Mark me with your come."

The hot wash of Nate's release erupted as he choked out a moan. "Fuck. God, Kyle, *yes*."

Even before his erection had subsided, Nate smoothed his come across Kyle's stomach, reaching to coat ribs and pecs and down below the waistband of the suit's trousers. Wherever he could touch. As much as there was to spread around. When he finished, he grabbed Kyle's clothed ass and used finespun wool to wipe off the rest.

"The trench will cover it," he said, out of breath. "And I'll like knowing that too."

Kyle smiled against Nate's mouth. "Me too."

"Will it be too humbling to say you were right? I never would've made it to the hotel."

"Quite the statement." Kyle began to do up the buttons that set his suit to rights. He held Nate's hands over the layers of fabric. "I like being right about knowing what you need."

The cab ride to the hotel was just as Kyle had imagined. At first they sat close together, wearing matched impish smiles of contentment, the spoils of their shopping trip at their feet. Kyle hooked his pinkie finger around Nate's. But one finger became all five. Hands became arms looped together, leaning into one another's heat. Then the teasing started. Quick touches along the inseam of jeans and wool trousers. Then presses, grabs, full-on clenching need.

Their need moved on to mouths, lips, tongues.

Screw the curious cab driver. Kyle was too far gone to give a shit. He only knew that breathing depended on kissing Nate. He craved his lover's taste and scent and quiet, greedy noises.

"You're being very naughty, Kyle."

"Yes, I am."

Their arrival to the hotel was barely in time. Kyle was hard. His chest felt constricted. No amount of inhales could calm his ragged pulse and the crazed thumping in his blood.

Just as he'd teased, he strode toward the reception desk with his usual confidence and bearing. Nate hung back, his shoulder propped against a support column, arms crossed. He wore the appreciative smirk Kyle had wanted to see.

"Reservation for Wakefield."

The pretty blonde wearing the hotel's swank uniform smiled at him as most women did—some combination of curiosity and the blush of being flattered by his attention. Kyle only flicked his grin toward Nate as the woman programmed the plastic key.

Soon, he said with his eyes.

Soon. More.

I'll never get enough.

He finished with the receptionist and met Nate by the elaborately decorated elevator. They waited side by side. He didn't know about Nate, but Kyle was about to crack the fuck up.

Face still forward, Nate snickered. "Yes. That was as good as you said it would be."

Only when the elevator doors closed behind them did Kyle let loose his laughter. They collapsed against each other in a festival of smiles, laughs, and greedy hands and mouths. They kissed right out of the elevator doors and down the hall, with Nate already stripping Kyle's trench coat and grappling with buttons.

Kyle had a tough time getting the damn key to work, mostly because both of Nate's hands grasped at his crotch. The shopping bag filled with pink unicorns crinkled against their thighs.

"At least let me get in the damn suite," he said on another laugh. "And don't you dare ruin our gifts."

Nate chuckled and backed off, pressing his forehead between Kyle's shoulders. The lock clicked open and they tumbled inside.

But when Nate tried to strip them ASAP, Kyle took both of his wrists and shook his head. "Oh no. We've already done it the down-and-dirty way. Gotta take turns or it'll get boring."

Nate pushed Kyle against the nearest wall, though his wrists were still immobilized. They kissed with the ferocity of a hurricane bearing down on their private sanctuary. "Boring? Seriously? I can't believe you managed that with a straight face."

"That's my job. Saying shit I don't mean."

Another kiss that left them both panting. "Then say something you do mean."

"I want a bubble bath."

Nate's surprise was unmistakable, especially when he started laughing again. "You fucking *queer*. Oh my God. Ruby purses and bubble baths. What other hella gay impulses are you hiding?"

This time Kyle didn't bother protesting. He was too happy smashing through old barriers. "I'm a sucker for the Pet Shop Boys. And Erasure. And the Scissor Sisters."

"Gonna take your mama out . . ."

"Oh, Christ, Nate. Don't sing."

"Spoilsport." He unknotted Kyle's tie. "But no musicals, right? Because I cannot stand musicals."

"The hills are alive . . ."

"God, you suck too. No singing!"

They kissed and touched and undressed each other, this time amid a heady buzz of happiness. At one point they accidentally stood facing one another, both rock-hard, both wearing nothing but socks.

"You have *got* to be kidding me," Nate said on a groan. "Get those damn things off."

Socks shed, they made their way to the bathroom, which was more like a palace than a room. Porcelain and brass gleamed everywhere. Two sinks. Arching, elegant faucets. The centerpiece was an eight-foot-round Jacuzzi tub shaped like a scalloped shell.

Nate whistled. "Damn."

"Best of the best," Kyle replied.

"I will have to make some requisite joke about the seashell thing, though. Like *The Little Mermaid*."

"Watch it. That was technically a musical."

After smiling at Nate's faux grimace, Kyle set about creating the most decadent bubble bath on the planet. Steaming water. Every bottle of bath products the hotel contained, which was quite a bit.

Suite for the win. Soon the air was scented with floral mist, and piles of bubbles completely obscured the water.

He was about to step in when Nate stopped him. "Wait. Come here."

Kyle did so with a mock-suspicious look, fascinated when Nate bent at the waist and licked up Kyle's bare abs. The come had dried into a slight film. Nate didn't seem to care. His tongue flattened and teased, taking in his own taste.

He stood and smacked his lips. "Seems like someone came on you."

"Damn. When did that happen?"

"Get in the fucking tub."

Kyle shrugged. "I was on my way before you felt the perverse, hot-as-hell urge to taste your own spunk."

"I taste good. Admit it."

"Busted."

The water was steaming hot, but a fabulous change from the cold he'd soaked into his bones throughout their night of snow-dusted shopping. Sitting down was tougher. He hissed as his balls broke the surface of water.

Nate stood with his legs braced in a defiant stance, his dick like steel. "I'm not getting in there if it's that damn hot." He glanced down at his erection. "Why risk the safety of something so impressive."

"Shut up, Mr. Stuntman."

Nate made the same hissing sound as he settled into the bath. "Jesus. Masochist much?"

"On occasion," Kyle said with a wink.

Loofah in hand, he began to work a heavy lather. Nate snatched it away. "You bathed me last time. My turn."

Kyle leaned back and spread his arms along the scalloped edge of the tub. "I'm all yours."

The scratching pressure of the loofah felt amazing, especially when Nate ran it along the tender skin of Kyle's inner thighs and at his nape. Kyle couldn't help a groan of pure pleasure. The tension he always, always carried began to seep from his pores as the man he loved washed him with such a heady mix of care and teasing.

When he couldn't stand nonchalant anymore, he reached out to softly touch Nate's cheek. The man stilled with the loofah poised between Kyle's pecs.

"Look at me, Nathan."

It always seemed to be an effort, but this time Nate's hesitation wasn't so gut-wrenching. Briefer. Less suspicious. Ice-blue eyes—eyes that could seem so cold and distant—were open and vulnerable with an emotion Kyle hadn't seen since they were fresh, hopeful kids.

Nate leaned against Kyle's hand where it cupped his cheek. His gaze never wavered. "Yes?"

"You are an amazing man."

Chapter Twenty-Six

Maybe, on some level, Nate was a coward. That level was pretty damn deep, and he used fast cars and dick-breaking stunts to make sure he didn't have to look at it, but there it was. Kyle scared him, because when this man called him amazing, all Nate wanted to do was believe him. Desperately.

Still, he did his damnedest to not let it show. His smile was genuine, since he really did want to be there. With Kyle. In too-hot water filled with girly bubbles and a hefty shot of ridiculousness.

He started the loofah up again, this time edging down toward the water and the taut perfection of Kyle's abs—which Nate had covered in come in an alley. "Aw, you're going to make me break into song."

Kyle smiled back, but Nate knew enough to see the wistfulness stuffed underneath. His fingers skimmed to the back of Nate's ear, where they set up tiny strokes and pets. "We promised no singing."

They hadn't made any promises between them, not this round, as if they'd been extra careful since beginning this redo.

Which had seemed perfectly natural to Nate . . . until recently.

Until he started to *want*. Want more. Probably more than he could have from perfect boy Kyle.

That didn't mean that everything was off limits. Bodies, those were safe. He leaned in to kiss his guy. When they kissed, nothing scary came out of their mouths. Good choice. Their kisses didn't stay soft for long. Kyle had been right about that too, the escalation and needing more.

But still, they held off. Kept their mouths fused, kept wet chests and stomachs plastered together. Nate's cock filled and swelled, only to meet Kyle's. If anything, Nate ought to be moving them along. He had a really big day tomorrow. The biggest of the entire shoot. He couldn't afford to be exhausted.

Yet he didn't leave Kyle's strong arms, which were wrapped around his shoulders and folded up his back. Their kisses spooled out like touching temptation.

The water had started to cool by the time they eased away. With their fingers laced together, Nate pulled them out of the giant tub. "Come on."

"So quiet," Kyle said, even as he obeyed.

Jesus, Nate wanted something easy and quippy to say. Nothing came. No jokes. Not even any growly come-on. The air had taken on weight in his lungs, counting down the minutes until dawn, until his flight, until he'd hold Kyle for the last time.

The towels were giant and ridiculously fluffy, as if guests would complain if they were less than two inches thick. Maybe they would. This place was certainly posh enough to cater to a clientele with high expectations. Not Nate. He was happy that he and Kyle were able to dry relatively quickly, except for the inevitable pauses for more kissing. And groping. Plenty of that.

In no time, Nate found himself on the bed in the giant suite. Though he stopped to fish out a condom and some lube from his jacket pocket, he didn't bother pulling down the chilled satin comforter before lying down and yanking Kyle on top of him.

He pushed Kyle's damp, dark hair back from his patrician features. "I like this."

Kyle's lips quirked on an endearing smile. He gave a little wiggle, as if to emphasize that their dicks were aligned. "What's not to like?"

"Absolutely nothing."

They were pressed belly to belly. Kyle's knees dug into the comforter between Nate's thighs.

They took each other. Claimed each other. Harsh kisses that neither tried to soften. Kyle settled his elbows into the bed by Nate's head. Sank down into it.

Funny to be the one on the bottom, technically enveloped by Kyle's big body, and yet Nate still felt like the one in control. His hands groped and stroked, finding the lube and beginning to open Kyle's ass for the taking. At the same time, everything inside Nate was spinning, slipping away. Something had shaken loose inside him, creating a feeling that had nothing to do with the tingling pleasure where his cock rubbed against Kyle's lower stomach.

This was something infinitely more frightening.

Infinitely bigger.

Kyle's strong hands rolled the condom down Nate's prick, and his fingertips dallied across the tender skin of Nate's balls. Then he rose up on wide knees with his hands on Nate's chest, and he took Nate into his body. The whole time, his dark eyes never wavered.

Nate couldn't look away. The solemn expression Kyle wore called to that hidden, scary thing awakening in Nate.

Or *re*awakening.

Because he knew. Even as Kyle began to rise up and sink down over Nate's cock, even as heat and clasping pressure overtook them. All of it was exactly what he needed. Wanted.

Loved.

He loved Kyle. Maybe still, maybe again.

Had he tried, he could've prevented it at some point, but only by locking off every happy memory and stopping this affair after their reunion fuck on the pool table.

Impossible.

That love wound inside him and had for so many years that he didn't want to look at it. Love was never a guarantee. For some lucky people it was a bright promise that lit up their entire lives.

For some people, it was hell on earth.

From want. From lack.

Nate couldn't take it any longer. He surged up to a sitting position, arms wrapped low around Kyle's back. He buried his face along a strong swoop of shoulder, bit the meat above Kyle's collarbones. Fucking with more intensity into such a willing body—at least Nate had this. At least he knew how to make Kyle moan.

He worked one hand between their bodies to add to the pressure on Kyle's cock. Timed their strokes. It didn't take much, and when Kyle came, pulsing in Nate's hand, the squeeze of his passage over Nate's cock did him in.

Pleasure was force and enticement at the same time, urging him to launch over some unknown edge. He battened down the harsh shudders that worked through his spine, pressed his closed eyes against Kyle's shoulder, and let go of everything while he clung harder. He didn't dare speak. Not a thing. Christ only knew what might come out of his mouth.

He was lost *and* found.

Taking care of the condom was the easy part. Easing his head down to the pillows where Kyle already waited was much more difficult. Not because he didn't want to be there. The very opposite.

He loved looking in Kyle's eyes that damn much. Once he'd gotten past his hesitations, he only craved more of the intimacy that bordered on self-destruction.

His jaw split on a huge yawn. "You don't look like you're ready to sleep." He didn't know how, considering the two orgasms each for the night. Unnatural for a couple of guys, but they'd always burned that hot.

"I have a surprise."

"It can't wait? I have a really big day tomorrow. You of all people know we can't fuck it up. The permits . . ."

"This won't take long." Kyle pushed off the bed and walked stark naked across the room.

Nate climbed up onto his elbows, the better to watch that firm ass make its way through the world. Beautiful. Everything else aside, Nate was a damn lucky man to have had the chance at knowing someone so much . . . *more*. More kind, more cultured, more charming than Nate had ever hoped to be. Kyle made Nate want to be more, just by being around him.

But when Kyle dug around in the small bag he'd carried away from the jeweler's, trouble pinged around the room. It landed in a tight knot in Nate's stomach.

The five-by-five wooden box Kyle brought back didn't ease that knot. He sprawled across the bed on his stomach, holding it out. "Technically it's past midnight. Merry Christmas."

Nate ignored the fact that his hands shook as he reached for the box. It hinged open from the center, two halves splitting to reveal a watch nestled in pale-green satin.

Except it wasn't just any watch. It looked priceless. The black leather band appeared deceptively plain, as did the white face. It wasn't decorated with anything so tacky as diamonds. Instead, its flawless quality practically glowed, as did the Bulgari emblem. The watch was precisely the sort of piece Nate never would have bought himself, even if he'd had the cash lying around. Yet he knew it would look fantastic on his wrist. Kyle operated five million levels above him. Always had.

His mind blanked. Flat-out blanked. Like swan-diving off a bridge and waiting for the bungee cord to jerk his brain back where it belonged. "Wow."

"Nice, isn't it?" Kyle lifted the timepiece from its nest. With sure, calm fingers, he wrapped it around Nate's wrist and fitted the band. "You'd mentioned mine so often that I figured it was time to get you one."

Nate gulped. "So you bought me a watch? What was it, another five thousand?"

Kyle laughed while shaking his head—enough of a pause that Nate could suck in a cool breath of relief.

"No," Kyle went on. "More than that."

"Oh fuck." He didn't need to ask for a number. Kyle's laugh told him enough to make his head swim.

"Thank you is more customary."

Nate sat up against the pile of white pillows, the ones he'd had thought they would sleep on, coiled together. Something like fury burned in his gut, made his bones creak and his tendons rigid. "It would be customary if I'm grateful."

Kyle's eyes hazed to a darker shade. His mouth dropped his smile. And right there, that's when Nate knew this was going down in flames . . . because he liked it. He liked that Kyle wasn't smiling anymore.

Because Nate didn't feel like fucking smiling either.

"I don't understand," Kyle said quietly.

After shoving off the bed, Nate yanked his boxers on. "I'm not a kept woman. No wait. I'm not a kept *man*."

"I never said you were."

"Then why did you buy me a kiss-off present?"

Logically, he heard how ridiculous that sounded, but he couldn't stop the train from slamming off the tracks. It was the only way he knew to express his rage. Kyle probably didn't mean it as any sort of goodbye, but Nate found himself absolutely unable to trust. He couldn't trust Kyle and he sure as hell couldn't trust himself. Even now, he was on the verge of ruining one of the best evenings of his life.

Kyle's arrogance came swirling back in the hold of his spine and the tilt of his chin. His eyes narrowed. "I bought you a watch because it's Christmas and I thought you'd like it. I didn't say one word about it being a kiss off. But you keep talking and maybe we can make that happen."

"Why not? Let's get this shit over with."

He had to turn away. He couldn't manage to say those words while looking at Kyle. He shook his head as he stepped into his jeans and hitched them over his hips. Before he could get them buttoned, a hand wrapped around his elbow and turned him.

Fierce. Kyle looked *fierce*. "If you want to run again, there's nothing I can do to stop that."

"Then get your damn hand off me."

Before he'd finished speaking, the import of Kyle's sentence sank through the whirling black void that was fast becoming Nate's mind. And his heart.

"Wait," he said. "Me? Run? Is that what you said?"

"It's what you did last time." Kyle was still completely, absolutely naked. His skin, so golden and shining. His muscles, bulging in striated relief on each rising thrust of anger. "Why break a pattern when it's worked so well?"

"Does that mean you're going to use daddy's connections to find me in another decade or so?" He bared his teeth in what felt nothing like a smile. He'd used that expression in prison when he'd meant to stake his space. "Give me some warning next time and we can get blood tests. Fuck raw. Really make this teenage nostalgia trip authentic."

"Why the hell not?" Kyle sneered. "It's not like that chip on your shoulder has gone anywhere."

That quick, Nate lost it. He swung his hand in an angered sweep and cleaned the nearby desk in a slam. Phone, blotter, room service book—all went flying. The notepad spun in flapping sheets. Rage boiled through his veins and crunched his hands into fists.

"What's the goddamned point? Restaurant reservations. Hotel. All to keep me quiet. Keep *us* quiet. So you tell me where that chip on my shoulder should go, Kyle. In the closet with you?"

Chapter Twenty-Seven

K yle had never been so cold. The cold had nothing to do with the fact he was still naked, with sweat chilling on his skin. Even the shocks of their youthful breakup hadn't hit him with this much shattering power.

He stood straighter, like a dare. Nate had looked ready to throw a punch, and Kyle welcomed the possibility. If they were going to hurt each other, he'd rather it be physically. Those scars would heal.

"Let me ask you something," he said, voice hushed. He managed to keep the quaver at bay, but that wouldn't last long. He was shaking too badly. "Pretend you were a scared eighteen-year-old guy with a radical plan to run away with the young man you loved. And let's pretend on the evening before that dreamed-of day, you waited with anticipation. The next morning, you waited with frustration. The day after that, you waited and worried. *Worried*, Nate. Where could he be? Turns out he'd stolen a car and bought some coke and fucked up *every* possibility of them being together."

"Old news," Nate growled.

"Fine. True. But stay with that kid. Because he was heartbroken. Devastated. Most of all, he was confused. Had it all been a lie? If those plans weren't important, maybe none of it had been."

That Nate didn't deny the bold statement stole Kyle's breath. He needed to gulp and swallow to get the next words out. "Eventually, Nathan, you would've made me strong enough and safe enough so that I could come out. I could've made for myself an honest life— with you. We had so many plans." He choked back the surge of hurt caused by memories of those naïve, broken days. "But after that . . . You wonder why I hide? What the fuck is the point of risking what I've achieved for a man who chose *prison* over me?"

Nate flinched, then stared him down. At least he had balls enough for that. Kyle was the one to look away as he grabbed his briefs and undershirt and tugged them on so hard that he could've ripped them into pieces.

"I didn't have the money," Nate said roughly. "Dad's semi had broken down in Arizona somewhere, so I wired him what I had. I wasn't going to be able to pay for my half of our room in New Haven."

"And you didn't tell me? What the *hell*?"

"I came by your parents' house during your party. Saw you inside. You looked so damn happy, as always. Center of attention. I couldn't do it. I couldn't live like some leech while you moved on and gathered new friends."

"Moved . . .?" It was Kyle's turn to want to fling things, throw punches. Instead he cracked his knuckles and realized he couldn't feel his fingertips. "Moved on? Jesus, Nate. Would you like to know why I was so happy that night?"

"Whatever. Give it to me."

"I was finally going to get away from my parents. *Couldn't wait.* I was drunk on the excitement that I wouldn't spend another goddamn night under their roof." He shivered, blinked back the emotion he couldn't hide. "I kept thinking how we'd spend the next day driving, and how we'd spend the next night under a roof of our own."

Nate's jaw worked. The ligaments along each hinge bunched. He was breathing faster, but he stood statue-still, eyes like glittering blue marble. To see that old wariness was too much. Kyle had thought nine years might make a difference, but Nate was the same scared, stubborn ass he'd always been.

"So you'd have paid for everything." Nate glanced down at the watch that glittered on his wrist. "Made it all better by throwing cash at things. But you know what? It still wouldn't have been our roof. It would have been your parents' roof, since they were still paying your bills."

"They don't pay my bills anymore. That watch comes from Pennfield money—money I've worked damn hard to earn on my own. But I'd throw every cent in the fucking sewer if it meant having the last nine years back." A headache struck Kyle's temples as if he'd been punched on both sides of his skull. "You know what I still don't get?

You could've plea-bargained. Six months and probation. I . . . Damn, Nate, I would've waited. Instead you sat there and let them slam you with three years."

Shaking his head, Nate seemed to make a decision. "Well, you see, that was your parents' doing."

Kyle sank onto the bed. Just like that, from standing to sagging. "What?"

"The DA and your parents came to me in jail. Offered roughly those same terms. I wouldn't be able to leave Virginia during my probation, but I'd be out in six months. Maybe four. Your dad played golf with the judge. Would've been etched in stone."

That headache was becoming death-metal rock in Kyle's brain. He couldn't think, as new pieces of the past aligned to form a grisly picture. "But."

"But they knew about us. They'd known the whole time, letting it slide because they didn't think it would last past high school. You'd—what was it your mom said? That you'd have scraped me off by then." Nate shrugged as if it didn't matter, but the move was stiff and riddled with pain not even he could hide. "The trade-off," he continued, "was that I was to cut off all contact with you. I'd lie to you. I'd tell you to head off to Yale without me because I didn't love you. How the fuck was I supposed to do that? So right to his face I told your dad to sit and swivel." He sneered, his face contorting around memories that stabbed them both. "Too bad it wasn't worth keeping my mouth shut."

Kyle shot up from the bed and surged within inches of the man staring him down. "What, so I'm supposed to take some blame in all this? I drove down to see you and you told me to fuck off. You never said a word about it."

"Like father, like son. Your look of disgust was exactly the same as your dad's when he made his little offer."

"Disgust? You're *sick*. I was staring through Plexiglas, where the man I loved was wearing a goddamn prison-orange jumpsuit. You'd ruined everything, and you'd told me nothing. Shields up. Checked out. What was I supposed to think? Or feel? I was barely more than a child. Only eighteen!"

"I was the same damn age, but I grew up fast," Nate said, grabbing his leather jacket and the shopping bag from Hamleys. That laughing, beautiful good time seemed like a lifetime ago—far more distant than the old hurts they hurled at one another. "As to what you were supposed to feel? Relief, maybe? True colors and all that."

"I really had no idea you were that insecure. Or that our love was so small."

"I didn't see you telling your parents the truth. They already knew, sure. But you didn't know that. You could've pleaded my case. You could've come out and at least proved you had some fucking balls. I needed a show of faith, Kyle—one a whole lot bigger than covering my rent and spinning pretty fantasies."

Pain bored like needles through Kyle's skin, down to bare bone. "Which would've been what, exactly?"

Nate swallowed tightly, as if he too was choking on this ancient muck. Drowning. It was the last thing they would do together.

"I wanted to be at that going-away party, but I didn't want to do it as your *friend*. I wanted to be your guy. I wanted you to storm out of the house if your parents couldn't get their heads around us being in love." He tugged the jacket around his taut, muscled body and lifted his chin. "I didn't choose jail over you, Kyle. I chose jail over being something shameful."

"And if I'd shown up three years later? When you got out?"

"An ex-con and the Yale grad? More things for you to hide or, worse yet, apologize for." He looked Kyle up and down with utter condescension. "So, nostalgia trip over. It's been a blast. See you on the set."

Nate slammed the door behind him, stealing the air from the suite. Bile pushed into the back of Kyle's throat. He was gasping, his mind spinning out of control. Now he couldn't remember the last kiss they'd shared, though it had happened only minutes before.

There sure as hell wouldn't be another one.

That Kyle could think in the morning was a goddamn miracle. That he'd dressed. That he'd shaved without taking off six layers of skin—it wouldn't have mattered. He already felt flayed and completely raw.

His heart was broken.

After taking a cab back to his room, he'd shut the heavy curtains, lain on the perfectly made bed, and stared into the darkness. He didn't think he'd slept, but he hoped he had. Throughout those endless few hours before dawn he hadn't heard Nate return to his room on the other side of their connecting door. If Kyle had accidentally caught a few winks, he might have missed it.

That didn't seem likely. Kyle had been able to return to his room—a small miracle because the space was filled with so many densely packed memories. He could barely breathe. For a man who'd been in prison, those same surroundings would feel more confined.

So where was Nate? What was he thinking? Bitterness and regret mashed Kyle into a wobbly pulp.

He looked ahead to a full day on the set, knowing he should eat something. Sour in-house coffee from a crappy single-cup coffeemaker only amplified the toxic sickness he couldn't shake.

Without conscious thought—no decision-making process motivating his action—he picked up his phone and thumbed a speed dial number.

His mother answered, although sleep still clouded her voice. "Hello?"

"Mother, it's Kyle."

"Kyle." Her surprise was obvious. "It's two in the morning. Is something wrong? Are you all right?"

"No."

The terse answer must've given her some warning because the line remained silent for long, nerve-wracking moments. "Then tell me," she said at last.

"I spoke with Nathan Carnes last night."

Another tense silence.

"Oh?" Her studied indifference was betrayed when her voice cracked. "He was that . . . that boy you knew, yes?"

"You know damn well who he was. *Is*. We slept together last night. And the night before that. In fact, we've been at each other for weeks."

"Kyle, there is no need to speak that filth to me."

He pressed on as if she hadn't spoken, although the word *filth* slammed behind his sternum. "Because I'm gay, Mother. Which you already knew."

It wasn't a question. But he did have one that needed to be answered.

"Is it true? Did you threaten Nate? Are you and Father the reason why he sat rotting in prison for three years?"

"Kyle, dear, it was for your own good."

"My own good?" The tide in his chest pumped out. "Do you have any idea what that's done to both of our lives? *Any* idea? And don't you dare fucking answer that because there's no way you could. I had a chance at being happy, and you stole it from me, like you stole three years of Nate's life."

"You need to calm down. You cannot talk to me like this."

"No? Fine. Get Father on the line and I'll tell him what a manipulative bastard he is too."

"Kyle!"

She sounded like she was crying, but Kyle was seeing red. He couldn't have discerned real tears from theatrics had his life been on the line, and he didn't give a good goddamn one way or the other.

Yet he was nearly as angry at himself. Since college he'd ordered neat little truths in his mind. He'd needed to stay in the closet because of his career? No, it was because his parents' opinion of him still mattered. He'd weathered their censure about starting a production company and their disappointment about his connection with a teenaged criminal. That had been exhausting enough—and enough of a blemish on their starry-eyed image of who he should be.

He'd always wanted people to like him, his parents most of all. Cold and distant, they had been hard to please. Nothing less than perfection would do.

Again, it was an easy out. Protecting his career. Craving approval from his parents. What if his compulsion to be liked was born of shame? Shame that he was gay?

Which would mean he'd locked himself in the closet. No one else to blame.

Enough was enough.

"What you did is unforgivable," he said, his voice as cold and brittle as a shard of ice. That shard had pierced his heart. Someone else deserved to feel his pain. "*Unforgivable*. I've spent nine years with this changing me, warping me into a version of myself that I can't stand."

"I'll admit, your father and I were doubtful of your career choices, but look at all you've accomplished. You never would've gone so far with that . . . that . . ."

"Pick a word and get on with it, Mother. Fag? Queer? Charity case? Or how about ex-con? Jesus, you can't even own up to what you think of him. And I thought I was the coward. You didn't say a damn word to me, just waded in with Father's connections and our overflowing coffers and made it happen—what you thought was best."

"That . . . *boy* would've ruined you. You were too oblivious to see that."

"I was too in love to see anything but how he was the most precious thing in my life. He wouldn't have ruined me. He would've made me happy."

"Now don't get so sentimental. That was a long time ago. Let's talk rationally about this." Her voice had become silky—the same cultured false calm he'd learned to imitate so well. "Fly back for New Year's, Kyle. It's already bad enough you're missing Christmas at home because of, what, this little film project?"

"Home. Little film project." He practically spat the words. His pulse was a thunderstorm in his ear. "That frozen mausoleum hasn't been my home for nine years, and this is my career whether you like it or not. And now that this tiny, inconsequential secret has come to light, don't expect me to set foot in your house again. I'm done trying to please you and Father because you don't deserve the effort."

Her protests became more frantic before he cut the connection.

He wanted to puke. But he had ten minutes to get on set. For Nate's big stunt. He glanced out the window, where the snow continued to come down.

No way. No way would they go through with it.

Kyle was the producer. He could call it off. Losing Nate's love was one thing. They would both carry on. Even if Kyle never recovered from this agony, at least Nate might.

But risking Nate's life? Fuck no.

That thought—hell, that *fear*—got him moving. He shoved away the pain, as he had for so long. It burned and scorched, but he needed a clear mind. Nate was so goddamn stubborn. All these years, he'd been working to prove himself. A snowy, beautiful Christmas wouldn't budge the chip on his shoulder one bit.

Which made that snowy, beautiful Christmas the most terrifying morning Kyle had ever faced.

Chapter Twenty-Eight

N ate hadn't realized exactly how high his hopes had gotten. Not until those hopes were destroyed. Ruined.

Leaving him a shit-ass mess.

He rubbed the heels of his hand across his burning eyes. He hadn't slept. Hadn't gone back to his room. Somehow he'd ended up knocking on Raney's door once the hotel bar was shut down.

The snow was still coming down, though at least it was lighter. They stood at the staging area. The Maserati was parked under a tarp, the better to keep the paint job shiny.

Watching warily, Raney snapped a wad of gum between his teeth.

Nate flipped through the schematics one last time. "Say it."

"No point."

"Stop being a bitch."

Raney's brows arched high. "Fine. You want it, I'll say it. Because I love speaking directly to brick walls. I fucking *told you so*."

"Not what you think." It felt like being trapped in an iceberg. No more warmth for him. The flame-resistant suit should have insulated him from the worst of the weather, but this chill came from the inside. From his own wrecked emotions.

"Really?" Raney made the word fairly drip with doubt. "You mean you and Mr. Producer Man didn't have a giant blowup necessitating you crashing in my room—not sleeping, mind you—the very day before you have to be completely on your game?"

"The stunt is going to be perfect." He'd stir burning barbeque coals with his dick before accepting anything less than perfect.

Raney couldn't lay into him full force because of the arrival of the very last knot of people Nate wanted to see. Steph. Pete Upton, director asshole supreme.

And Kyle.

His heart squeezed on a sickening clench. He wanted to reach for him. Needed to touch.

Can't.

At least some petty part of him got to enjoy the fact that Kyle looked like shit. His suit coat was unbuttoned, his shirt wrinkled. Worse than that were the pitch-dark shadows under his eyes. The drawn aspect of his features made his ears seem bigger.

He looked like someone who'd been roughed up and pushed around.

Nate had done that.

He crossed his arms over his chest and tucked his hands under his elbows. Hopefully he'd come off as intimidating rather than obviously curling into himself. Hell, he still wore that stupid, goddamned watch—proof that Kyle meant something to him. He had no reassurance in return. He wanted the right to claim him, somehow, anyhow, there in front of everyone.

But that had been their problem all along.

Stephanie started first, one hand patting Upton's shoulder. "We're a little concerned about the stunt."

Nate ground his teeth. Maybe he was worried too, but that didn't mean he liked hearing it out of anyone else's mouth. "It's all under control."

Upton gave a single sharp nod. "See? Told you we'd be going forward."

Kyle didn't seem too happy with that idea. "It's not too late to back out. We can do some wire-work and CGI back at the studio—"

"Bullshit," Nate gritted out, at the same time Upton started making yippy noise about the budget. Nate only had eyes for Kyle. The worry there was almost enough to sway him. Almost.

Kyle's shoulders shifted. "Can I talk to you for a moment? Alone?"

That easily, any sympathy was burned away in a hot rush of new anger. Alone. It was always *alone*. He pulled his cheeks tight so the corners of his mouth turned up into a fair approximation of a smile. "Mr. Wakefield, if you're worried about production, please allow me to assure you, *again*, that Second Chances is the best. We'll get this done."

"Good," Upton interjected with a fair amount of cheer.

It gave Nate half a second's pause to be on the same side with Upton, but occasionally crazy shit happened. There was no chance in hell he was going to abort the stunt. They had three allotted takes, and the permits specified they each had to be completed in an hour's time. Traffic was only shutting down for the briefest glimpses.

He had to launch the Maserati off a ramp. Simple. It was the angle of the camera that made this difficult, because they wanted a shot of the undercarriage of the car and Big Ben at the same time. All to show a bomb with a digital readout strapped to the driveshaft.

Most days, Nate could have done it in his sleep. Which was a damn good thing considering he could barely blink. So fucking tired. Of all this shit.

"Don't be like this." Kyle's eyes were big. Filled with hurt. He'd better be careful or he was going to spill his own damn secrets.

"This is business. I'm keeping it to business."

Steph was shooting daggers at Kyle. "See? Everything's running as smooth as can be. Now let's let these guys have their space so we can be on time. The bobbies are waiting to block traffic."

She tugged on Upton's arm, trying to get him to turn away, but the man wasn't budging. That suspicious look had returned to the features half-concealed by his dumb-ass baseball cap.

"Nate." Kyle's harsh voice lost most of its moneyed posh. "Stop. Please."

Nate's stomach knotted. He only shook his head. There was nothing else to say.

Except Kyle . . . He flattened his lips, then ran the tip of his tongue over the bottom one. "Nate, I'm begging you. As someone who loves you."

Nate's heart swelled—but clenched down just as fast. That could mean anything. Love like brothers. Like good friends.

Not how he wanted to love and be loved by this man.

"You don't have any room to ask anything of me. Not anymore."

"I don't get any consideration for wanting you to be safe?" Kyle couldn't seem to help a darting glance toward the director, who was watching. Flat-out watching with a gleeful expression, like he should be holding a tub of popcorn. "Or for this past month? Or our whole lives?"

"What do you want me to say?"

"I don't want you to say anything. I want you to listen." There was a good little hit of that arrogance, the stuff Nate loved. Kyle as prince and near god.

Nate scowled to hide his confusion, his hurt. "I certainly can't prevent you."

"I love you."

Kyle's voice was clear and true, loud enough to carry all the way to the Second Chances crew. Raney's head jerked towards them, and he wasn't the only one.

"What are you doing?" Nate growled.

"I don't care anymore—not about what anyone says or thinks. I don't care who hears. No, more than that. I *want* them to hear. I want the whole fucking world to know what I feel and to hear what you deserve to hear."

"By throwing around 'I love you' so that it sounds like begging? So that maybe you'll get me to do what you want?"

"I love you," Kyle said again, even louder, like a statement of liberation.

Sweet Christ. That wasn't what he'd expected. Not at all. He was left . . . *blank*, unable to think of anything.

No, that wasn't true. Unable to think of anything that was more than a syllable or two. The word *yes* echoed over and over in his head. His chest was sucking into itself, crushed by the twin pressures of anger and hope.

"I'm not asking you for anything more," Kyle said. "I know how messed up everything is. Last night . . . Last night was pretty hardcore."

It had been, but up until their fight it had been perfect. They'd found the easy, relaxed openness that he'd always hoped for with Kyle, which is why it had hurt so much to feel like something lesser. Someone smaller than he ought to be, given expensive presents rather than hope for a future.

"Jesus," he said after a heavy swallow. "Is this really the time?"

"Maybe. Maybe not."

Kyle closed in tighter. Steph gaped at them. She finally managed to tug Upton away, although the director's gaze remained riveted to them both. Raney had . . . disappeared, blending into the background in the way that had made him an excellent conman once upon a time.

"Nathan, I love you," he said, with undeniable intensity. "This is how one lover says it to another. With respect and dignity. Without fear or hesitation. Whether completely alone or in the middle of London."

Nate and Kyle were very publicly *not* alone. The whole crew was watching them, either surreptitiously or with open interest. Some were probably making notes to sell the story to the gossip bloggers, though Nate wasn't sure how much they'd get off a story about an up-and-coming producer and a stuntman.

But it was Hollywood. And it was still a gay man coming out. Very, very publicly. A PR rep's story would likely make its way to Andrew and Vanessa Wakefield. God only knew what they'd do next. Fuck with Nate's reputation even more? Call their lawyers and write Kyle out of their wills?

Would Kyle care?

Nate finally realized that his brain was spinning out into ridiculousness. He rubbed his temple as if that would order his thoughts. "I don't understand what you're doing."

Kyle laughed, a little helpless sounding. He shrugged and spread his hands as he looked out at the crowd. "I'm coming out. Kind of for you, but mostly for me. I'm tired of feeling unlovable."

"You're not," he said without thought, without a goddamn bit of sense. But hope was undeniable now. It sizzled under Nate's skin. He tried to rein it in. "What about your company?"

"We'll work with those who know the meaning of the word *professional* and who mind their own business, and we'll support those who support us."

"Us?"

"The LGBTQ community. The whole alphabet of people who deserve a lot better than I've been parsing out for us."

"Jesus, Kyle." He was spinning. He was gathering every second as if this was a dream that would slip away if he didn't pay attention to every tiny detail—not the least of which was the unerring earnestness in Kyle's deep brown eyes. "What about your parents?"

"I burned that bridge this morning when I told my mom to fuck off."

"You didn't."

"Did. Both barrels. I'm exhausted from pretending to be who I'm not—some juvenile need for their approval. I respect myself, and you, and us. No one else matters."

He came one step closer. Nate wanted to reach for him. Hold him. Yet even now he didn't fucking dare.

He'd never pushed their boundaries in public. Never stretched what Kyle would accept, because he hadn't wanted the blowback of shame. He stayed motionless. Breathless.

And so very frightened.

When Kyle finally touched his skin, Nate flinched. Kyle saw it, probably felt it. His expression filled with sorrow. "That. I did that, didn't I? I don't think I can ever tell you how sorry I am."

Nate reached up, hooking his fingers over Kyle's strong wrists. His thumbs brushed the light dusting of hair. Talking seemed beyond him. He only shook his head.

"No," Kyle insisted. "I am sorry. I hurt you, and I made you feel like a nasty thing, and I'm not sure there's any way I can make up for that."

Nate couldn't stop a helpless chuckle. "This helps."

Yup. Still the center of attention.

Kyle's touch scaled up, over Nate's shoulders. For the first time in his career, Nate loathed the flame-resistant safety suit that could potentially save his life. It deadened the contact he needed so much.

"I don't know where we can go from here," Kyle said. "Maybe nowhere. I know I've broken your trust. Not only when we were kids—because you're right, I shouldn't have tried to sneak out of town. I should have held your hand and left with my head high. But lately . . . It hasn't been nostalgia for me."

Nate swallowed the frightening joy that was clawing up his throat. "Me either. Not really. I shouldn't have said that."

"Then I'm begging you. Please." Kyle cupped Nate's cheeks with cold fingers. "Let's shut this down."

Nate almost took him up on the idea. But outside the tarp, past the cherry-red sports car, the snow had stopped. Eased. This was their chance.

Silently, he unbuckled the expensive watch he couldn't wear during the stunt. Kyle was confused, which was apparent in the furrow between his brows and the way his mouth drew down. That expression didn't ease when Nate pressed the watch into Kyle's hand.

He looked down at the gold and black, then back up at Nate's face. "I don't understand."

"You've gone and pulled your little stunt. Now it's my turn."

"You can treat this like a joke, but I won't."

Kyle grabbed Nate by the shoulders and tightened his hands around Nate's shoulders. A heartbeat later, they were kissing. With smooth lips and the nearness of his body heat, Kyle seduced Nate in no uncertain terms. He was insistent and damn—the kiss was so very *right*. Everyone could see it, and Nate felt every beautiful nuance. Their mouths opened. Their tongues touched. Their breathing went nuclear. He couldn't resist spiking his fingers through the chilly strands of Kyle's hair, down to the scalp, refusing to permit any little bit of space between them.

There was no more space to claim. Kyle had him, and Kyle was setting the terms. Normally that would've pissed Nate off to no end, but this was radically different. If Kyle wanted to kiss him like long-lost lovers in front of a thousand pairs of eyes, Nate would willingly let him. He smiled into his kiss, dug deeper with his fingertips, and felt Kyle's smile in return. One gorgeous, heady kiss disintegrated into a dozen smaller kisses, and they tasted each other and laughed with each other.

They were exactly who they were supposed to be.

No more hiding.

Nate wasn't stupid. He owed his own apologies. More than that, probably, if they had half a chance at making something work. At least they *did* have that possibility.

He was tempted to keep kissing, if only to glory in Kyle's lack of inhibition. His passion—there in front of the whole damn city—was as genuine and unabashed as when they were alone.

This was no dream. This was the first moment of the rest of their lives.

"You weren't joking," he said, trying in vain for nonchalance. "But I like that you were smiling."

"I'll keep smiling if you see sense. Now, Nate—"

"Nope. Hold this for me, will you? I'll be back in a minute." He stepped back and couldn't hold back another huge grin. "Because this? This is gonna be awesome."

A few words to Raney set the team off in a flurry of activity. Extras to their places. Policemen prepared to halt traffic.

Nate slipped into the sweet beast of a car—low-slung and bone shaking when its engine kicked on. He gunned it once, twice, before slowly guiding it out of the berth and into position at the end of the vacant street.

The radio nodule in his ear crackled with a flurry of last-minute coordination. Then came the voice Nate was hoping to hear, both then and over the next few decades. Kyle's voice.

"Nate?"

"Here."

"Don't die before I'm done with you."

He grinned again. Wider. Big enough to pinch his cheeks. His heart was floating, like this goddamned Maserati was going to if he had anything to say about it. "I wouldn't dare."

Chapter Twenty-Nine

For the umpteenth time in the last twelve hours, Kyle felt ready to hurl. He'd done what had been completely impossible four weeks ago. He'd come out on a goddamn movie set—a set that was actually the whole of London.

It had been worth it. Nate would always be worth it. Hell, Kyle was beginning to feel—genuinely feel—that *he* was worth it. He'd do whatever he needed to have Nate back in his arms, and to continue where they'd left off. Their kisses and matched smiles weren't preludes to sex; they were promises for so much more.

Now he adjusted his headset as if he had a nervous tic. Not too far from the truth. His eyes burned from heavy emotion and lack of sleep. He couldn't tear his eyes away from the blood-red Maserati as Nate drove north on Parliament Street.

"In position," came Nate's voice. Everyone heard him, of course, but it didn't feel that way. Nate was speaking right to him. They were connected now in a way that was intense, fraught, and so damn tenuous.

This fucking stunt.

Kyle had to suck it up. It was Nate's job, and it would be no matter what future they patched together.

Various voices checked in. Those responsible for clearing traffic, for placing the extras, for pushing the CGI-ready ramps into place. Specially designed scaffolding, also painted that unnatural CGI green, had been constructed along each side of Parliament Street to protect the buildings from harm should anything go wrong. Fire trucks waited behind substantial, protective rubber blocks. Those precautions would keep any runaway Maserati from speeding past the roundabout that circled Parliament Square.

Wouldn't want a flying car to take out a statue of Churchill.

They'd been allotted official traffic stoppage on the surrounding streets for fifteen minutes per shot. Each shot took forty-five minutes to stage, all devoted to preparation.

Nate had it down to a science. His whole team did.

That didn't ease Kyle's gut-sick fear.

He stuffed a hand in the pocket of his trench coat and gripped Nate's watch. "Come back for this, you asshole."

"I heard that," Steph said at his side. "That was awesome, by the way. Like . . . *awesome*."

"You're repeating yourself."

She shrugged. "Out of adjectives. Guess that means I should put out an ad for a roommate."

"Let's not get ahead of ourselves."

"What's my favorite cuss word, Kyle dear?"

He raised his brows. "Bullshit?"

"Bingo."

Kyle's pulse sped at the idea of living with Nate. He hadn't let his mind go there, not while everything was so unsettled. Now the image was crystal clear and so radiant that he needed to push it away. Possibilities that amazing were blinding.

"Last check complete." The stunt coordinator sounded confident. "Everything in place."

Upton called for quiet, then, "Action!"

From the high perch in Parliament Square where Kyle and Steph waited, away from the precisely placed cameras, they had a perfect view down the quarter mile to where a red Maserati growled into the winter air.

On a squeal of tires, Nate gunned it.

He hadn't driven for more than three seconds before the word "abort" was shouted into everyone's headsets. Nate slammed his brakes. More burned-rubber squeals. He'd stopped the car a good two hundred yards before the jump ramp.

"What the fuck is going on?" Upton screeched. "Someone tell me! Now!"

"Camera seven's offline. There's ice on the damn cables."

"Oh, for chrissake," Kyle spat. He was too tired for this. Too edgy.

"It's only one of the two most important cameras on this shoot," Upton said tersely, his frustration turning deadly mean. "And I'm on the other one. Who the hell do I have to fire? Somebody give me a goddamn name!"

Kyle was thinking the same thing.

"We've missed our traffic window," Steph said. "Shut it down and reset."

Fuck.

Two hours passed. Nate had gotten out of the car, walked around to stretch his legs, but he stayed with Ethan Raney and his team. For the best. Nate's safety was paramount, with his head one hundred percent in the game. Kyle didn't need to make things worse.

A second attempt was aborted too, even before it started. The team responsible for setting up the ramps took too long, and the police couldn't keep the curious out of harm's way. Their hour sped by like the tap of a toe.

Kyle was going out of his goddamn mind.

The words "last check complete" told everyone to bring their A game. Last chance. They had run out of day.

"Action!"

The Maserati shot down the road like a jet with four wheels. Less than three seconds later, the tires made contact with the ramp. A cylinder in the passenger seat shot air through a hole in the foot well, like a cannon exploding. That downward force, coupled with Nate's fantastic skills, propelled the car off the ramp, flying, spinning on its axis. Red tape on the scaffolding showed how high the car needed to be in order for it to be centered against Big Ben.

Nate had achieved the perfect height, which meant the Maserati was three stories above the street.

After a complete three-sixty revolution, the car touched down on the landing ramp. Kyle felt as if he held his breath on behalf of the entire production crew. His lungs were stuck. Not working.

It looked . . . flawless.

Until the Maserati raced from ramp onto asphalt. The tires made a sick spinning noise as they struggled for grip.

"Ice," Steph whispered.

Thoughts raced—useless thoughts. Salt. Chemicals. Heaters and fans. They'd done everything to keep the street dry and safe.

Yet the gleaming red beast of a car slid out of control. It fishtailed wildly before spinning in circle after circle toward the foam pads and fire trucks. Smoke from the agonized tires trailed out in spiraling arcs. The engine sounded like a screaming, dying animal.

The nose of the car barely missed the left side of the scaffolding, but the back end wasn't so lucky. As Nate seemed to wrest control from the limits of physics, a rear wheel pinged off the metal framework. The Maserati bounced like a pinball, taking hit after hit until it slammed sideways against a support pole. The whole scaffold shook.

The car burst into flames.

"Nate!"

Kyle jumped down from the platform at a flat-out run. Fire shot up, taller than the fire engines and foam pads. The smell of burning metal and rubber filled his nose, pumping in and out of lungs that worked furiously. He still wore his headset—a circus of shouts and orders, none of them comprehensible. They could've been in Swahili for all Kyle could understand.

Nate. God, no. Not like this.

He ran until he reached the safety barrier, where even his status as producer didn't gain him access. All he could do was stand by as the firemen did their jobs. The wreckage of the sports car was barely visible beneath layers of white foam, which began to asphyxiate the flames.

Distantly, he heard Upton's voice. "Status on the shot. Do we have it?" The radio waves were littered with commands and coordination.

Kyle couldn't look away from the car, unblinking, praying as he listened to the reports. Every cameraman gave an affirmative. Upton was hollering again, but this time in celebration. Kyle was going to stride over and knock the man's goddamn head off if he didn't shut up.

It wasn't time to celebrate.

Mouth dry, he inhaled and did his job. "Close down the set," he ordered. "We're fined for every minute. Close it *down*."

People worked like ants in a hive. Everything was cleared away and back in place, which provided space for emergency workers to swarm in. A firetruck and an ambulance pulled alongside the wrecked sports car. Safety inspectors patrolled the scaffolding to look for places weakened by the accident.

A collective cheer went up, jerking Kyle's attention back to the mangled Maserati.

Between them, two EMTs pulled Nate out of the car. They'd already affixed a stabilizing collar around his neck. Slowly, they lowered him onto an awaiting stretcher.

The police were as fascinated with the scene as everyone else, but no one had as much to lose as Kyle. He shoved past the barriers and sprinted toward the ambulance. Nate's expression was nauseatingly slack—until he saw Kyle.

A slight smile. "Did we get it?"

Kyle growled when he really wanted to rail and smash his knuckles against concrete. Anything to relieve the tension. "You are the worst human being on the planet." To allay the words spoken so harshly, he took a shaky breath and brushed a strand of sweaty hair back from Nate's brow. "Yes," he said tenderly. "We got the shot."

"Fuckin' A." Nate smiled wider. "*Aaaand* I can still feel my wiggling toes. Win."

Kyle huffed a painful sigh of relief. "Worst. Human."

One of the EMTs began to guide the gurney toward the ambulance. "We have to get him to hospital."

"I'm going with him," Kyle said.

"No, you're not." Nate's voice was a rasp, but it was filled with conviction. "I did my job. You go do yours. We'll both come out of this employable."

"And alive."

"Yup." Nate looked haggard and incredibly tired. "Got it covered."

"I'm not through with you." Kyle thought his voice sounded way too desperate. It was either that or grab and hold and never let go.

Soon.

Nate offered one last smile as he was loaded onto the ambulance. "I hear ya, college boy. Now scram."

Kyle spent the next six hours on the telephone. It would've been three times that many without Steph and a whole cadre of assistants. Every financier wooed by Pennfield on Saturday night had to be wooed all over again, this time with high-speed downloads of the dailies. No, the stunt hadn't gone according to plan. Yes, the cleanup was going to be costly. But hell yes, the footage was incredible.

The insurance and PR guys were glad Nate hadn't been killed. The wrong sort of publicity. Steph had been gracious enough to handle them.

Kyle's neck ached. His ear had that hot, numb feeling of having been pressed against a phone for an eternity. The burn in his throat didn't seem to be going anywhere, rasped to shreds by fast talking. Forced smiles made his lips feel rubbery.

The absolute last person he wanted to see striding toward him was Peter Upton. Rubber lips, activate.

Upton surprised him, however, by holding out his hand. "Nice work, Wakefield."

"You're not going to rake me over the coals about the money? Or about Second Chances?"

"The money's your problem. I'm just the humble director." He said it with a cockeyed smile. "As for Second Chances, I'll tell you a little secret—since you shared such a big one this morning."

Kyle didn't bother hiding a scowl.

"I know, I know," Upton said. "But here's the truth. With just about any other crew, we would've done that on a studio."

"Is this your version of Christmas spirit, Upton? Your heart growing three sizes?"

"Best it gets. I'll see my cardiologist as soon as I'm stateside."

As Upton walked away, he was already shouting at a new, hapless victim.

"Hey." A soft feminine shoulder bumped his arm. "You still here?"

"Yup."

"When you should be at the hospital."

"You sure?"

She nodded, then looked at the fire opal bracelet draped over her wrist. "I think you've earned it. And I'll square it with everyone in Bangkok that you won't be on set until February."

"What?"

"*Late* February. You know. Recuperation time. Then you can cover me. I plan to make the most of my time in Bora Bora."

Kyle hugged Steph and whispered his thanks against her hair. "You're the best."

"I know it. Now go."

It took a half hour for the cab to drop Kyle off at St. Thomas's Hospital. Had he been the sort to chew his nails, he would be missing ten of them. Instead he wondered if it was possible to wear a hole in Bulgari leather. He clutched Nate's watch like a talisman.

Through the corridors, through the doors, through the wards that blended together.

Until he found Nate's room.

"You don't look like you cheated death," Kyle said.

Nate sat halfway up, relaxing against two fat pillows. His color was back, and he'd been cleaned up. The hospital gown wasn't the most flattering garment ever worn, but it was a damn sight better than a neck brace.

"Yet here I am. I missed my flight, but the doctors have cleared me to receive congratulatory hugs and kisses." He assessed Kyle and shook his head. "But that's not going to happen yet, is it?"

"No."

Kyle approached slowly, beset by a sudden case of nerves. He grabbed the nearest chair and pulled it close to the bed. "Why did you do it, Nate? Choosing prison over being made into something shameful . . . There's a certain fucked-up eighteen-year-old logic to that. But today? You walked away from me after I'd put everything on the line." He shoved his hands through his hair, realizing he hadn't slept in nearly forty-eight hours. "You're a hard man to trust."

"Do you have my watch?"

Kyle did a double take, frowning. He handed over the timepiece without a word. It looked so right against Nate's strong wrist.

"I did it because you've always been the best. You demand the best. I've never thought I measured up to those standards. Even when we were kids, I was the scholarship charity case and you were the golden boy. No one understood our connection, least of all me." He petted a thumb over the leather strap. "That's why I needed to know why you'd hired Second Chances—for me or for what I could do. And that's why I boosted that car ten years ago."

Kyle wet his lips. Waited. He needed this more than he needed to touch Nate. He literally sat on his hands to keep from reaching out.

"I was scared. Sure, I didn't want to share space in your closet. But closer to the truth, I was convinced you'd get tired of me. It was easy to get our kicks when the pickings were slim, there in school. But Yale? And the whole world after college? How the hell was I supposed to live up to what you'd need?"

"By flying a Maserati?"

Nate smiled and let his head sink back into the pillows. "There's my clever college boy. But here's the thing. I always wanted to be worthy of you. Today . . . Kyle, you proved you're worthy of *me*. I didn't think that'd ever be the way it went."

Kyle was blushing in that way of his, where the apples of his cheeks matched the tips of his ears. "And how does that feel?"

"Feels like I'm the best there is. I won't have to prove it again, to me or you or anyone. I got you to come out and I caught fire in the shadow of Big Ben, all on Christmas Day. No one can compete with that."

Unable to help himself, Kyle chuckled softly and shook his head. "I've created a monster. There won't be any living with you."

"No? I was definitely hoping our living arrangements would change. I like waking up with you too much." Nate exhaled. "I think I need more of those kisses now. Come closer and I'll tell you secrets."

Kyle sat on the edge of the bed, his legs shaking. His hands shaking. Hell, if it was part of his body, it was shaking. He leaned close, running his touch up Nate's arms as he stretched along the man's chest.

They kissed. Softly, as a hello.

"You said secrets," Kyle whispered. "Spill it."

"I didn't only keep your pictures while I was inside. I slept with one under my pillow."

Kyle inhaled softly, his heart melting into a scalding puddle.

"And Jaime? My ex?" Nate touched Kyle's cheek, his ice-blue eyes more open and expressive than ever. "We broke up because he accused me of sleeping with your memory more often than I slept with him.

I've missed you for years, Kyle. I've loved you the whole time. Never stopped."

Inching forward on the bed, Kyle pressed his forehead against Nate's. They shared the same heartbeat, with their fingers knitted together.

"Say it again, Nate. I need to hear it."

"I was a scared, idiot kid nine years ago—"

"We both were."

"—but I'm not scared anymore. What you did . . . coming out like that. Kyle, you took my breath away. I love you too."

They held each other, arms tight, emotion edging their hands and kisses with desperation. Not as if they were going to lose one another, but as a reassurance that this was really happening.

"I can breathe," Kyle whispered against Nate's temple. "I can finally breathe."

"And I'm not afraid of a damn thing. How could I be? *You're* here." Nate stroked his nape and kissed him with heart-stopping tenderness. "We're both free now. And free to love each other."

"Promise it'll be forever this time."

"I promise, Kyle. Forever is *our* Christmas present."

Epilogue

H appiness seemed to be a state of body rather than a state of being. Supreme relaxation. Nate had never felt easier in his own skin. Practically all of that had to do with the man sitting next to him.

The man who was wound so tightly that he might pop like a bottle rocket out the sunroof of the limo.

"Hey." Nate scooped the hand between them into both of his. Kyle's fingers were chilled, so he lifted them to his lips. "It'll be fine."

Kyle managed a small smile. "Oh, I know it'll be *fine.*"

"Then what's wrong?" Except Nate had a feeling he knew.

"I don't want fine. I want awesome."

So many mixed-up but wonderful emotions. Pride in Kyle's amazing determination, and in the fact that Nate had called it right. Plus a little amusement at their predictability. Only three months of marriage and they were absolutely boring.

He hid his smile behind Kyle's hand. Boring. Right. Once upon a less enlightened time, Kyle would've dropped millions on an Upper West Side penthouse, just to establish their residency and get married in New York. Instead, they'd chosen to say their vows in a little Colorado town. No press. A few friends. And a shared gratitude that they could be *who* they were no matter *where* they were.

They still had the penthouse, though, for when life in Hollywood got too batshit. If it weren't for all the offers rolling in to Second Chances, Nate might still indulge in the paranoia that he was the kept man. Fuck that. He was loved and in love. Sometimes he could hardly believe how damned lucky he was.

Kyle sat rigidly on the black leather seat next to Nate in the limo. Every limb radiated tension. He wore a three-piece suit Nate wouldn't have known how to put together. And after a ton of cajoling, he'd talked Nate into letting Kyle pick his clothes—which turned out to be more expensive versions of what he normally wore. Fashion was stupid.

Yet it pleased Kyle to make sure they both looked their best. Nate had put up the bare minimum of fuss because he liked his man happy.

His husband.

Damn, that was still nice to think.

The limo stopped, then inched forward a few feet. Kyle leaned to look out the black-tinted windows. "We've got a good crowd. And the publicity department didn't need to inflate it with extras. God, listen to those screams." His grin was so wide and bright that it made Nate want to drag him home.

"It's your big night."

"Yours too."

"Come here and kiss me before it's too late." Nate tugged Kyle closer and curled his fingers in the satiny material of his lapel.

Their mouths were practically one, a blend of silent words in the slick of lips and curl of tongues. Kyle cupped the back of Nate's head, while Nate bit the bottom lip between with steady intent. A promise to hold Kyle's desperation at bay.

He pulled back slowly. No taking. Not now. Instead, their foreheads pressed together, and Kyle's breath shivered over Nate's lips. "Later I'm going to have you," Nate whispered. "Raw and rough. Or maybe not. Maybe we'll do it the slow, sweet kind. Either way, we're going to fuck until we see stars and collapse on our bed."

The soft grin Kyle offered wasn't exactly what Nate had expected, but it was beautiful nonetheless. The tip of his arrogant college boy ears turned red. "Our bed. Of that entire promise, those are the two words that sank in."

"Damn, Kyle. Stop that shit." The limo pulled forward again, and the screaming voices outside surged in volume. "You're on."

An assistant opened the car door in a move that was practically invisible in its smoothness. Nate ducked out first, then eased toward the crowds pressed up against temporary fencing. Kyle wasn't the primary target of the paparazzi, but he got his fair share of attention.

The incredibly handsome, incredibly moneyed producer who'd come out in an incredibly public way.

All for the picture's lead stuntman.

They'd even been on the cover of a couple of magazines. Nate had been conflicted about gaining attention from something that had been a bone of contention between him and Kyle for so long. But they'd talked it over—several rounds, best done when naked and sated—and decided screw it. They'd work that publicity for all it was worth.

Sure enough, the phones of both Second Chances and Pennfield rang until the batteries died.

Which made it completely worth hitching his thumbs in the pockets of his dark jeans and watching Kyle play to the cameras. The whole time, Nate got to think about how he'd have the man stretched out and open later—in their bed. Just like Kyle had said.

A minute later Kyle returned for him. Hand out. A soft smile curved his mouth into something unbelievably appealing. His smile broadened, real and shining. "Nothing smart-mouthed to say?"

Nate shook his head. Thousands watched them, lots of them screaming and so many cameras with their black, shining lenses. And Kyle's warm fingers intertwined with his. "Nope. This is . . . perfect."

Except he was wrong. When Kyle leaned up an inch and kissed him—that was perfection. A soft cushion of mouth on mouth. Enough. Exactly what Nate had always wanted, all those years ago.

He'd been unable to believe in either himself or Kyle. That wasn't the case anymore. There, on the red carpet, they were together. It was Nate and Kyle on film in public. A declaration of forever and of love they'd always shared, even if they'd gone without for far too long.

They denied themselves nothing now. That's what counted. And Nate was never giving up another second of Kyle's love.

Explore more of our holiday stories for charity!
riptidepublishing.com/titles/collections/2017-
holiday-charity-bundle

Riptide's 2017
Charity Bundle

Benefiting
The Russian LGBT
Network

Featuring:
Roan Parrish
Katie Porter
Cecilia Tan

Dear Reader,

Thank you for reading Katie Porter's *Came Upon a Midnight Clear*!

We know your time is precious and you have many, many entertainment options, so it means a lot that you've chosen to spend your time reading. We really hope you enjoyed it.

We'd be honored if you'd consider posting a review—good or bad—on sites like **Amazon, Barnes & Noble, Kobo, Goodreads, Twitter, Facebook, Tumblr,** and your blog or website. We'd also be honored if you told your friends and family about this book. Word of mouth is a book's lifeblood!

For more information on upcoming releases, author interviews, blog tours, contests, giveaways, and more, please sign up for our weekly, spam-free newsletter and visit us around the web:

Newsletter: tinyurl.com/RiptideSignup
Twitter: twitter.com/RiptideBooks
Facebook: facebook.com/RiptidePublishing
Goodreads: tinyurl.com/RiptideOnGoodreads
Tumblr: riptidepublishing.tumblr.com

Thank you so much for Reading the Rainbow!

RiptidePublishing.com

Acknowledgments

The process of writing a book can be like tucking bits of life into a time capsule. A particular era. A particular state of mind. *Came Upon a Midnight Clear* was a safe place for us when those bits of life whirled in a tornado of uncertainty and loneliness. For that, we will always think back on this story as being very dear. Helping us along the way, both creatively and personally, were Sasha Knight, Sarah Lyons, Fedora Chen, Patti Ann Colt, Kelly Schaub, Ami Silber, and The Group That Shall Not Be Named. That our families supported us and kept us steady *could* go without saying, but no one has families as amazing as ours. They deserve all the love and gratitude we have to give.

Also by Katie Porter

About the Author

Katie Porter is the writing team of Carrie Lofty and Lorelie Brown, who've been friends and critique partners for more than ten years. Both have been nominated for RITA® awards, and are multi-published in several romance genres. Carrie has an MA in history, while Lorelie is a US Army veteran. Although apparently high-strung, Carrie sings lead in a women's a cappella choir, scares the pants off people as a haunted house actor, and starts every holiday season with *Die Hard*. She's successfully raised her two daughters to defend its place in the Christmas movie canon. Seemingly laid-back Lorelie is obsessed with Washi tape, loves true crime, and gets off on running—a fact that still surprises her on a regular basis. For her family of three boys, only Rizzo the Rat in *The Muppet Christmas Carol* is required holiday viewing.

To learn more about the authors who make up Katie, visit katieporterbooks.com or follow them on Twitter at @carrielofty, @LorelieBrown, and @MsKatiePorter.